Praise for Alex Prentiss's
NIGHT TIDES

"[Alex] Prentiss has created one of the most imaginative heroines ever.... She's both powerful and vulnerable, and truly compelling.... An intriguing mystery with deep and complicated characters."
—*Romantic Times Book Reviews*

"A fascinating paranormal suspense thriller starring an interesting protagonist whose special skill brings a special freshness to the mission of saving abducted college-age females. The story line is fast paced from the onset, while the romantic subplot enhances the amateur-sleuth inquiry. Fans will appreciate *Night Tides* due to a heroine whose connection to the spirits of the lake makes for a unique enjoyable read."
—HARRIET KLAUSNER

"With a plethora of characters, *Night Tides* is a fresh and exciting debut novel by new author Alex Prentiss. The pacing is quick, and the plot is addicting. The characters are well drawn and a bit quirky...[and] the tension is palpable. The erotic content is plentiful but tastefully done.... Delve into this mesmerizing read that will keep you captivated long into the night."
—Romance Reviews Today

DARK WATERS

BY ALEX PRENTISS

Dark Waters
Night Tides

DARK WATERS

Alex Prentiss

BANTAM BOOKS
NEW YORK

A Bantam Books Mass Market Original

Copyright © 2010 by Alex Prentiss

Published in the United States by Bantam Books, an imprint of The Random House Publishing Group, a division of Random House, Inc., New York.

BANTAM BOOKS and the rooster colophon are trademarks of Random House, Inc.

978-0-553-59298-6

Cover design: Marietta Anastassatos
Cover illustration: Frank Petsch © redbrickstock.com/Alamy

Printed in the United States of America

www.bantamdell.com

9 8 7 6 5 4 3 2 1

To my mom, Grace West,
who really liked the first book

Special thanks to:
Anne Groell
Marlene Stringer
David Pomerico
Sjolinds Chocolate House
Caroline Aumann
Valette, Jake, and Charlie

DARK WATERS

CHAPTER ONE

THE NIGHT WAS hot and wet, but Rachel Matre felt oddly distant from it as she stood naked on the edge of Lake Mendota, her bare feet sinking in the warm mud. Her belly fluttered with nervousness, and she wrung her hands unconsciously. But what was normally something she desired—something she craved and couldn't live without—now felt tentative and uncertain.

I almost failed them; what if they no longer want me?

Rachel was thirty-four but looked younger, with a body kept trim and firm by regular jogging. She had unruly blond hair and full lips, and a haunted look in her eyes that spoke of past traumas hidden deep and well.

She was in tiny Hudson Park, hidden from view by the effigy mound of a water spirit. It had been built by an ancient, now-vanished Native American tribe called the Lo-Stahzi, and the park existed to protect it. The park, and the rest of downtown Madison, Wisconsin, occupied a narrow isthmus between Mendota and its sister lake, Monona. Here was where she met her spectral lovers.

The spirits of the lake, ancient and inexplicable, had saved Rachel from drowning when she was a teen. Ever since, she had returned to their amorous, erotic, and insatiable embrace. She came to them naked, in the middle of the night, and they pulled her beneath the surface and enveloped her in sensual safety. They took her to heights of passion she never dreamed possible, and in return she helped them right wrongs in the surface world. She had no idea who they were or why they were here, only that they loved her and protected her.

Or at least they had once. But did they still want her, after what had happened? Not only had she failed in her task to protect a young woman named Patty Patilia from danger, but her own body was now marked by another man. The outline of a tattoo covered her torso from breasts to below her navel, placed there against her will by the madman Arlin Korbus. As she stepped into the water, she wondered if the spirits would even want her this way. Her body had been used against her will, but she still felt guilty for it. At weak moments she thought that if she'd just allowed him to do the tattoo in the first place, perhaps he wouldn't have gone on the rampage that left one woman dead and four others marked for life. She knew rationally none of it was her fault, that Korbus acted for his own reasons, but that knowledge did little to stem her own sense of responsibility for what happened. She hid her shame at her violated flesh from everyone else, but the spirits would know. They always knew.

She took another step. Soft silt squirted up between her toes. A wave broke against her thigh, splashing across her abdomen and the evidence of her recent ordeal. Korbus had kidnapped her, along with four other girls, and planned to mark their bodies with designs they'd once refused. Rachel had fought back, ultimately killing Korbus with her bare hands. But only Ethan Walker's timely arrival had saved Patty from the effects of a black widow spider bite.

"Please," she whispered. "Please take me. I did the best I could. Please."

She needn't have worried. The first touch came gently—an unmistakable caress along her calf that raised glorious goose bumps. The fingers trailed up her leg, across her knee, and then along the inside of her thigh. They faded as they neared her most intimate place, and for just a moment she feared it was a farewell, not a welcome.

Then the hands were everywhere, just as they'd always been, and they pulled her beneath the surface. As always, even though she was underwater, their magic allowed her to breathe in safety.

We have missed you, the voices said in her head as watery lips closed over her nipples. *We have ached for your body.* Hands pushed her thighs apart, exposing her in a way that would be grotesque in any other situation. But here, floating in a world with no up or down, she welcomed it. Already she was wet inside before the slippery, liquid tongue began stroking her, and teeth just firm enough for the purpose nibbled at her clit.

It was all it had ever been, and more. She would've screamed with relief and delight if she'd been above the surface.

Another tongue traced the still-sensitive line of her new tattoo. *We will always treasure you. You will never be defiled to us. Bring us your pain, your troubles, and drown them with us.*

She felt a rush of emotion too powerful for words.

It was like an amorphous orgy with her at the center. All attention focused on her needs, sensing when things grew too intense and she required a moment to recover. Yet the passion never really abated. She was caressed, kissed, sucked, and penetrated. It went on for so long that she began to wonder if they ever intended to let her go. Could she die this way? she thought, after innumerable orgasms. And would she care?

But the spirits had more than sex on their minds. When they finally released her and she stumbled, exhausted and rubber-legged, to the bank, she collapsed on the grass and realized her skin tingled in a new way. She looked down at her naked body glistening in the pink illumination from nearby streetlights. It took a moment to realize what had changed.

The tattoo was gone.

The outline of Arlin Korbus's insane image—a forest scene with half-naked dancing girls that covered her torso—had vanished. No evidence remained that it had ever been there. Only her original tattoo—a small, simple outline of the park's effigy mound just below her navel—remained.

She went from shock to delight to relief so quickly that she could only express the emotions through tears. She ran her hands over her body again and again, checking for any indication that she'd imagined it. But there was no doubt that the tattoo was gone.

Suddenly she thought, not of herself, but of Patty Patilia. The girl the spirits asked her to protect, the one they called a "treasure." Patty was marked as well, and she faced weeks of painful laser procedures if she wished to remove the visible signs of Korbus's violation. But if the spirits could so easily remove Rachel's tattoo—

"Wait!" Rachel cried. Her voice rang through the silent darkness, causing a nearby dog to bark. But by then she'd already dived back into the lake.

She kicked along the bottom, her mind screaming, *Please don't go. Not yet!* She'd never issued this kind of demand before, and had no idea if the lake spirits would respond.

But with no warning she was enveloped, spun onto her back, and pressed down into the silt. She was penetrated deeply and completely, and brought to orgasm with no time to prepare.

As the waves of feeling faded, she formed the thought that had driven her back into the water. *Please help Patty. She's got no one here who can save her the way you saved me! You called her your treasure, remember? She needs you.*

Hands caressed her everywhere at once, and a voice whispered, *You are kind, and caring, and we love you for it. We will protect our treasure. Her need shall be answered.*

Thank you, she thought. *Thank you!* And then, exhausted, she climbed from the water.

PATTY PATILIA SAT on her bed in her favorite sleep shirt, wide awake. Her skin still crawled from the violating hands in her dream. She could rationalize everything that had happened to her consciously—especially the certainty that Arlin Korbus would never harm anyone ever again. She'd seen him die, after all. But that did nothing to stop her subconscious from resurrecting him.

In her dreams she was still bound by duct tape, her screams muffled and her struggles useless. She felt the cold touch of the knife's flat edge sliding against her skin while the sharp side sliced away her clothing. There was no escaping the thoughts of shame, terror, and helplessness; they lived as vividly as if they'd just happened moments before. And when she dreamed of the spider, she always woke up screaming.

The hardwood floor creaked as she walked to the bathroom and drank some water. She had the upstairs studio in an old house that was divided into three apartments, and as she looked around at her meager belongings, she felt a rush of disappointment. *I graduated a year ago,* she thought, *and here I am still living like a student, playing my songs in coffeehouses basically for tips. My CDs sound like crap. Maybe my dad is right. I'm just another whiny bitch with a guitar. Nothing special at all.*

She picked up her guitar from its stand by the bed. Music had always been her voice when words failed her. She put the strap over her shoulder and began to pick softly as she paced the room. As she fumed, the gentle strumming changed to a grind of great raw chords that, even with an acoustic instrument, sounded loud and violent. She continued until there was a knock at her apartment door.

She froze, and saw by the clock that it was nearly two in the morning. She pulled on her robe and opened the door as far as the security chain allowed, prepared for the irate neighbor she knew stood outside.

Instead, it was a young man she'd never seen before. A reflexive jolt of fear went through her.

"Hi," he said. "I, uh . . . heard you playing."

She choked down the lump in her throat. Strangers never used to terrify her. "I'm sorry, I know it's late, I just got carried away. It won't happen again."

"No, it didn't bother me at all. In fact, I really liked it." He smiled and ducked his chin demurely, and she felt a totally unexpected tingle that dissipated almost all her fear. "My name's Dewey, by the way. Dewey Raintree."

She giggled. "Really?" Although she could see only half his face through the opening, she was almost instantly infatuated. He was *exactly* the type of boy she always fell for like a skydiver with a bad parachute: slender, about her height, with disheveled dark hair and round John Lennon glasses. His smile was open, kind, and apparently came easy. The twinkle in his eyes woke the dormant butterflies inside her.

He smiled bashfully. "Yes, really. I know it's a little silly."

"No, I'm sorry, I just . . . It sounds kind of like a

character on a TV show. *The Adventures of Dewey Raintree.*"

"Would I travel the country in a van solving mysteries?"

Again she giggled. "With your semiverbal Great Dane?"

"Named Ramlet?" he said in a Scooby-Doo voice.

Now she really laughed, and so did he. When she paused for breath he said, "The reason I knocked on your door was that I thought maybe we could play together." He raised his own guitar case so she could see it. "I'm not very good, though. They say rock and roll is three chords, and the truth? I know two chords and some gossip."

He's a musician, too, she thought, and her knees grew weak. All the emotions and feelings she feared gone forever surged back, apparently determined to make up for lost time.

"I know you don't know me, and I don't expect you to let me in," he said quickly. "I thought maybe we could sit on the porch downstairs. The two guys in that apartment are gone for the summer, so we shouldn't bother anyone if we're quiet."

She hesitated then, the butterflies suddenly replaced with the buzzing, beelike terror. Before Arlin Korbus, this would've been a no-brainer; she had thought the world safe, and that people were basically good.

As if reading her thoughts, Dewey said, "Tell you what. Call or email someone and tell them you'll be with me if you want. Heck, take a picture with your cellphone. I promise, I have no ulterior motives." He grinned shyly. "Okay, that's not *entirely* true, but I promise to be a gentleman."

Close and lock the door, her fear said.

Bite me, she said to her fear. "Give me two seconds to get dressed and send that email. I'll meet you downstairs."

He actually blushed with delight. "Great. I'll see you there."

RACHEL LAY AWAKE in bed, her hair still damp from her post-swim shower. She was naked, staring up at the ceiling, her nerve ends still janglingly alive. Her hands ran slowly, lightly, over her skin. Her cat Tainter slept on the floor beside the bed, his light feline breathing the only sound.

Mainly she felt relief. The spirits still wanted her, and they loved her enough to use their magic to remove the ghastly marks of her captivity. The medical procedure to do the same thing was long-term, expensive, and painful. And when she'd asked for help with Patty, they'd promised to do so. She wondered how that would manifest.

Then with no warning, her thoughts turned to Ethan Walker and their single night together. Ethan of the strong, supple body and melting blue eyes, who accepted her tale of the lake spirits and responded to the magical call for help sent through them. She'd killed Arlin Korbus on her own, but without Ethan's aid escaping from that basement, Patty Patilia would have died.

The spirits had accepted Ethan; if she brought him

to the water and made love to him there, she could be like any woman with her human lover. It was something she'd wanted ever since she understood the nature of the lake spirits' power over her. And what had she said to him? *I'm afraid if you stay around right now, every time I see you it'll remind me of what happened. And I don't want that. Not for me, and not for you.* That hadn't been the truth, though. The truth was that she wanted him desperately, but she still hesitated and wasn't at all sure why. What was she *really* afraid of?

Still, her hands changed from reassuring caresses to something more purposeful. She should've been exhausted, all desire burned out by the spirits' ravishing, but at the memory of Ethan's touch it roared back at full intensity. She knew she couldn't achieve orgasm, but neither could she stop, and she squeezed and touched herself urgently, moaning softly so as not to wake the cat. She writhed on the bed, one hand clamped between her thighs, the other cupping a breast, content to be awash in mere desire after the series of shattering climaxes in the water.

AND ACROSS THE isthmus, in bed beside Dewey Raintree, Patty Patilia felt a very similar satisfaction.

CHAPTER TWO

POSTED BY THE Lady to the *Lady of the Lakes* blog:

> Summer's here, and the time is right for dancing on the isthmus. With the kidnapper dead and gone, we can enjoy the street fairs, neighborhood festivals, and other good times without looking over our shoulders. But remember to keep your eyes open, and if anything strange or dangerous happens, let the Lady know.

ETHAN WALKER LOOKED out his office window at the capitol dome. The seat of Wisconsin's government loomed large over him in every sense, its fingers reaching more and more into the private sector as it sought to stem the worsening economic chaos that gripped the whole country. Ethan's company, Walker Construction, had avoided the worst so far; he'd downsized a bit, and some anticipated contracts had fallen through.

It was a whole hell of a lot better than the situation faced by some of his competition, and Ethan wished he could take credit for it, but it was really just the luck of the draw. Soon he'd need work just like the rest of them, and he had no idea where it might come from.

Ethan was a big man, broad-shouldered and muscular. He'd served in the army during the first days of the Iraq War, and had avoided the stop-loss trap that snared so many of his fellow enlistees. He'd kept in shape since returning to civilian life, channeling a lot of unruly emotions into his gym routine. It kept him focused on what really mattered.

He had dark hair that tended to flop boyishly over his forehead, making him look younger than his twenty-nine years. But he also had the calm center instilled by his youth spent learning responsibility and trustworthiness on a large dairy farm. It was that center that kept him from the excesses of war and led him to help bring a fellow soldier to justice for rape and murder. Some from his unit—the kind of men who laughed when human beings died—considered him a traitor and a coward. But he lost no sleep over that, or over their threats of vengeance.

Now he tried to keep his thoughts on work, and not on the thing that he *did* lose sleep over: the aching loneliness he'd felt since Rachel Matre broke up with him. "Broke up" was probably an overstatement: They'd had one date, one night of amazing sex, and then she'd been kidnapped by Arlin Korbus. To help rescue her, Ethan had contacted her lake spirits, baring himself emotionally and physically to their ministrations. The whole experience had been overwhelming, and he still awoke sometimes in the middle of the night, rock-hard and sweating, as the intimate touch of that watery mouth returned in his dreams.

Of course there was no one with whom he could talk about it. His father would simply tune him out. His brother Marty the cop would have him committed. And his former girlfriend Julie . . . well, the less he saw of her, the better. He did not trust her, or himself when he was around her.

He looked at his appointment book and frowned. He didn't remember seeing *this* on the schedule yesterday. He went to his office door and said, "Ambika, what's this ten-thirty appointment?"

"That would be Mr. Garrett Bloom," his office manager said in her lilting Hindi accent. "The phone was ringing when I got here this morning. He was most insistent that he see you today."

Ethan's stomach plummeted. "Garrett Bloom? Really?"

"Oh, yes. The immensely important Garrett Bloom wants a few minutes of your time for something that might benefit the community as a whole. Those were his exact words, and all I could get out of him."

"Did he sound angry?"

"Oh, no, he was perfectly charming. And he has the knack of filling up any silence so it's hard to get a word in." There was both annoyance and professional admiration in her voice; Ambika prided herself on keeping control of any verbal exchange. "I told him you could spare fifteen minutes. I have no doubt he can talk that long without pausing for breath more than once."

"He's a local legend, Ambika. And he does a lot of

good work." *And he gets in the way of lucrative projects like the ones* I *need to get,* he added in his head.
*And he isn't above showing up with a TV crew in tow
to put "greedy profiteers" on the spot. Oh boy.*

"I have no opinion," she said, her opinion coming
through very clearly in her tone, "but he did not sound
angry. Rather pleased with himself but not angry."

Ethan smiled. "Okay. Send him right in when he
gets here."

He went back into his office and opened his laptop
almost gratefully. Preparing for a last-minute meeting
with someone like Bloom should certainly keep his
mind off his broken heart. He typed Bloom's name into
the search engine. He knew Bloom's background, of
course, but wanted to be fresh on the details.

He clicked through the splash page with the letters
PBN in a Java logo. Then the man's face popped up on
his business's main webpage: tanned skin, immaculate
hair, tie knotted to perfection. His mustache was so
even it looked as if it had been drawn on with a pen.
He radiated trust and benevolence, which befitted the
motto written beneath the image: *This is our community, and we should have a voice in how it changes.*

Ethan methodically checked the links along the
bottom: About, Projects, Comments, Contact. Bloom
called himself a "community activist," battling at-
tempts to alter the basic nature of Madison's downtown isthmus. He'd unsuccessfully fought the condo
project Ethan's company was now building, and suc-
ceeded in getting Walgreens to relocate its newest store
to avoid tearing down a street's worth of old buildings.
There was a PayPal link that solicited donations, but

Ethan knew Bloom didn't hurt for working capital. After all this time working with the Madison power structure, the man was as connected as a male octopus in mating season.

Under the Current Activity tab, Ethan found links to a pollution cleanup, a drive to distribute free soap to the downtown homeless shelters, a push to overcome the state attorney general's religious-based resistance to sex education in schools, and a petition asking the local Catholic bishop to apologize for inflammatory remarks about victims of priestly abuse. He seemed to have no bone to pick with any current construction projects.

Ethan closed that window and clicked the bookmark for the *Lady of the Lakes* blog. This was the unofficial source for everything on the isthmus, and its anonymous Lady seemed to know everyone's dirty laundry. He put Bloom's name in the search box and read the half-dozen entries that mentioned him. Four praised his efforts on behalf of local residents; two criticized his alleged womanizing, but numerous women jumped to his defense in the comments.

On a whim, Ethan put his own name into the search box. There were no results. He couldn't say why, but this annoyed him. He was involved in those controversial condominium projects, not to mention his role in rescuing the victims of Arlin Korbus, the mad tattooist. The news had mentioned him, although only tangentially, focusing instead on Rachel Matre's heroics. Wasn't he worth at least a comment?

He shook off those thoughts and returned to the

immediate problem. *Why* did Bloom want to see him? Was he coming as a friend or as a foe?

ETHAN CAME AROUND his desk and shook Garrett Bloom's hand. In person, he was as tall as Ethan, and as neat, tanned, and slicked into perfection as he was in his photograph. "Congratulations," Bloom said at once.

"And why is that?"

"Because I've chosen you for my newest project."

Ethan raised his eyebrows. "Really?"

"Oh, yes. Do you know the old mental hospital on Atwood down by Olbrich Park? Just past the gardens, down the hill from the road?"

"Yeah, I know it. It was called Parkside, right?"

Bloom snapped his fingers and touched the tip of his nose. "That's the one."

The building always looked more like a prison than a hospital to Ethan, which reflected the attitude toward mental health care during its years of operation. The Mendota Mental Health Institute on the north side eventually absorbed Parkside's patients, and the building stood vacant for several years, gradually falling into disrepair. It was now little more than a shell, used by addicts and others for illicit activities.

Bloom continued, "We've bought it, and we want it renovated into a community center. That whole area is underserved, and deserves more than it's got. And you're the contractor we've chosen to do it."

"Really? Don't you need to take bids, or—"

Bloom waved his hand as if shooing flies. "Not with

private financing like we have. We can hire whoever we want, and we want you."

Ethan was speechless for a moment. "I'm flattered," he said at last.

"Don't be," Bloom said with a smile. "It's going to be a mess, politically and publicly. There's a reason nobody's done this before."

"Which is?"

"The land is tied up in litigation over its possible Native American significance. But I'm pretty sure I can get around that in a way that will benefit everyone."

Ethan knew the difficulties that came with this sort of project. After centuries of disenfranchisement, Native Americans were not hesitant to use the courts to stop what they perceived as desecration. Truthfully, Ethan didn't blame them, but he had no desire to get tangled up in it. "'Pretty sure' still leaves an awful lot of leeway," he said guardedly.

Bloom turned serious. "I'm 'pretty sure' enough to have raised twelve million dollars in funding. I wouldn't waste my time doing that if I thought it would fall apart. I respect the native tribes and what's been done to them; I have no interest in profiting at their expense."

"Me neither," Ethan said. *Twelve million dollars,* he thought, and tried not to smile.

"Then we're on the same page. Have your lawyer contact my lawyer and we'll get the contracts drawn up."

"Okay. But I have to ask: Why me?"

"We want a solid local firm with a history of

conscientiousness. The only thing is, I'd like to get started almost immediately. Can you do that?"

"Do you have the plans?"

"I'll have the architect send them over."

"Then I'll look at them immediately and get back to you."

Bloom smiled and touched his nose again. "I knew you were the right man for the job, Ethan. May I call you Ethan?"

For twelve million dollars, Ethan thought, *you can call me Princess.* "Sure."

"Now, I'll need some biographical information for my website and the press. Stuff to show how environmentally conscious you are."

Although he never deliberately tried to destroy anything he didn't have to, Ethan certainly met no environmentalist's definition of *green.* "Who said I was?"

"It's just image. I know you're conscientious, but we want to accent it. Not," he said with sudden seriousness, "*lie* about it. I won't tolerate that. But you employ legal immigrant labor, you've worked to keep the character of neighborhoods, you've kept your buildings within environmental codes . . ."

"None of those were my ideas, though. It's just what the jobs entailed."

"Still, you did them and they count. And didn't you grow up on a dairy farm?"

"That's right, over in Monroe."

"And there was something else. . . ."

"I served in the Iraq War?"

"Yes, that's definitely a positive. But it was something else. . . ." At last Bloom snapped his fingers and touched his nose again. "Your brother, that's right. Well, your *adopted* brother."

"He's my brother," Ethan said with certainty.

"Of course, of course. Isn't he Asian?"

Ethan nodded. "He's Hmong. Originally from Laos."

"And he's gay, right?"

Ethan tried not to wince at the thought that Bloom knew so much about his family. Of course the man would've checked him out, but still . . . "Yes. But seriously, I don't want him brought into this."

"You're not *ashamed* of him, are you?" Bloom said with sudden outrage.

"No!" Ethan almost shouted. Then he caught himself. "He's a cop, that's all. He's got his own job to consider."

"Oh," Bloom said. "I'm sorry. I misunderstood."

"But he *is* off-limits," Ethan repeated.

Bloom waved his hands. "Of course, of course. We have plenty to work with anyway. This will be a pleasure. We'll be in touch soon. As I said, we want to move quickly on this."

After Bloom left, Ethan sat behind his desk, staring into space, wondering if the meeting had really happened. Twelve-million-dollar contracts didn't just fall from the sky, yet this one did. And it was attached to a public figure whose notoriety might push Ethan's firm to the front of a lot of lists.

When he looked up, Ambika stood in the doorway, her arms crossed. "You're happy to get this man's business, aren't you?"

"Of course. I'm happy to get *any* business. Why?"

"I don't trust him."

"Really? Why not?"

"I can't put my finger on it at the moment. But there's something . . . off about him."

"He's a politician. Maybe it's just the company he keeps."

"No, it's him. I'm sure. I have a good sense for these things."

He looked at her dubiously, but she only raised her chin and looked at him with faux seriousness. "Others have thought as you do, sahib. They have learned not to underestimate my powers."

ETHAN WALKED DOWN State Street to Michelangelo's Coffee Shop, got a latte, and sat in the corner with his laptop. He tapped in Bloom's name again and pulled up some of the past projects the man had been involved in, wanting to get more detail than his earlier cursory examination. He hated to admit it, but Ambika's warning had him a bit spooked; it was out of character, and therefore significant.

Before he could get started, though, a new voice said, "You shouldn't look at lesbian biker porn in public, don't you know that?"

Ethan looked up. Standing over him was a tall, athletic-looking black man in a business suit. "You know me too well," Ethan said, and stood to shake the offered hand.

Kenny Hickman turned the chair opposite Ethan's and straddled it. "I came by your office, and Ambika said I'd find you here. I think she's starting to like me; she only rolled her eyes at me once."

"She's actually very nice. She's just protective."

"Like a mama wolverine. So what's been happening?"

Ethan had known Hickman long enough to trust his discretion. "Apparently I just won the contract for a new lakeside community center on the site of the old Parkside Mental Hospital."

" 'Apparently'?"

"I didn't even know it was on the drawing board, or that I was in the running for it. I'm still not sure it's for real."

"How long has that place been sitting empty anyway?"

"Years. They don't even have flea markets in it anymore. I'll have to check to see if an asbestos crew needs to clean it up first."

"And who's behind this pleasant surprise?"

"Garrett Bloom."

"Wow," Hickman deadpanned. "Did he let you feel the holes where the crucifixion nails went in?"

"What?"

"He's got a savior complex. Or a martyr one."

"You don't believe somebody can just *care* about other people and want to help them?"

"No."

"Well, I do. Besides, I'm just tearing down one building and putting another one in the same place. I don't even think the zoning needs to change."

"Just don't sign anything without reading it," Hickman said.

"I never do."

Their discussion turned to sports, then inevitably to women. After Hickman left, Ethan got online again and read through the critics of Bloom's methods. Yet they were overwhelmed by his seriously high-profile supporters, from Wisconsin's most liberal senator to that great beacon of hope and justice, Angelina Jolie. And his projects had ushered in a new era of environmentally friendly building that truthfully had bedeviled Ethan ever since he started his own business.

He switched back to the *Lady of the Lakes* blog and read through the latest posts. Minor scandals, a reported series of burglaries, nothing he couldn't also find in the newspaper or other legitimate sources. Had Madison simply calmed down in the last two months since the Korbus affair, or had the Lady's thumb slipped from the isthmus's pulse?

And then, unbidden as always, came thoughts of Rachel Matre. His body responded to her memory as it always did, and he had to uncross his legs to stay comfortable. His torrid encounter with her seemed as fresh and vivid as if it had happened last night, not two months ago. Her mouth, her breasts, the soft curls between her thighs, all filled his senses with desire and longing more intense than any he'd ever felt before. Worse still were the emotions they wrought—feelings that he could neither express nor endure.

And yet he'd promised to stay away. She needed time, she said, to recover from the awful things Arlin Korbus had put her through. And Ethan had agreed, because he imagined it would take weeks, not months. Now he had to face the very real possibility that she might never call, and he would never again be allowed to touch her.

And for some reason, that made his belly knot up with anxiety harder than even the worst firefight he'd experienced in Iraq.

CHAPTER THREE

FOR THE FIRST time since she'd been abducted and forcibly tattooed two months earlier, Rachel got through a whole breakfast shift without catching anyone staring at her.

When she first came back to the diner after being released from the hospital, the scrutiny had been startling. She knew there would be some interest: She'd been on television, in the papers, and on the Internet. It wasn't every day a mere diner owner, let alone a female one, single-handedly killed the man who'd terrorized the city with his kidnapping spree. It made sense that people would want to look her over.

And look they did. The diner was packed for that first week, with people lined up outside the door, waiting for seats. The regulars, deprived of their usual positions at the counter or tables, simply stopped showing up. The very faces that would've comforted her most were replaced by strangers, most of them from the university, and all of them with the social skills prevalent in the Internet age. They stared and talked about her as if she couldn't hear them, the way they would've if she'd been a video on YouTube.

This gave the diner a brief economic boom. Helena had hired a new waitress named Clara while Rachel recuperated in the hospital; the surge of business upon Rachel's return forced them to bring in another, a tall, dark-skinned girl named Roya. Jimmy the cook dragged in a friend, a fellow recovering addict who rose to the challenge and kept the food coming. They found their rhythm quickly, and for a blissful fortnight the diner ran at the absolute limit of its capacity.

During that time the patrons treated Rachel like radioactive porcelain. No one wanted to "bother" her with requests for food or drink, or "trouble" her with the questions they were dying to have answered. Often they *did* ask them, of one another, while she was within hearing distance. Did she still have nightmares? Had she been raped? Was she post-traumatic? *Yes, no,* and *a little* were the answers, but she never got to utter them because no one questioned her directly. This meant the rest of the waitstaff had even more work, and eventually even they grew resentful of the whole china-doll approach.

Finally, Clara snapped.

"Look," she announced to the full dining room, her apron covered with freshly spilled coffee. She and Rachel were on duty, but since no one wanted to bother Rachel, Clara covered the whole floor, both the counter and the tables. "I'm just one woman, with two hands and two legs. And one last nerve, which *all* of you are now on. If you want me to wait on every single one of you, I will, but it'll take a while and I won't be too damn happy about it. Rachel is *fine*. Just watch."

She made an elaborate show of poking Rachel in the shoulder.

"See?" Clara continued. "She won't break. She can pour coffee, and write down orders, and walk and talk at the same time. So how about some of you letting her wait on you, okay? *Okay?*"

It didn't help Rachel's sense of being conspicuous when the local community radio station, WART, began playing a tribute song by fellow kidnappee Patty Patilia. Patty certainly intended no harm, but the insanely catchy chorus rapidly became the bane of Rachel's existence:

And on the date you'll
See your Fate bring you Rachel
You'll know just how late you'll
Be to your own funeral . . .

She finally had to ask—beg, really—Patty not to perform the song. She even offered to buy the rights so she could refuse them to anyone else, forever. Patty said she understood, although Rachel saw the hurt in her eyes; it was intended as a tribute, after all. Patty certainly had talent, and even the lake spirits said one day her music might change the world. But surely not "Fate Brings You Rachel."

But now, with the tattoo magically gone, the worst was over. She was close to being just plain old Rachel Matre again, head cook and bottle washer of Rachel's diner. And that should have made her very happy indeed.

But she still couldn't bring herself to call Ethan Walker.

THE MORNING AFTER Rachel's reunion with the lake spirits, Patty Patilia bounded into the diner, giggling like a little girl with a secret supply of candy. She propped her guitar case against the counter, sat on her favorite stool, and waved to Rachel and Helena. "Hi, ladies. Beautiful day, isn't it?"

When Rachel arrived with water and silverware, Patty added, "And how are you this fine morning?"

Rachel smiled as she arranged the fork, spoon, and knife. At last, this was the Patty she'd first met after the concert at Father Thyme's, bright and open and seeing only the good in the world. She smiled and said, "Not as good as you, apparently."

"That's because . . . well, I can't tell you about it here. Can we go somewhere private?"

Rachel looked at Helena, who nodded. Rachel said, "Sure. Let's step outside."

Practically bouncing with eagerness, Patty followed Rachel out into the parking lot. They stood in the shade beneath one of the trees. "So what's up?" Rachel asked.

Patty sighed. "Last night I met a boy."

"Really?"

"Yes. He heard me playing my guitar and asked if we could jam. And we did." She leaned close and

whispered, "In every sense. It was amazing. And—"
She stopped and blushed.

Rachel grinned. *Her need shall be answered,* they'd
promised. "What?"

"Well, he saw my . . . tattoo. The one you and I
both got. Did I ever tell you about why I turned it
down when he first showed it to me?"

Rachel shook her head.

"It wasn't that I hated the design. I didn't. I simply
couldn't afford it, and I was too ashamed to say so. So
I pretended not to like it." She looked down at her
shoe scuffing in the dirt.

Rachel reassuringly touched her shoulder.

"Anyway, Dewey saw it. And he said it was beautiful. That it suited me."

"Did he know how you got it?"

"He didn't mention it, but it made me think. And
I've decided I'm going to keep it. And have it finished.
That way, it won't feel so much like a mark of violation
anymore. It'll feel . . . like *me.*"

"So when do I get to meet this Dewey?"

"Never, I'm afraid. It was his last night in town before he headed off to do charity work in Africa or
something. I probably won't ever see him again. But
that's okay, you know? Ever since the whole kidnapping thing, I've been . . . skittish. But he showed me
that I didn't have to be. Just because one man was a
psychopath doesn't mean they all are. Right?"

Rachel laughed and put her arm across Patty's
shoulders. "I'm very happy for you."

"I'm happy for me too. Before, it was like I was

inside Tupperware looking out. Now . . ." She giggled. "Somebody popped the lid."

Rachel kissed the top of Patty's head. She deserved to know. . . . Didn't she? Maybe not the explicit truth about her miraculous one-night stand but definitely about the spirits that brought him to her. Rachel was their avatar, but they called Patty their *treasure*. If anyone should know about them, it was her.

And wouldn't it be wonderful to finally have someone, a friend and a sister, to share this secret with?

She said to Patty, "Let's take a walk, okay?"

Patty shrugged and smiled. "Sure."

After alerting Helena and Clara, Rachel and Patty walked in silence down to Hudson Park. Rachel led her carefully around the effigy mound, not wanting to disrespect it, to the big gray rocks at the water's edge. They sat.

After a long moment gazing out at the sun-sparkling waters of Lake Mendota, Patty said, "That's weird."

"What?"

"The smell. That watery pond smell. I didn't notice it at the time, but that's what Dewey smelled like."

Rachel nodded and asked, "Do you know what lives in this lake, Patty?"

"Fish, I guess. Frogs, snakes. Those little lobster-looking things, what are they called—crayfish? Why?"

Rachel looked around to make sure they wouldn't be overheard. It was a hot summer day, and the lakefront houses on the opposite shore shimmered slightly in the haze. In the distance, a Jet Ski bounced along the waves. Children played out of sight in a nearby backyard, and an old man in black socks mowed the grass around his flower beds.

"What would you say," she began carefully, "if I told you there were also spirits living in the lake?"

Patty turned toward the mound behind them. "That's what those effigies are meant to represent, isn't it? Water spirits?"

Rachel nodded. "But I mean there are spirits in the lake *now,* as we speak. And they . . ." She trailed off, suddenly afraid, worried about how the words would sound. It was one thing to tell her lover in the dark, after sexual intimacy connected them, as she had done with Ethan Walker. To tell a girl who was to all intents and purposes still a stranger seemed impossibly daunting.

For twenty years Rachel had kept her relationship with the lake spirits a careful, deep secret. Now she'd told two strangers about it. Or at least that would be true if she went ahead with this conversation.

Twenty years. Almost as long as Patty had been alive.

"And they what?" Patty prompted, all wide eyes and encouraging smiles, bringing Rachel back to the moment.

Rachel took a deep breath. "Let me tell this all the way through before you say anything or ask any questions, okay?"

"Okay."

"There *are* spirits in the lake. They're related to the effigy mounds, but I'm not sure how, and I'm not sure if they're ghosts or have *ever* been human. When I was fourteen they saved me from drowning. They also became my first . . . lovers. I don't know who they are, or how it works, but when I'm underwater with them I don't need to breathe, and they treat me the way I want to be treated. As a woman, I mean. They connect with me , , , sexually."

She paused. Patty's expression hadn't changed: She was still open, waiting, sincerely accepting.

Rachel plunged ahead. "The water that seeped into the basement where Korbus had us all tied up? It was lake water, and by doing what I did"—*I masturbated in front of three other women,* she thought, and felt herself blush—"I was able to contact the spirits, and they passed the message on to Ethan."

"Ethan was the big man with the police when they broke in?"

Rachel nodded.

They sat without speaking for a long moment. The sounds of waves, wind, and traffic enveloped them. Rachel couldn't look at the girl, and couldn't believe she'd actually told her this story. Next she might as well post it to the *Lady of the Lakes* blog.

At last Patty said, "It does sound a little crazy, but I believe you."

Rachel laughed. "Is that right? Why?"

"Because you used it to save my life."

"A crazy woman could still be in the right place at the right time to be a hero."

"But I already believe in spirits, and faeries, and an unseen world. I believe I have a muse, and she sings to me when I can quiet my mind. Spirits are not strangers to me, so I have no problem accepting yours as real."

Rachel smiled at the girl's sincerity. "And you'll

keep this to yourself? Not tell your friends, or my friends, or anyone?"

"Of course." She made a sign of locking her lips and throwing away the key. "Magic is supposed to be secret, isn't it?"

"Yeah," Rachel agreed. "It is."

She was about to reveal her request to the spirits on Patty's behalf when the girl said, "Can I ask you something about them, though?"

"Sure."

"Have you ever felt like they meant you harm?"

"No, never. Why?"

"In all my reading about nature spirits, they all harm people. They don't always mean to, it's just that their priorities are so different from ours." She looked out at the lake, and then indicated the chemical foam that edged the shore. "We haven't treated their home very well. They have every reason not to like us."

"I've never felt any danger from them," Rachel said with certainty.

"That's good. I'd be too scared, I think, to let them do that to me."

Not if it was the only way you could have an orgasm, Rachel thought. She looked back at the water; where her eyes fell, the surface suddenly swirled, for an instant creating the illusion of a face gazing up from beneath. Then it was gone.

The moment must've been longer than she thought, because Patty said tentatively, "Is there anything else?"

Rachel smiled. "No, that's all," she said ironically. It wasn't, of course. But no one else, *no* one, knew that diner owner Rachel Matre, who claimed she didn't even own a computer, was secretly behind the gossipy and notorious *Lady of the Lakes* blog, where she passed on the secrets given to her by the lake spirits by hiding them among tidbits gleaned from conversations at the diner. And no one else ever *would* know.

As they walked back to the diner, Patty said, "I have some more good news. I have a gig this weekend. A *paying* one."

"Congratulations. Where?"

"I'm part of an all-star lineup of people you've never heard of." She giggled at her own joke.

"Is it time for the Atwood Street Festival again?"

"Nope, this is a one-off at Olbrich Park. Some kind of civic thing they want to be fun instead of boring. I'm right after the opening speaker, so I don't have to stick around all day. You want to come with me?"

"I'll have to check the schedule. Our weekends are pretty busy. But if it's at Olbrich, it may draw off a lot of our traffic. But only if you promise not to play that song about me."

Patty raised her hand and said, mock-seriously, "Musician's honor."

"Musicians have no honor," Rachel teased.

"Okay, Girl Scout's honor, then."

Rachel was about to ask if Patty had ever really been a Girl Scout but caught herself. Of course she had. That insane optimism would've made her perfect for it. "Then sure, I'll go. But I get a lifetime supply of free cookies if you're yanking my chain. Thin Mints."

"Those are the best, aren't they?" Patty agreed.

CHAPTER FOUR

EARLY SATURDAY MORNING, before sunrise, Kyle Stillwater stripped down to his swim trunks and stepped into the water of Lake Wingra. Although he chose this place and time for its privacy, secretly he was always disappointed that no one was there to see.

He was twenty-three, in tremendously good shape, and handsome enough that women were the least of his problems. His long black hair and high cheekbones spoke of his Native American ancestry, while his blue eyes were so light that some people assumed he was blind when they met him. And yet his acting career refused to take off.

He'd been stuck in Madison for three years since graduating from college. He'd made forays to both coasts, but despite a flurry of auditions, his best-paying gig had been posing for a series of romance-novel covers. That is, prior to the one coming up later today—*this* gig paid more than all his other acting jobs combined.

He sliced through the water, his muscles moving with ease. *An actor's body is his instrument,* one teacher said, *and he must keep it tuned at all times.* He reached the opposite shore and crawled out into the woods to a small clearing, where he did twenty minutes of calisthenics as the sky lightened above him. He'd be on public display for today's job, so he wanted his body firm and tight. He went over his lines in his head, ensuring that he had the speech down properly. It wasn't a long one, but his employer had stressed that precise wording was key.

Then he swam back. Halfway across the lake, something brushed his bare belly from below. It felt for all the world like a hand, and it brought him up short. He stopped, treading water for a moment, then decided he'd been mistaken.

Still, he felt a tingle of uncertainty deep in his belly. Lake Wingra, smaller than either Mendota or Monona, had a reputation for strangeness. He'd never experienced anything weird here before, but now the dark forests along the shoreline seemed filled with menace. Out of the corner of his eye something moved in the water, but by the time he turned it was gone.

He struck out for the shore again. He was barely ten feet from safety, in water no deeper than up to his knees, when the watery hands grabbed him and pulled him under.

THE WEATHER WAS perfect for the ground-breaking ceremony for Garrett Bloom's new community center: sunny, a comfortable seventy-five degrees, and a nice breeze off Lake Mendota. Olbrich Park, which abutted the old Parkside Hospital grounds, had been turned into a sixties-style hippie carnival for the day. Vendors, political booths, and street performers amused the attendees, and children played among bubbles and streamers. The resemblance to the Summer of Love was not planned; it was simply the way a certain segment of the isthmus population expressed themselves.

Mayor Joe Ciarimataro, district alderman Dora Flass, and two city court judges attended in their official capacities. The local media had turned out as well, but most of the crowd came from the neighborhood the center would ultimately serve. Longtime residents were delighted to be rid of the old eyesore of a building and to have it replaced by something that might actually help the area.

A flatbed trailer served as a stage, its unsightly parts hidden by a rippling banner that proclaimed "PBN: Progress Begins Now!" Logos of various sponsoring companies competed for space along the edges. On the trailer itself stood a lectern with a microphone and a row of empty metal folding chairs, each prominently marked "reserved."

"Great googly-moogly," Rachel said. She and Patty had walked the twenty or so blocks from the diner, and now stood on the sidewalk, looking down at the park. "All this just to tear down that old heap of bricks?"

"It's not just that. It's to break ground on a new community center," Patty said. "All these people will benefit from that."

"Uh-huh," Rachel said skeptically. "And the people getting the money to build it will benefit more."

"You're too cynical. Garrett Bloom is behind this, and he wouldn't do that."

Rachel said nothing. She didn't know Bloom, but she distrusted anyone with loads of money who tried to speak for the great unwashed.

Rachel followed Patty to the backstage area, a big plot of ground blocked off by a yellow plastic mesh fence. A serious-looking man in a crew cut checked a clipboard for Patty's name, then nodded for them to go through. For some reason, his presence annoyed Rachel; he seemed too *much* somehow, more security than an event like this needed. Or, she revised mentally, *should* need. He wouldn't have been out of place standing at the door of one of the Hollywood parties she saw on TV.

"Thanks for coming with me," Patty said as they approached the green-room tent. She wore a big floppy sun hat and her usual black performance dress. "I know it's probably going to be a bunch of boring speeches, but it'll be nice to see at least one familiar face in the crowd."

"Thanks for asking me," Rachel said. Her sundress rippled in the breeze, caressing her smooth legs. She wore almost nothing under it, and her skin adored the sensation. "This is my neighborhood, too, after all. And I needed to get out of the diner."

She looked up at the old mental-health hospital squatting beyond the trees, its empty windows like the eyes of some monster waiting to pounce. It was a rectangular structure built into the side of a hill, so that the second story had its own opening on the far side. Its white concrete walls were faded, cracked, and covered with gang-related graffiti. No glass remained in any of the barred windows. Local teens still used it for illicit activities, despite the fact that some of them had been found wounded or dead on its grounds. But then, that was teenagers for you. Every one of them thought themselves immortal.

"I *am* glad someone's doing something with that place, though," Rachel added. "It's been empty for too long."

Inside the backstage tent, young men and women in bow ties and tuxedo shirts, their armpits circled with sweat, dispensed drinks to the people milling about. Rachel recognized two local poets, several well-known businessmen, and at least one longtime occasional patron of her diner. Patty got herself and Rachel two bottles of water from an ice chest, and Rachel was just about to take a drink when she spotted the absolute last person she wanted to see.

"Shit," she said aloud before she could stop herself.

A tall blond woman stood with her back to them, speaking to a pair of men in suits and ties. She wore a sleeveless summer blouse and lightweight skirt, and her hair was brushed straight and shiny. She was clearly at ease with both their professional and personal attention. In fact, one of them blatantly appraised her rear end, shaking his head in admiration and winking at a friend across the room. The friend flashed a thumbs-up.

"Oh," Patty said. "It's that reporter, isn't it?"

"Julie Schutes," Rachel almost spat. She was an unethical news reporter and, more important, a former (and for all Rachel knew, current) girlfriend of Ethan Walker. "Let's get out of here before—"

Julie turned and spotted them. She quickly masked her moment of surprise behind cheery faux delight. "Shit," Rachel and Patty said in unison.

Julie excused herself from her admirers and sauntered over, champagne flute in hand. The two men appreciatively watched her walk away. She stopped before Rachel and Patty, one hip cocked like the silhouette on a summer beach novel's cover. Her press pass hung on a lanyard that dovetailed through her pushed-up cleavage. "Ms. Matre, Ms. Patilia," she said coolly. "I'm surprised to see you here."

"Yes, apparently they'll let any old riffraff in," Rachel said with a cold smile.

"Oh, that's right, Ms. Patilia is on the program, performing one of her little songs," Julie said. "And you're here for moral support, then?"

"Is this off the record?" Rachel snapped back. "You have a problem with that, as I recall."

Julie sipped her champagne and said, "Ms. Matre, your fifteen minutes are over, I'm afraid. There's no longer any 'record' where you're concerned. But," she added as she turned away, "I'll be sure to tell Ethan I ran into you."

Rachel was glad the light in the tent hid her blush. Patty shook her head and said, "Why do all the beautiful ones turn out to be such bitches? Shouldn't they be a little more kind and grateful? Isn't life easy enough for them?"

"They do it because they can." Rachel seethed quietly. She suddenly realized she'd clenched her fists so tightly that she'd crushed the water bottle, which leaked onto the grass by her sandals.

Patty took her arm. "Come on, then. Let's go out and mingle with *our* kind of people. We may not be cover models, but you can trust us not to stab you in the back."

Patty led Rachel out of the tent, around the stage, and into the expectant crowd milling out front. Rachel waved to Michelle, Helena's long-term partner, who sat behind a table selling homemade cellphone holders. Michelle was thin, with sharp features and close-cropped black hair, and she and Helena had the most stable relationship Rachel had ever seen.

Patty also waved to people she knew, and introduced Rachel several times. Rachel dutifully smiled and nodded, but five seconds later couldn't recall a single name. She was too busy fuming over Julie Schutes and the implications of her final words: *I'll be sure to tell Ethan I ran into you.*

So in the weeks since Rachel had seen him, while she'd thought of him almost constantly yet avoided the simple act of picking up the phone, Ethan had returned to the arms of his former lover. No doubt Julie had worn him down with well-timed bait-and-switch encounters, casual "oh, look who's here" moments at zoning meetings, fund-raisers, and whatever the hell else building contractors and reporters had in common. Perhaps she'd blithely offered to meet for coffee, or maybe a drink after work. An incautious word, a strategically undone button, and she would've set the hook, blissfully falling on her back as he dove in with all the enthusiasm of a kid at a toy store.

That had to be what happened. Because the alternative—that Ethan had sought out Julie because Rachel brushed him off—was too much to bear. She knew the lake spirits wouldn't abandon her, so once again her conscience demanded to know: What was she *really* afraid of?

"Let's go back to the tent," Rachel said suddenly.

Patty looked surprised. "Why?"

"Because that's where the free booze is, and I need a real drink."

Patty shrugged. "Okay."

Just before they reached the crew-cut sentinel, Patty spotted another friend, a tall girl with a ring through her nose and a tiny stud beneath her lower lip. Her name was Skyler something. Rachel dutifully shook hands and accepted the obligatory "Wow, you were the lady on TV, weren't you?" Then she rather rudely grabbed Patty's arm and turned to pull her out of the crowd. This was not getting her closer to the alcohol.

As she did so, she ran smack into Ethan Walker.

CHAPTER FIVE

ETHAN EMERGED FROM the backstage tent. He was oblivious to the admiring looks from the women in his immediate area. Clad in a suit and tie that fit his muscular body like they had been molded to it, he was a lone beacon of no-nonsense masculinity among the paunchy or effeminate elite.

He nodded at the crew cut–sporting guard, wondering anew at the need for his presence. Normally a scruffy college kid would do fine, and be much cheaper than this sort of muscle. Ethan recognized the body language as ex-military, and the hard little eyes as indicative of someone who enjoyed inspiring fear. But if the guard noticed anything about Ethan, he gave nothing away.

"Ethan!" a voice called, and he turned as Garrett Bloom approached. Even in the summer heat, he looked cool and perfectly groomed.

Ethan shook his dry hand and said, "Quite a soirée

you've put together here, Garrett. Must've cost a fair bit of change, for a charity event."

"Not so much as you would think. Most of it's donated or provided at cost. Besides, it's important to use occasions like this to foster a sense of community. We're all so tied in to our iPhones and PCs that we forget what human contact is like. Wouldn't you agree?"

"I never thought that hard about it," Ethan said honestly.

Another man joined them, and Bloom said, "Ethan, have you met James Red Bird?"

Red Bird was short and dark, and wore his long black hair tied back in a ponytail.

Ethan held out a hand. "Mr. Red Bird."

"Please, call me Jim," the man said as they shook. "Mr. Red Bird was my venerable ancestor." He winked, then smiled.

"You'll see a lot of Jim over the next few months," Bloom said. "He's going to be my contact person for this project."

"The Lo-Stahzi, ancestors of my own Karlamiks people, once lived on this land," Red Bird said with a sweep of his arm. "We can't get it back, but if we're involved with what happens to it, perhaps we can renew a bit of our identity. This community center is a good thing."

"I thought you said there were no Native American ties to this land," Ethan said.

"No, I said I could get around it in a way that benefits everyone. Jim isn't a flunky; he's a tribal representative and has a Ph.D. in Native American history."

"And I bowl two-seventy," Red Bird deadpanned.

"He can handle any heat from the Native American troublemakers."

"'Troublemakers'?" Ethan repeated.

"We have our own Al Sharptons and Gloria Allreds," Red Bird said. "They like to jump in front of cameras. The truth doesn't much concern them."

Bloom noticed someone else inside the green-room tent and said, "Ethan, if you'll excuse us, there's someone else I'd like Jim to meet."

As Ethan watched the two men depart, he recalled Ambika's suspicions. There was no reason both Red Bird and Bloom couldn't be sincere, but when someone claimed to work for the common good, their *own* good was often a big part of the equation. But did that really matter to him? He was just the damn builder, after all.

Lost in thought, he walked past the security point, anxious for some fresh, nonpolitical air. He bumped into someone coming backstage and said "Excuse me" out of reflex. Then he froze as he recognized Rachel Matre.

RACHEL STARED UP at Ethan openmouthed, as if some deity had appeared from the skies. He was certainly handsome enough for it, and the instant of contact, even cushioned by their clothing, was enough to send a jolt of excitement through her body. "Ethan," she said needlessly. Her voice sounded ragged inside her head.

He looked as flummoxed as she felt. "I, uh . . . Hi, Rachel," he said, and turned to the girl beside her. "Patty."

"Mr. Walker," Patty acknowledged.

Ethan turned back to Rachel. "Um . . . how are you?"

She had to lick her lips, which had gone dry. "Fine," she said. "And you?"

Patty leaned close to her and said, "I'm going over by the T-shirt booth." Rachel clumsily reached to stop her, but the girl disappeared into the crowd, leaving her alone—or as alone as she could be under the circumstances—with Ethan.

"I'm doing pretty well," Ethan said in response to her question. "I got the contract to build this new community center."

Okay, Rachel thought with relief, *we can talk about work. That's a safe topic.* "Not a bad score in this economy."

"No. A lot of people are out of work, that's for sure."

"And a lot more will be before the country recovers."

"That's what they say."

The conversation trailed to a halt, but they continued to gaze at each other. *I wonder what Julie sees in those big blue eyes when he looks at her,* Rachel thought.

Finally he said, "So how's business at the diner?"

"Doing great. Had to hire two part-time waitresses, in fact. And another cook."

"That's great news. Do you ever hear from those other girls?" He meant, of course, the two surviving college students who, like Rachel and Patty, had been kidnapped by Arlin Korbus.

"No. We're not a sorority, and we don't have re-unions. Last I heard they were all doing as well as can be expected under the circumstances."

He smiled and nodded. After another awkward silence, he said, "Well, I should go. I have to round up the shovels for the ground-breaking ceremony." He held out his hand. "Nice to see you, though."

She took it reflexively. "Likewise."

It had been a shock when they'd bumped into each other before. Now the moment their bare skin touched, it was as if it flipped a bank of switches inside her. Her knees grew weak, the bottom of her stomach dropped, and her nipples strained against the sheer sundress. The world around them paused, and she felt the tingles that signaled the buildup to her body's most intimate response.

Then he walked away and she stared after him, mouth open once again, glad that he couldn't hear the unmistakably throaty gasp that escaped her.

She looked around for Patty. Now she *really* needed a drink.

ETHAN'S FACE BURNED bright red and he feared his sudden, unexpected erection was visible to everyone he passed. He left the backstage area and hurried through the crowd, uncomfortably aware of all the other women dressed for summer around him. He kept his eyes straight ahead and his suit jacket closed until he found a clear space at the water's edge away from the frolick-ers. He closed his eyes and tried to think the most unerotic thoughts possible, desperate to deflate his urgent manhood. A visible bulge in the day's news photos would not send the right message to future potential employers.

The soft lapping of the water at his feet had the opposite effect, though. It vividly brought back his first (and so far only) night with Rachel, when she'd told him the story of her lake spirit lovers. It had been his idea for the two of them to go into the water together, and now he remembered the way she had clung to him, legs locked around his waist and arms wrapping his shoulders as she thrust wantonly against him. He stood waist-deep on the silty bottom, precariously balanced yet certain somehow that he wouldn't fall. She'd come then, loud and emotional and overwhelming, in what she told him was the first time ever with a man inside her. And he'd come into her as well, without protection but again secure in the inexplicable knowledge that there was no danger. He no longer needed porn; that encounter had fueled his masturbatory fantasies ever since.

He wiped his sweaty face with his handkerchief. This was *so* not the time for this, but the memories wouldn't stop. And now, after seeing her again, Ethan realized two important things.

First, he was in love with her. The real thing. The kind all the songs were about.

And second, since she'd never bothered to make contact with him since, she must feel differently. Hell, all she even wanted to talk about was work. If that wasn't a polite brush-off, then what was?

With that, his erection faded, and he closed his eyes against the despair that washed over him.

"Penny for your thoughts," a familiar voice said.

He turned to see Julie Schutes. "What are you doing here?"

She gestured with her champagne flute at the crowd behind them. "Working, what else? This is a big above-the-fold kind of story. A positive message about the power of neighborhoods and families, blah, blah, blah." She smiled—a dazzling display that would've brought a lesser man to his knees—and did a little turn for him that made her skirt flare just enough to flash her thighs. "And it gives me a chance to dress up."

He knew she was beautiful, so it wasn't a surprise. He also knew how her mind worked, which negated any of the beauty's effect. "If you went to all that trouble, shouldn't you get to it?"

She leaned against a tree, arching her back slightly so that her formidable breasts were on prominent display. The breeze rustled the branches above them, making patches of sunlight sparkle on her golden hair. "Ah, I can write this sort of thing in my sleep. I'm more concerned about you." Her voice grew serious. "How are you doing these days?"

"Fine. Busy. Making it. Why?"

"Because I *miss* you." She lowered her chin just enough to emphasize her blue eyes as she added, "Don't you miss me at all?"

"Sure. But you're always there in the papers, aren't you?"

She raised her hands. "Okay, okay, I can take a hint. I'll leave you alone. But seriously, Ethan, if you ever need to talk or . . . anything else . . . just let me know.

My feelings for you haven't changed, and I'm beginning to think they never will."

She gave him a tiny pout—so small she could deny it if he tried to turn it against her—and walked back into the crowd. She swung her hips with an extra bit of emphasis, and he couldn't help recalling other times when she'd moved them with equal skill.

And yet he felt nothing. His heart, and his body, belonged completely to Rachel Matre—as doomed as such dedication might be.

No, dammit, he thought. *I'm not just accepting this. I've got to talk to her about it.*

BEHIND THE STAGE, Garrett Bloom rattled off instructions to his assistant. She was tall and slender, yet her eyes radiated intense seriousness behind wire-framed glasses. She nodded along as he spoke.

". . . and make sure that Councilman Hawthorne is sober enough to get up the stairs. I don't want him falling down and making a scene like he did that time at the Mallards game."

"Already under control," Rebecca Matre said. "I had the waiter cut him off after one beer, and then sent that pretty little intern, the brunette with the big rack, over to talk to him. That seems to have kept him distracted," she added with wry distaste.

Bloom grinned and kissed her cheek. "Becky, I don't know what I'd do without you."

"Call the employment agency," she said simply.

"Not possible. You're irreplaceable."

"And you're late to start the show."

He looked at the clock on his BlackBerry. "Shit! I've got to hit the Porta Potti before we start." And he rushed off without another word.

JAMES RED BIRD sipped bottled water and watched Garrett Bloom's blond assistant. She showed enviable legs beneath the hem of her skirt, and a fine, firm bosom. She wouldn't likely turn to fat after childbirth the way his own wife had, he mused. Of course, she also probably wouldn't be as gullible as Helen Red Bird; few women, of any race, were. Or perhaps, since he was always traveling, Helen was just too tired from rearing three kids essentially as a single parent to put up much of a fight. He considered himself a reasonably faithful husband, but when the right morsel crossed his path, he wasn't above sampling the fare. And Bloom's assistant looked delectable.

Bloom emerged from one of the blue portable toilets and walked over to Red Bird. Red Bird nodded toward the blonde and asked, even though he knew, "Who's that again?"

"My assistant, Becky," Bloom said. "You've met her before."

"Oh, yeah. She's very pretty."

"She is that. And I can trust her, which is worth a lot more."

"But 'very pretty' isn't bad. . . ."

Bloom caught his tone. "Do not turn your Great Plains charm on that one, Jim, I mean it. I need her close to *me,* not distracted by the noble savage. Don't make me open a can of Great Spirit Whoop-Ass on you."

Red Bird grinned. "I cannot begin to tell you how many actionable offensive statements you just uttered, but I bet my tribal lawyer can."

"I'll see you in court, then. Now make yourself available for photo ops, will you? People need to remember you if our plan is going to work. In the meantime, I have to get this show on the road."

Red Bird bumped fists with Bloom, and the activist went off to coax the mayor to the lectern. Red Bird continued to mingle, but kept a surreptitious eye on Becky as she spoke into her Bluetooth and worked her iPhone's touch screen. He wondered if her skin was as smooth everywhere as it seemed to be on her calves.

BECKY FINISHED SENDING an email on her iPhone, then turned and let out a little yelp of shock. Her older sister, Rachel, stood right behind her. They both froze; neither had expected to see the other here.

Finally Rachel said, "This is a surprise."

"An unpleasant one for you, I'm sure," Becky snapped.

Rachel patiently ignored her tone and turned to the girl beside her. "Becky, this is my friend Patty Patilia. Patty, this is my sister, Rebecca."

"Nice to meet you," Patty said with a nod. "I've heard a lot about you."

"No doubt," Becky said disdainfully.

"All good, I promise," Patty said with a forced laugh.

Becky suddenly recognized Patty's name. "Wait, you

were another victim of that crazy tattoo artist, weren't you?"

Patty nodded. "Your sister saved my life."

"Oh, she's always trying to save people," Becky said bitterly.

Rachel forced a smile. "Well, good to see you, Becky. We'll let you get back to work."

"What makes you think I'm working?"

"You're backstage, you're dressed up, and you have a Bluetooth," Rachel said patiently.

"Yes, well . . . enjoy the ceremony." With that, Becky turned and walked away.

PATTY LEANED CLOSE to Rachel. "She seems very tense."

"She was born that way," Rachel said drily. But she shivered despite the heat as a premonition of danger rippled through her. Becky's slender feminine form, weaving among these powerful men, suddenly looked very vulnerable. And as she'd repeatedly demonstrated throughout her life, she had no capacity for recognizing imminent disaster. When they were children, Rachel had protected her as best she could; now no one looked out for her.

"It must be hard on you," Patty said.

Rachel shrugged. "It is what it is."

Patty noticed the flow of people out of the backstage area. "I think we're getting ready to start. I'll see you after my number, okay?"

"Okay," Rachel said. "Break a leg."

Patty scampered off, and Rachel joined the nonparticipants as they filed out to watch the show.

"LADIES AND GENTLEMEN, I'd like to thank you for coming to our little ceremony today," Garrett Bloom said into the microphone. He stood at the lectern and looked out at the motley crowd, waiting for their polite applause to die down. Hippie commerce continued at the booths, as the merchants showed no inclination to listen to speeches.

Mayor Ciarimataro had introduced Bloom following his own comments about the importance of community efforts, the verbiage all recycled from his reelection speeches. He called the center a "boon to its neighborhoods" and claimed the effort was actually part of his own long-range plan to revitalize neglected parts of the city. Bloom sat quietly through this, smiling and nodding along. The mayor could certainly claim credit, as long as he remembered it the next time Bloom came to him with a project.

"This new community center," Bloom now continued, "replaces an institution symbolic of society's past neglect of its most vulnerable members. It will be a beacon to the citizens of the isthmus, reminding us that neighborhoods still exist, and that moving forward into the future doesn't have to mean destroying the fabric of the past." There was more polite applause at this, one of his best-traveled tropes.

He glanced back at the dignitaries. The mayor and aldermen had on their public faces, but Ethan Walker looked uncomfortable. Inwardly, Bloom sighed; he'd picked Walker for his media-friendly status as a veteran and a local, but it was clear he'd have to work extra hard to get the man polished if he had no more public grace than this.

RACHEL STOOD NEAR the front of the stage and tried not to look at Ethan. She also tried to ignore the presence of Julie Schutes off to one side, listening intently as she scrawled notes. And she fought the urge to search for Becky behind the yellow fence. Which left her with nothing to focus on except Garrett Bloom's speech.

"And now, before we have the actual breaking of ground, I'm proud to present local musician Patty Patilia," Bloom said. He gestured dramatically as she emerged from backstage, carrying her guitar.

Patty stepped up to the same microphone and adjusted it to her height. Then she strummed a chord and began to sing.

Her song, "Give Thanks to the Waters," was about the need to respect the lakes and not treat them as trash receptacles. She rhymed "sturgeon" with "bludgeon," making it work vocally. She was preaching to the choir for most of the audience, and if the presence of the political bigwigs behind her made her nervous, it didn't show.

When she finished, the applause was polite, with pockets of genuine enthusiasm. Patty bowed slightly and said, "Thank you, ladies and gentlemen. And now I'll turn things back over to—"

She was interrupted by a woman's startled scream.

CHAPTER SIX

THE CRY RANG out across the park and silenced all conversation. It even startled a flock of birds from one of the big cottonwood trees. Everyone turned to find its source.

Then Patty, from her elevated position, muttered, "Oh my goodness." The microphone picked it up, and everyone followed her gaze.

A man stood at the very edge of the water, his back to the lake. Two huge trees framed him as if he were a statue in a shrine, and the sunlight glistened from his wet skin. His body was sculpted like some Greek god's, and his face was sharp-featured and aristocratic. He was bronzed and dark, with the unmistakable hues of Native American ancestry. At first he appeared to be naked and carnally impressive, but a second glance showed it was really one end of his wet loincloth hanging almost to his knees.

The only thing that spoiled the Native American effect was his hair. It was long, straight, and snowy white. The wind blew it back from his face, dramatically highlighting a sharp widow's peak.

He remained perfectly still, hands on his hips and chin high. If the scrutiny affected him, it didn't show. Rachel had the same thought as every other woman present: *I bet he's used to being stared at.* Certainly she felt a little catch in her throat as she took in his physical perfection.

He strode across the park toward the stage. He passed within touching distance, and Rachel had the almost unbearable urge to run her fingers down the broad muscles of his back. She had never felt such instant, powerful physical desire for a total stranger— not even for Ethan. And as he went by, his eyes flicked up and met hers for just an instant—a contact that she had not seen him make with anyone else. Her breath caught in her throat.

She turned away, certain that her lustful thoughts were visible, but realized at once that she was neither alone nor conspicuous. A teenage girl moaned audibly and squeezed her upper arms together, making her breasts thrust forward. Her nipples were visibly erect. Beside her, an older woman breathed rapidly and fanned her face with a program.

Patty remained frozen in place at the microphone, one hand against her chest as if she was short of breath. Garrett Bloom eased her aside and said into the microphone, "Ah . . . Hello, sir. I'm sorry, but I don't believe we've met. Can someone help you?"

The man stopped on the grass before the stage, again put his hands on his hips, and announced, "I am here to say . . ." he began, then faltered. "To say . . ."

Then his expression changed. He looked around as if waking from a dream. He took in the crowd, the lectern, and the old mental hospital. He turned and froze when, across the lake, he saw the distant dome of the state capitol rising above the city.

His brows knitted in fury. In a voice deeper and more mature than before, he said, "What has happened here?" Then he looked up at the lectern. "You. Are you the chief of this tribe?"

Bloom looked as confused as the man in the loincloth. "Am I what? Er . . . Yes, I suppose." He glanced back at James Red Bird, who shrugged.

"Then you are at war with the Lo-Stahzi," the man snarled. "This is *our* land, *our* home. And you have desecrated it. You have carved into the land and sent its spirits into exile. You have piled stones higher than the greatest trees, and for what purpose?"

This broke the spell for Rachel. *An activist,* she thought wryly, *who definitely knows how to work the crowd—or at least the female part of it.* But she knew the Lo-Stahzi had vanished long before the current tribes appeared, and even longer before the Europeans had settled the area. This had to be some publicity stunt, because there was simply no way this beautiful man could represent that long-dead civilization.

"Is that right?" Bloom said. "Well, sir, I don't mean to be rude, but there are no more Lo-Stahzi. The tribe is extinct. Now, who exactly are *you*?"

The man started to speak, then he got the same confused expression. When he spoke, his voice had returned to its original youthful sound. "I am . . . Artemak. No, wait, I'm . . . Kyle Stillwater. And I . . ."

He shook his head and said in the deeper voice, "I am glad you can understand me. Our languages are not so different, then."

"What?" Bloom demanded. He seemed more annoyed than angry. "What the hell are you talking about? Yes, I can understand you, but I think you're crashing the wrong party. This is the ground-breaking ceremony for the new community center; we're not desecrating anything."

"No, I'm supposed to be here," the man Stillwater mumbled in the younger voice. "Aren't I?" Then the outraged elder returned. "'Ground-*breaking*'?" he said, his eyes wide with horror. "You break the ground at your *whim*? You drive your implements into the soil with no regard for what exists there?"

"You're a member of Save the Moles?" Bloom said with a derisive chuckle. The dignitaries behind him laughed uncertainly. "Look, sir, don't make me throw you out. This is supposed to be a day of celebration. Just go on your way and we'll forget this happened, okay?"

Stillwater pointed a finger at Bloom. "This land you now desecrate with your very presence was once a sacred place where we, the Lo-Stahzi, communed with the spirits of the lakes."

Rachel gasped in a way that had nothing to do with Stillwater's sexual appeal. Was that mere rhetoric, or did he truly know about the lake spirits?

"Sir, I don't know who the hell you are, but I've invested all my time and energy into this project, into this place and these people, and I won't see it derailed by some hippie lunatic in his underwear."

"There is no spirit in your heart," Stillwater continued, smiling as if this realization pleased him. "It is an empty vessel. And it may have its uses."

"Okay, we really don't have time for this," Bloom snapped. "*Security!* Please escort Mr. Stillwater off the premises and into police custody."

Two big men—one of them the guard Rachel and Patty had encountered earlier—strode from backstage and started pushing through the crowd. The tightly packed women near Stillwater inadvertently impeded them. The men muttered apologies as they tried to work their way through without roughing anyone up.

Stillwater saw them coming and strode back toward the water, just evading the two security men. He walked into the lake without a backward glance and vanished beneath the surface. The security officers reached the shore just as he went under, but he did not reappear.

Rachel joined the crowd of fixated women at the water's edge, although she was more in control than most. If he knew about the spirits, was it possible that he *was* a Lo-Stahzi? And if so, did he possess more information about the watery beings who had possessed her body for all these years?

One of the security men pushed her aside. Rachel saw the flash of a small gun in the man's paw of a hand, but he quickly tucked it out of sight. "There's no sign of him," he said into the Bluetooth attached to his meaty ear.

As the security men retreated, two TV cameramen rushed to the edge of the lake and filmed the water's surface, waiting for Stillwater to reappear. But there was no sign of him, and the only boat visible was too far away for him to reach while swimming underwater. And if he'd hidden scuba gear, there would be telltale bubbles.

"Holy crap, who was that guy?" one cameraman said to the other.

"Some lost Chippendale dude who fell into the lake," the other said wryly. "Man, would you look at the way these chicks are panting after him?"

"Didn't look like an Indian to me, that's for sure," the first one said. "And where the hell did he go?"

Local news reporter Betsy Basker rushed up to the second cameraman. "Quick, I need to film some bookends with the lake behind me." She peered at her reflection in the camera lens and adjusted her hair.

"Your face is red," the cameraman said, amused.

She fanned it quickly. "It's just the heat."

"And your high beams are on."

"Then just zoom in tighter!" she snapped.

He smiled. "Uh-huh. Are you ready? In five, four, three . . ." He silently mouthed *Two, one,* and nodded for her to begin.

"This is Betsy Basker with *Channel Twelve News,*" she said, her on-air voice deeper than her normal one. "The mysterious interloper who called himself Kyle Stillwater vanished into the lake behind me, but his disruption of what should have been a celebration has left many involved red-faced." She stopped, silently counted to three, then said, "Betsy Basker, *Channel Twelve News,*" as a tag for the story when it was edited together.

Rachel stepped aside to let the newsmen past. They

would no doubt descend on Garrett Bloom next. She wondered if they would try to interview Ethan as well. Then she scowled, remembering that he had his own personal news reporter these days. Julie would cover him in every sense.

Through the din of murmurs, Rachel heard a nearby woman's voice distinctly say, "*Artemak* is here." She said it with such wonder and feeling that Rachel scanned the crowd for its source. She spotted a tall woman with dark hair standing at the front of the watchers, her face hidden from Rachel's position. Something told her this was the source, but before she could pursue it, the woman vanished back into the throng.

The crowd dispersed back to its carnival, leaving only a few people, all women, staring out at the water. Rachel headed back to the stage area to locate Patty.

JULIE SCHUTES STOOD in the shadow of a tree, scrolling back through the pictures on her camera. Kyle Stillwater was almost unbearably handsome, and just looking at his digital image made her insides quiver a little. It had been weeks since she'd been intimate with anyone, and that occasion had been nothing to write home about. But even her undeniable physical attraction to this trespasser didn't overcome her reporter's instincts. Who the hell was he, and why would he show up in nothing but a glorified jockstrap at this public occasion? If he really wanted to stop Bloom's little project, his choice of method left a lot to be desired. So what was he really up to?

She put the camera in her bag and took several deep breaths. The desire did not diminish, though. There was only one thing to do, and that was to find someone to help her satiate it. She knew, of course, exactly who she wanted to try first.

GARRETT BLOOM GLARED at James Red Bird and hissed, "What the *fuck* was that all about?"

"I don't know," Red Bird said with equal urgency. "It wasn't the script I gave him!"

"He's a damn activist, isn't he? *Swimming* here in his *underwear*! I tell you to get a goddamned actor, and you get Crazy Horse!"

"That's a racial—"

"Don't change the subject! The plan has now gone down the crapper. So what are we going to do about it?"

Red Bird shook his head. "I don't know."

"Well, you better pray I come up with something. And in the meantime, find that idiot and keep him out of sight!"

Red Bird, clearly annoyed at being the target for Bloom's rage, said sarcastically, "I'll tie him up in my wigwam."

"Whatever. And don't speak to the press about it. I'll handle them today and get a prepared statement out tomorrow."

Red Bird walked away muttering to himself. Bloom shook his head, then turned and let out a startled yelp. Ethan Walker stood right behind him.

"Was that a friend of Jim's out there?" Ethan said.

"What? No, it's—" Bloom took a deep breath,

pasted on his best smile, then put a hand on Ethan's shoulder. "Ethan, I'm really sorry. I guess we'll have to skip the whole ground-breaking thing."

"Why?"

"Well, for one thing, half the media's gone. They're all rushing back to file stories on that half-naked jackass."

Ethan nodded but made no effort to hide his skepticism. "Yeah, I guess they would be. Did you know anything about it ahead of time?"

"What? Of course not! Why would you say that?"

"Your whole spiel about getting around any Indian troublemakers. It seems like you might've suspected something was going to happen. Was that why you were reading Jim Red Bird the riot act just now?"

Bloom waved his hand. "It's completely unrelated. Now if you'll excuse me, I have to speak to what's left of the press and make sure they understand that this won't slow us down." A great shout rose from the remaining press corps as he ascended the steps to the stage.

THERE WAS SOMETHING off about this whole situation, but Ethan couldn't quite put his finger on it. It felt like theater, not like real life. Yet why *would* Bloom disrupt his own ceremony?

A woman engrossed in her iPhone walked past him, and he jumped a little, momentarily thinking it was Rachel. There was a definite resemblance in this woman's body shape and the way she moved. But when she paused in mid-step to listen to something on her Bluetooth, he realized who she was: Rebecca Matre. He'd seen her picture at Rachel's apartment.

For an instant, no more than a nanosecond, he pondered approaching her as a replacement for Rachel. Then he mentally kicked himself for even considering such a thing. Men *were* scum.

PATTY CAME DOWN the steps from the stage, pushed through the people milling there, and rushed up to Rachel. Her pale décolletage was flushed pink. "Wow, did you see that guy?"

"I think everybody saw him," Rachel said.

"Was he as gorgeous up close as he was from the stage?"

"He was easy on the eyes," Rachel agreed.

"The wives of all the big shots were looking at him the way a dog looks at a steak," Patty said. Then she noticed Rachel's distraction. "Are you all right?"

Rachel shook her head slightly. "Yeah, I'm sorry. It's just . . ."

"What?"

Rachel looked around to make sure they weren't overheard, then leaned close to Patty. "Do you remember what I told you about the lake spirits?"

Patty nodded. "He mentioned them, didn't he?"

"Like he knows about them," Rachel said. *Like he* knows *them,* she wanted to add.

"Maybe he was just being poetic," Patty said. " 'Spirits,' you know, like a nature religion, like paganism."

"Maybe," Rachel said. Then, gathering herself with an effort, she added, "Come on, let's get out of here."

"I'll get my guitar," Patty said, and scurried off.

Rachel wrapped her arms around herself. She felt different—wrong, somehow—as if the encounter with the strange man had upset her internal bearings. But she hadn't touched him or even spoken to him; all they had shared was a momentary glance.

In that moment, though, she felt as if she'd been laid bare for him. And perhaps the discomfort swirling in her now was because he had seen her for what she was.

CHAPTER SEVEN

RACHEL AND PATTY parted at Duncan Street. Patty walked up the tree-lined avenue to her student apartment, blithely whistling "Indian Reservation," and Rachel headed back to the diner. By the time she got there, Helena and Roya had already cleaned up and prepared for the next day, and Jimmy was just locking up. There was too much competition for the dinner crowd, so the diner served only breakfast and lunch. Rachel took a cursory look at the register receipts, saw no problems, and went upstairs.

After carefully locking her door, checking her blinds, and feeding Tainter so he'd stay off her lap, she took the computer from her closet and got online. The Lady posted a quick recap of the events at the park, and she was careful to phrase it so that it sounded like it might have come from someone involved, not just a spectator.

When she finished, she reread what she'd written and yawned. Then she deleted most of the adjectives, leaving only "handsome" and "scantily clad" to describe Kyle Stillwater. Otherwise it read like the overheated writing in a romance novel.

Yet even as she did this, she felt her own body shimmer with attentiveness. Just the memory of the way he'd walked across the grass, his body gleaming, his white hair billowing behind him, got her blood racing. She wondered if all the other women and girls were experiencing the same thing. If so, there were going to be some awfully lucky husbands and boyfriends reaping the benefits.

But not for her. Not yet, at least. She glanced at the clock and sighed. It would be hours before she could do anything about the nagging desire coursing through her. *Hours.*

ETHAN BOUNCED THE basketball against the ground and made an easy jump shot from what would have been the top of the key on a real court. He'd gotten better at it since his tour in Iraq; in high school he'd set an unofficial record for missing the most open layups.

He turned as the gate on the privacy fence squeaked open. A dark-skinned Asian man, much shorter and slighter than Ethan, entered the enclosed yard behind Ethan's house. He wore jeans and a faded Milwaukee Brewers T-shirt.

"Hey, Marty," Ethan called to his brother.

"Got a beer?" Marty Walker asked.

"In the fridge."

Marty went inside and grabbed two bottles. He

gave one to Ethan. "I hear you had some fun at the ground-breaking today."

"Yeah, you could say that. Some lunatic in a diaper tried to disrupt things."

"I also hear you ran into Rachel Matre."

Ethan frowned suspiciously. "And who told you that?"

"I'm a cop. I hear things."

"Yeah, well, I did, but that was all it was."

"So you didn't talk to her?"

"I was *working*, Marty."

Marty's face remained deadpan, but he clucked loudly like a chicken.

Ethan turned and shot the ball at the hoop, but it bounced impotently off the rim. "She said she'd call me when she was ready, Marty, and she hasn't called."

"Was she with anybody?"

Ethan caught the rebound, shot again, and this time missed entirely. "I don't want to talk about it, okay? I also saw Julie there, so why aren't you asking about her?"

"Because I thought you were smart enough to stay away from *that*." Marty set his beer on the patio table and caught the hard pass Ethan tossed at him. "I just can't believe you haven't at least called her. You're taking the whole keeping-my-word thing a bit too far, if you ask me." He jumped, shot, and hit nothing but net.

Ethan caught the ball on the first bounce. "Yeah, well, nobody asked you." But Marty's words only reinforced his own decision. It was time to stop waiting and take action. He dribbled to what would've been the three-point line on a real court, turned, and shot. This time, like his brother, he hit nothing but net.

PATTY PATILIA LAY on her bed in her underwear, the window open and an oscillating fan blowing across her sweaty skin. The afternoon had grown hot and still, and the scent of the lake drifted up from the shore. It reminded her of Dewey, and that in turn reminded her of their night together. It also brought back the vivid memory of the mysterious man who'd interrupted the ground-breaking ceremony. But even more, it recalled Rachel's story of the spirits living in the lake.

Patty had not been simply polite when she said she believed Rachel. As a child, Patty had regularly seen ghosts and faeries, and even as an adult she tried to stay open to the presence of the unseen. If someone as levelheaded and apparently normal as Rachel Matre believed there were spirits in the lake, then Patty had no problem accepting that.

And the *kind* of spirits Rachel described excited her. She wondered, if she approached them and offered herself, if the spirits would come to her in the same way. The thought was alternately exhilarating and terrifying, but after her experience with Dewey, she *wanted* to have a regular lover. Her sexual experiences had been infrequent and seldom matched her expectations. Now she was ready to be shown again how a woman *should* feel under her lover's hands.

She rolled onto her side and retrieved her cellphone from the nightstand. She pulled up Rachel's number and was about to dial when she changed her mind. It seemed like the wrong subject for a mere phone call: *Hi. . . . Whatcha doing? . . . Oh, really? . . . Say, do you think your supernatural lovers might have some available friends?*

Instead she sat up, stripped, and went into the shower, turning up the water as cold as she could stand it. She was supposed to accompany another songwriter at a local coffeehouse near midnight, and at the moment she was too distracted to concentrate. As the icy water pattered against her skin, she took long, deep breaths and tried to think of nothing but music.

THE AFTERNOON GAVE way to an evening that, for Rachel, seemed to draw on forever. At this time of year, it stayed light until nearly ten o'clock, and people stayed on the streets—and in the parks—until even later. There was nothing to do but wait it out—which was more and more difficult as the darkness fell. She felt both tense and lethargic, and the desperation for contact with her spirit lovers was tempered by a sense of impending, inexorable doom.

Her cellphone rang at ten-thirty. She recognized the number and said, "Hi, Becky," as cheerily as she could.

"Hey," Becky said neutrally. "I hope it's not too late to call."

"I'm wide awake."

"Me too." She sighed—a sound that Rachel knew very well. "I've been going over the disaster in my head all day."

"'Disaster'?"

"At the park," Becky said impatiently. "In case you

didn't know, that was a big deal for my boss, which makes it a big deal for me."

"I'm sorry, I wasn't thinking. Have they found that guy yet?"

"No, he hasn't popped back up. And he hasn't made any statements to the media."

"Maybe it was just a prank."

"No. Garrett has a lot of enemies, and I'm sure one of them is behind it. We just have to be ready for the next offensive."

"I'm sorry, sweetie."

There was a pause. When Becky spoke again, her words had their normal bitterness, but the tone was somber. "I have a problem of my own too. I don't know if you want to hear about it."

"Of course."

There was another pause. "I think I'm . . ."

The connection hissed so long that Rachel was afraid they'd been cut off. "Becky?"

"Nothing." Becky sighed wearily. "It's my own problem. I'll deal with it. I'm sorry to bother you, Rachel."

"No bother," Rachel said, but Becky had already hung up.

She stared at the phone in her hand and considered calling her back. But their relationship didn't work that way. They spoke when Becky wanted, and only about Becky's problems.

And at the moment, Rachel had enough problems of her own.

CHAPTER EIGHT

DETECTIVE LAYLA MORRISON sent the uniformed officer to the back of the apartment building to watch the patio doors. She'd seen too many suspects bolt out the back door when cops knocked on the front, and wanted to be certain this one wouldn't escape. Mayor Ciarimataro had personally told the chief to handle this quickly, and lucky Layla got the job.

She knocked firmly—the cop knock that everyone in these low-income apartments knew all too well. "Mr. Stillwater," she called, "it's the police. Open up."

It took a moment, but eventually the porch light came on and the door opened. A young man, clearly Native American, squinted out at Layla. "Yeah?" he said sleepily.

She held up her badge. "Detective Layla Morrison. Are you Kyle Stillwater?"

He looked puzzled. "Yes. Why?"

"May I come in?"

"Um . . ."

"I come in, or you come downtown."

"Okay, okay. It's just . . . I wasn't expecting company."

That proved to be an understatement. The tiny apartment was filled with pizza boxes, fast-food bags, and soda cans crushed flat and placed in paper bags. There was a TV, an old Xbox, and a few paperback copies of famous plays. On one wall hung the only decoration: an 8×10 professional glossy of Kyle Stillwater, his shirt open to show his chest and his long, shiny black hair. Across the bottom, written in bright blue ink, was the word "Super!"

Stillwater, dressed only in tight blue jeans, kicked aside enough detritus to expose the couch. "Have a seat."

"No, thanks. Is anyone else here?"

"No."

"Are you an actor, Mr. Stillwater?"

"Yeah."

"Do you own a white wig?"

He blinked. "Huh?"

"How old are you?"

"Um . . . twenty-three."

He looked it, too. The man who disrupted the ceremony, though, had been at least ten years older. Could it have been makeup? "Where were you this afternoon between twelve and three?"

"Here. I was sick, I think."

"You think?"

"No, I was sick."

He didn't sound guilty or stoned, just sleepy and

confused. He also wasn't anything like the sex god described by the women who saw him at the park. Then again, he was an actor. "Someone who called himself Kyle Stillwater disrupted a civic event in Olbrich Park."

Stillwater looked like he had trouble following her statement. "Someone . . ."

"There aren't a lot of Kyle Stillwaters in the area. In fact, there's precisely one."

"Well, it wasn't me!"

"Can anyone corroborate that?"

He looked confused at the word "corroborate."

"Can anyone give you an alibi?" she repeated patiently.

"No, I've been sick. I told you."

He wasn't old enough to be the guy from the park, she thought, and he certainly seemed legitimately sick, or at least out of it. She could haul him in for questioning, see if he was on drugs, but her gut told her this wasn't the guy. "All right, Mr. Stillwater, it looks like some weird case of identity theft. Someone used your name. But I'm going to leave my card so if you hear anything you can call me. You'll do that, right?"

Stillwater took the card and looked at it. "Yeah, sure."

WHEN THE POLICEWOMAN left, Kyle Stillwater put the card under a magnet on the refrigerator, stumbled back to the bedroom, and was unconscious before he hit the mattress. In his dreams he swam without any need to breathe, past the faces of others similarly engaged.

AT MIDNIGHT, RACHEL could stand it no longer. For discretion and safety she wanted to wait until later, but the need was simply too great. She'd been pacing her apartment, naked, for an hour.

The parks all closed at eleven, and since the Korbus kidnappings, the police had been extra-diligent about chasing people away. They also made frequent patrols during the night, but that wasn't a problem. She needed only a small window of time unobserved. Once she got into the water, she'd be fine.

She put on her T-shirt, running shorts, and tennis shoes; locked the door behind her; and started down the street toward Hudson Park. The air shimmered with humidity, making halos around the pink streetlights. Insects swirled about them, and when she began to jog she felt tiny midges against her legs and face.

The sidewalks were deserted, and most of the houses were dark. She ran silently through the neighborhood of big lakeshore homes, breathing methodically and enjoying the feel of fresh sweat on her skin. The whole Arlin Korbus affair had made her slightly paranoid; she checked often for pursuit and perused shadows for unexpected movement, but she could accept this small-scale PTSD. Korbus was dead by her own hands, and the chances that another of his ilk lurked nearby were astronomical.

"Rachel!" someone called out.

She jumped, startled, and would've sprinted away

had she not recognized the voice. A young man emerged from one of the side streets, also dressed for running. His hair was dyed jet-black with lighter tips, and he had huge hoop modifiers in his earlobes. She'd met him once before, on a night when she was too busy to stop and talk. "Ace, right?"

"That's it," he said with a grin. His inherent shyness overcame his attempt at blasé cool. "Ace is the place. Mind if I run with you?"

Something about his boyish friendliness made her smile. "Okay, for a bit. But part of the reason I run at night is for privacy."

"I understand. Me, too."

They ran three blocks without speaking, their feet making smack-slip noises on the concrete. A carful of teens passed and hollered something, but it was drowned out by their thumping bass. When Ace and Rachel reached Williamson Street, where Father Thyme's coffee shop and the Sparkler pizza place were still crowded, Rachel stopped, put her foot on a fire hydrant, and stretched her calf muscles. Ace did the same, and she caught him surreptitiously trying to peer down the neckline of her T-shirt.

She laughed. From most men it would be either threatening or insulting, but it endeared this boy to her even more. "Ace, do you really think my boobs are that different from any other woman's?"

He looked down. "Well, they're all beautiful in their own way."

She mussed his hair like a child's. "Ace, really. I'm too old for you. You should have a girlfriend your own age."

He still didn't meet her eyes. "I did, sort of. We just broke up. She just seemed so . . . immature sometimes."

"She'll grow up. And so will you." She nodded toward the street that led eventually back to the lake. "This is where we split up, okay? I'll see you around." She crossed the street before he could say anything else.

Still smiling at the smitten boy's sincerity, she passed the looming trees of big Martyn Park, where dozens of people lounged in the shade or tanned beneath the sun during the day, and continued around the curve to her precious refuge, Hudson Park—barely larger than the low effigy mound it existed to protect. Soon she would be naked, caught in the carnal embrace of her waterborne lovers. She began to tingle with anticipation.

But suddenly she froze. In the night's silence, the squeak of her sneakers against the pavement as she stopped might as well have been a scream.

A tall silhouette stood at the top of the hill—*her* hill—beside the effigy mound. He gazed down at the hidden spot where she undressed and entered the water. And the stranger did not move or look back, even though he must've heard her approach.

The broad shoulders and narrow hips were thoroughly masculine. Her first hopeful thought was *Ethan!* If it *was* him waiting for her, knowing she would come to this park, she would throw herself in his arms and make love to him right there. And never let him go.

But the instant she had the thought, she knew it was wrong. The silhouette *did* look familiar, but it was definitely not Ethan Walker. It was also too broad and muscular for Ace. Who was it, then?

Except for breathing, she did not move. And for a long time, neither did the stranger. Then he crouched and did something with his hands near the effigy mound's head. She drew breath to shout, but sweat trickled into her eyes. In the brief moment as she paused to wipe it away, he vanished into the shadows.

She walked slowly forward, alert for any movement. She crossed the damp grass and reached the spot by the effigy mound, every muscle tense. In the faint illumination from the streetlights, she saw a dozen small rocks arranged in a circle a foot in diameter. She picked up one and held it toward the pinkish lights. It was a normal rock—the smooth kind found in any garden, or pulled from any stream or lake—but painted on it was a strange symbol.

She carried it up the hill to see it better. It resembled the Christian ichthus symbol but instead of graceful curves it had sharp edges and points. When she touched it with her finger, she saw that it was drawn on with mud. Her touch smeared one line.

She was about to toss it aside but at the last moment felt a powerful compulsion to return it to the ring on the ground. After she did so, she took several deep breaths and looked out at the water, which was normally inviting and irresistible. Now, though, it seemed subtly repellent. Encountering the stranger here had somehow broken the mood.

She could still swim, she knew. Chances were the spirits, with their intimate knowledge of her moods and responses, would have her moaning within minutes. Or she could go to another part of the lake. The spirits would be there wherever she swam, but she just couldn't muster the desire to act on those certainties.

Who had the man been? And why did he look familiar? She knew many men socially, most through the diner, but she could not place this one.

Then as a little shudder ran through her, she realized who he was: *Kyle Stillwater.* She'd watched the half-naked Adonis stride into the lake, and he'd looked exactly like this man in silhouette. But why in God's name would he be here? And what did that circle of stones mean? Had he built it or just examined it as she did?

It was all too weird. She turned and jogged back the way she came, then cut up three blocks before turning back toward home. Her feet echoed oddly, as if someone followed and matched her stride precisely, but whenever she looked back, the sidewalk was empty.

CHAPTER NINE

POSTED BY THE Lady to the *Lady of the Lakes* blog:

> Those of you who were there know what I'm talking about. The big ground-breaking ceremony for the new community center was hijacked by one fine piece of manhood who came out of the lake in a temper and very little else. The Lady isn't sure about his claims regarding the plot of land, but she does agree that he can protest anywhere he wants to.
>
> Does anyone have any good pictures to share?

THE STORY OF Kyle Stillwater's startling appearance at the park was on the front page of the Sunday *Capital Journal* and was the lead on the three local TV stations. Missing from them all, though, was any picture of the man himself. Owners of every electronic recording device—digital still cameras, video cameras, or cellphones—found that any images were hopelessly corrupted.

Even Julie Schutes, who had checked her photos right after she took them, had found them pixilated beyond any possible use once she returned to her office. Only one picture—a distant one that showed Stillwater as a mere silhouette standing in the lake and taken from her stall by a seller of hemp products—survived.

Most interesting were the photographs taken on actual film by a couple of camera buffs. In these, Stillwater's features were both blurry and distorted: His eyes were round and black, his nose and chin elongated, and his mouth a death's-head grimace.

These photos did not run in the papers, and the photographers were unable to scan them and post them online. When they tried, the hardware and software refused to cooperate.

The newspaper's staff researcher did find the photograph of a local actor known as Kyle Stillwater—a one-quarter Ho-Chunk Native American who'd done some modeling and commercial work. He resembled the man who'd crashed the ceremony, except that he was ten years too young and his hair was jet-black. And when shown his picture, all the women who'd been at the park that day were absolutely certain it wasn't the same man, because this mundane Kyle Stillwater just didn't affect them the same way. At all. It *couldn't* be him.

No one could reach the actor for comment. His agent in Chicago said he would pass along any media requests but could assure the authorities that his client had no paying jobs at the moment.

_____

WHEN ETHAN WALKER got to work Monday morning, Garrett Bloom was already there, pacing in front of Ambika's desk. Her expression indicated just how long that had been going on. "I thought you got here at ten," Bloom snapped without preliminaries.

Ethan clenched his teeth in annoyance; he didn't like being scolded, let alone in his own office before he'd had his coffee. He glanced at the clock. "It's five after."

"That's still late."

"Since I'm the boss, no one usually complains about my punctuality."

"On most days," Ambika muttered.

Bloom scowled at her, then said urgently, "I have to talk to you in private. _Now._ It's important."

"Okay. Ambika, hold all my calls until Mr. Bloom and I are finished."

"Of course, sir," she said coolly.

Bloom barely waited for the inner door to close behind them before he said, "You've got to start doing the serious construction _now._ Today, if at all possible. Bring in a crane, knock down some walls, that sort of thing. Stuff people can _see._"

"Why is that?"

"Momentum, son. A body at rest tends to remain that way, but one that's moving is hard to stop."

"That's 'inertia,' not 'momentum.'"

"Well, whatever it is, we need it."

"Because of what happened at the ceremony?"

"_Yes!_" Bloom exclaimed as if it was the dumbest question in the world. "It has nothing to do with whether or not he's right, or legitimate, or anything. He's drawn attention, and that's what's important. I expect a half-dozen Native American activists in my office before the day's over."

"Isn't that what James Red Bird is supposed to handle?"

"Jim is a good man, and loyal, but he's a behind-the-scenes worker. This has changed the whole game plan."

"Why?"

"Because even if that lunatic was right, it's immaterial, because it can't be proved without a full-on archaeological dig that could take months, even years."

Ethan hoped his sinking dread didn't show. "That's true."

"But there's no *evidence*, Ethan, and I'm certain no elected official in his right mind would shut down something that provided jobs for hardworking Americans. In this economy, jobs outweigh history."

"Except to stray Native Americans."

"Exactly!" Bloom almost shouted, missing Ethan's irony entirely. "That's why we need to get the ball rolling."

Ethan thought hard before speaking. "The soonest I can do what you're asking is next week."

"Next *week*?"

"Yes. And you'll have a hard time finding anyone else who could do it faster—and frankly, I wouldn't trust anyone who said they could."

Bloom thought for a moment. "Then that's the best you can do?"

"It's the best *anyone* can do," Ethan said firmly. "I

promise, a week from today there will be a procession of very visible big trucks carrying debris while we gut the building. And then we'll very publicly knock it down."

Now it was Bloom's turn to ponder. "All right, then. If that's the best that can be done, that's what we'll do. Thanks, Ethan. I'm sorry this has all gone to hell this way."

When Bloom departed, Ambika came in, crossed her arms, and said, "He is *not* a nice man. Before you arrived, he stepped out in the stairwell to make a phone call. His voice was very loud. He called someone a 'dumb Indian.' For a moment I thought he was referring to me, but it was the person on the other end of the phone. I do hope he won't be a frequent visitor."

Ethan assured her he wouldn't—and then, when Ambika had returned to her desk, he dialed up the State Archaeological Commission office. He had a friend on staff there and knew he could get straight information.

"Yeah, I saw that on the news," Lannie Boyd said when Ethan reached him. "They didn't have a picture of the guy, though. I was curious to see if he was someone I knew."

"Is that likely?"

"I cross paths with a lot of so-called activists. Some are legitimately concerned with tribal dignity, and some are just out to see their names in the papers."

"So his claim *could* be legitimate?"

"As a matter of fact, I did some proactive checking on that very thing, just so I'd know where to find the information in case anyone needed it."

"And what did you find?"

"Nothing. When that old mental hospital was originally put up, a standard survey revealed no trace of former Native American habitation on that patch of land. Of course, they called them American Indians then, but you know what I mean. It was classified 'clean and pristine,' as we say unofficially."

"So I have nothing to worry about?"

"We have better technology now, and I'm sure if you dug down far enough and sifted every square inch of dirt, you'd find some trace of human activity. These lakes have been around for a long time, after all. But those guys back then knew their stuff, even without computers and DNA analysis, so until there's hard evidence to the contrary, I'm inclined to think they got it right."

"That's not just you sticking up for your profession, is it?"

"Maybe a little. But if there was serious doubt, we'd get out there and look around. Fieldwork is fun."

Ethan tapped his fingers on the desk. "I'm supposed to start tearing down the building next week, Lannie. I really don't want to get blindsided."

"I can understand that. If you like, I can come over and check it out, unofficially officially, if you know what I mean."

"That'd make me sleep better," Ethan said.

"I thought that's what that blond reporter was for."

Ethan felt his cheeks burn. "Ah. She's old news."

"Really?" Lannie said with mock interest. "So she's on the market?"

"She'd eat you alive, Lannie."

"A man's got to die of something."

After the call, Ethan retrieved the survey maps of the lakefront and studied them. How exactly had Bloom gotten title to such a prime piece of real estate? For that matter, why had it lain undeveloped for so long in the first place? Lakeside property in Madison was in sky-high demand.

He scanned the lakeshore to either side of the parcel. There were effigy mounds in three nearby city parks, but they made no pattern implying one might have originally been located at the hospital site. Still, if Stillwater was part of some fringe group—and God knows Madison had plenty of those—his performance might be the start of something darker and more dangerous. People with environmental blinders on thought nothing of doing things that resulted in human injuries or death.

He gazed out the window at the capitol dome and went over his options, but he knew there was only one real choice. And he'd made it when he shook hands with Bloom.

IN HIS OWN office on the west end of the isthmus near the university hospital, Garrett Bloom continued to pace. It was his preferred mode of thinking. He'd worn the carpet in a circuit from his desk around the guest chair, to the door, and back. "Maybe it's Seth Golfine," he said at last.

"No," Rebecca Matre said. She sat on the edge of the desk, legs crossed below a tight skirt. She knew he frequently checked out her legs, and she liked it. Then again, he checked out every woman's legs. "If he was against it," she continued, "he'd do it in public. Remember the hissy fit he threw when you wanted that homeless rapist released on bail?"

"Homeless *accused* rapist," Bloom corrected. "And that scene at the lake was pretty fucking public."

"But *he* wasn't there. He's too much of a media whore to let someone else take the spotlight." She smiled. "And personally, I'd just as soon never see him walk around in a loincloth."

Bloom barked a laugh at the image. "You're definitely right about that." He paced some more, then snapped his fingers. "Maybe it's Asshole Anspach."

"And why would *he* do it?" Becky asked wearily. They'd spent the morning this way, as Bloom went down his list of enemies, trying to figure out who might be behind the ceremony's disruption. It was a long list, and Becky was already exhausted. But so far they'd identified no one who seemed likely to concoct such a bizarre stunt.

"Why would he do it?" Bloom repeated. "To make me look bad, that's why. To get revenge for all those times I've pushed things past him to get them approved by the full city council."

"It seems out of character for him. He's more the slash-your-tires-in-the-parking-lot type."

"Ah, you're right. It's silly. Still . . ." He stopped at the window and looked out at traffic on University Boulevard. "It looks like the only way to find the brain behind it is to find the body first. We have to locate that guy—the one who came out of the lake."

"Kyle Stillwater?" Just saying the name sent an

intimate flutter through Becky. She'd been awake a good part of the night fantasizing about him. It was out of character for her; Becky just didn't lust after good-looking men like that. She preferred men of substance, with brains and goals and power. Like Garrett Bloom. But her body had certainly pursued its own ideas, leaving her with no choice but to indulge them. Her cheeks reddened at the memory.

Bloom was too preoccupied to notice. "That's not his real name, I'm sure. 'Stillwater'? Give me a break. But just to be safe, can you do some of that Internet hoodoo that you do so well? See if you can find out anything about him?"

"I already started," Becky said. "There's a local actor, a Native American, by the same name and who vaguely resembles the man we saw. I Photoshopped white hair on him, though, and it just wasn't him. I'll keep looking, though."

As she stood, she bumped into Bloom during one of his circuits, and he caught her awkwardly in his arms. Their faces were inches apart.

Becky gasped with delight. She enjoyed the way his hands felt through her blouse, their long fingers promising nimble foreplay. His left palm rested over the clasp to her bra, and she wondered if he could undo it one-handed. She felt his body against hers, lean and hard from regular exercise.

She looked into his eyes. *Kiss me,* she thought desperately, wishing she was telepathic. *Bend me over your desk, or push me to my knees before you. It's all right, I'll do anything you want. Anything.*

"Anything," she said, sighing.

He leaned close. His breath was minty. Then he released her. "Sorry, Becky, I should've watched where I was walking. Let me know if you find out anything."

Then he sat back behind his desk and pulled up something she couldn't see on his computer. Her skin tingled where he'd touched her through her clothes, and she seriously considered throwing herself across his desk and begging him to have his way with her. He was everything she admired: strong, committed to a cause, and mature. She wanted to be his lover, his student, his slave.

But she said, "No problem," and went back to her own desk outside his office. She closed the door behind her, knowing he preferred privacy.

CHAPTER TEN

ON TUESDAY MORNING, Rachel's diner was as busy as ever. Rachel, Helena, and Clara waited on the customers. Clara, dressed in tight shorts and a push-up bra, was a hit among the young men, and even old Professor Denning let his eyes follow her a couple of times.

Marty Walker sat at his usual counter stool, immune to the perky breasts repeatedly passing by. He wore his lightweight summer suit, which did nothing to hide the bulge of the gun beneath his left arm. When Rachel brought him a coffee refill he asked, "So how's the tattoo removal going?"

"Surprisingly well," she said with no irony. "I think I'll be done early, in fact."

"I have a friend on the force who had to get his ex-wife's name taken off his arm. He said it was the second-worst pain he's ever felt."

"What was the worst?"

"Marrying her in the first place."

They laughed, and Rachel tried to make the next sentence sound as casual as possible. "Oh, by the way, I ran into your brother over the weekend. Literally, in fact. At the ground-breaking for the new community center."

"Oh, yeah, I heard about that."

Her blush hit before she could do anything to stop it. "He told you about it?"

"No, I mean I heard about what happened at the park when Aquaman came out of the water."

Rachel's blush deepened. "Oh. Of course. Yes, it was quite a show." *Just walk away,* she told herself, but her feet stayed resolutely put. "Ethan looked well," she prompted.

Marty shrugged. "He's healthy."

Don't do it, her common sense warned. But she said, "And I saw his girlfriend, too."

Marty frowned. "Girlfriend?"

"Julie. The reporter."

Marty laughed. "No, they're not back together. She's chasing, but he's on full evasive maneuvers. He knows better than to get caught up in *that* drama again."

Her knees grew weak at the rush of relief. "Really?"

He reached across the counter, took her hand, and said gently, "Rachel, you asked him to stay away, and he *will* until you tell him not to. He gave his word, and that's the most important thing he has. It's stubborn and ridiculous and old-fashioned, but that's what he's like."

"I know," she murmured, like a child caught in a fib.

Marty released her. "And I know he'd love to hear

from you. I know it the same way I know the sun comes up in the morning. But one of you has to make the first move here."

"I know," she repeated, and rushed away to take another order as fast as decorum allowed.

MARTY CAUGHT HELENA'S eye across the room. The two of them had conspired to bring Ethan and Rachel together in the first place. Now they were working desperately, if delicately, to get them to at least talk to each other.

Helena shrugged. Marty nodded.

IN HIS EFFICIENCY apartment on the city's north side, Kyle Stillwater winced as he opened his eyes. He lay atop the covers on his bed, in nothing but his white briefs. The hangover rattling through his brain was the worst he could remember. As he stared up at the ceiling, he heard a fly buzzing against the window glass and Spanish-speaking children playing outside.

He swung his legs off the edge of the bed and sat up. What the hell had happened to him? His last clear memory was of swimming in Lake Wingra. He certainly hadn't been drunk then. In fact, he hadn't been drunk in six years—no mean feat with the alcoholism in his family. He fumbled for the remote on the nightstand and turned on the TV.

The smug weatherman said, "The forecast for today, Tuesday, is sunny and hot, with a slight chance of—"

Kyle sat up straight, his head suddenly clear.

Tuesday? What happened to Saturday? Or Sunday? Or Monday?

He tried to stand, but his head swam as soon as he did, and he landed back on the bed. His stomach churned with nausea and panic. He crawled to the bathroom and vomited, then lay curled on the floor for a long time, too sick to even flush. He tugged a lock of his black hair over his eyes. At last he rose to pull the handle and glanced into the bowl.

He froze.

The contents of his stomach looked like lake water, algae, and silt. There was even a dead fish floating on top.

He vomited again and passed out.

WHEN THE BREAKFAST rush ended, the diner settled into the slow, comfortable space before lunch. The summer sun blasted through the windows and off the white walls made of dry-erase board. In addition to the day's menu, some of the panels sported elaborate customer artwork, including some leftover "Welcome back, Rachel" messages that hadn't yet been wiped away.

Helena's shift had ended at ten-thirty. Clara was the only other waitress on duty, and she was clearly exhausted. She went into the kitchen and wiped her neck with a wet paper towel. "I thought," she said, "that the summers weren't as hot in the north."

"No, they're not as long," Rachel said. "They're plenty hot. And we have wonderful humidity."

"I'll say. I used to spend my summers doing volunteer

work on an elephant sanctuary in Tennessee, and this reminds me of that. Without the smell of elephant manure, of course."

"They have an elephant sanctuary in Tennessee?"

Clara nodded. "For abused zoo and circus elephants. They have all this acreage to roam on however they want. People can't come and stare at them, either."

"Sounds pretty freaky," Jimmy the cook said. He scraped leavings from the griddle and dumped them in the garbage. "I wouldn't mind wandering around on a big nature preserve. Seems kind of wrong that elephants get to do that and people don't."

"The elephants only get to do it because of the way people have treated them," Clara pointed out.

"Yeah, well, some people have treated me pretty badly, too," Jimmy mumbled.

Rachel's eyes fell on Jimmy's lean forearm. The muscles rippled beneath his skin, and Rachel suddenly recalled in uncomfortable detail the muscles across Kyle Stillwater's back. He'd passed so close on that first day that she'd felt the heat from his body, every muscle hard and perfect. It was a memory that had replayed itself endlessly in her mind and dreams, especially since she'd glimpsed the man at the park. Had it *really* been him?

Yet her reaction was not entirely one of lust, although that was definitely a component. It was, instead, a kind of cruel fascination, reminding her that twice she'd missed the chance to touch him. And it made no sense, since she was still fully and desperately in love with Ethan Walker.

But it was no longer images of Ethan that filled her head in the darkness. For the past two nights, she'd writhed in a tangle of damp sheets, alternately frenzied and lethargic. She felt taunted by her own body and the powers that possessed it, but sleep never came in any restful form.

Now a haze of feverish, unhealthy desire settled on her whenever she let her attention stray from any immediate task. She wondered if any of the other women from the ceremony had experienced the same thing. Certainly they'd stared as hard.

Oswald Denning sighed and stretched, his fingers threaded together over his head. The ancient tweed jacket that he wore in all weather revealed a split seam beneath one arm. "I think I shall adjourn to the library," he said as he stood. "Even at my age, 'publish or perish' still applies. Good day, ladies."

As he went into the sun, a surge of AC-defying heat pushed its way inside. Clara fluttered the front of her apron. "I wish we had one of those airlock double doors like they have at Denny's."

Rachel looked up sharply. Before she could snap back, Jimmy said, "Don't tell me I just heard the D-word!"

Clara saw Rachel's expression. "Yikes, I didn't mean anything by that. They have the same doors at Walgreens too."

Rachel said, "We just try to live in a Denny's-free environment. They're our main competition. If we pretend they're not there long enough, maybe they'll go away."

Helena came in through the kitchen door. She wore

a white button-down shirt over a bikini top, and tight black denim shorts. "How's it going?"

Rachel frowned at her and said, "What are you doing back here?"

"I just wanted to check on Clara," she said.

Clara, clearing Professor Denning's dishes, sighed loudly but said nothing.

"She's doing fine," Rachel said, loud enough for both women to hear.

"*I* like her," Elton Charles said from his corner table. "She's very perky."

Clara winked at him.

"You see?" Rachel said to Helena. "You have to cut the apron strings sometime."

Helena grinned conspiratorially. "I know. She's just so serious, it's fun to pick on her."

"I can hear you," Clara called. She did not sound amused.

Helena poked Rachel playfully on the arm. "By the way, Michelle just told me she saw you at the park for that male-stripper show on Saturday."

"Yes, I went with Patty," Rachel said. "It was quite a sight."

Helena snorted. "Honey, to hear her go on about it, you'd think she was straight."

So it even affected Michelle. "He *was* handsome, but I'm sure it was all just some stunt to get attention."

"Then I think it worked."

Rachel felt a rush of shame and snapped, "What does that mean?"

Helena's eyebrows rose. "It means that in all the years I've been with her, I've never seen Michelle turned on by a man before. She's the gayest woman I know."

Rachel sighed. "Sorry. It must be the heat. Excuse me for a minute; I'll be right back."

She went into the ladies' room and splashed cold water on her face. She felt like she needed a shower—not the cold kind but one that was hot and soapy and cut through grime. Yet as she studied her reflection, she saw that she was flushed even now across her shoulders and neck. She could blame it on the heat and humidity for the sake of others, but it did nothing to make her feel less . . . *skanky*.

And that bugged her the most. No one had any claim on her, and she could find any man she wanted attractive. So why did lusting after the mysterious Kyle Stillwater feel so fundamentally *wrong*?

I need my lake spirits, she thought as she wiped the water from her cheeks. *I need them tonight.*

CHAPTER ELEVEN

KYLE STILLWATER STOOD at the edge of Lake Wingra, in a little cove hidden from the main body of water. He was deep in the Arboretum, a nature preserve at the heart of Madison. Here the forest remained as thick as when his people had first found it, even if the traffic noises from the nearby beltline ruined the overall effect.

He stared at the water, shaking like an addict going cold turkey. In a sense, he was; the urge to return to the lake had grown exponentially throughout the day until he simply couldn't fight it any longer. And now that he stood at its edge, another desire overwhelmed him: to dive naked into its waters.

Everything in his world was wrong. He felt like he was in one of those *Star Trek* episodes in which the characters slipped into a parallel universe where everything looked the same but was the opposite of how it should've been. First his voice mail was filled with calls from his agent, the same agent who hadn't returned a message in six months, telling him they needed to talk about his recent performance. Then the paper said that a man named Kyle Stillwater had interrupted a huge ground-breaking ceremony on Saturday—which, granted, he had been hired to do—yet he had no memory of anything between waking up that morning and the last time he swam in Lake Wingra.

He hadn't called his agent, or his mother, or any of the other relatives who'd left messages wondering what the hell he was doing. He had tried to reach Henry Hawes, an old man who'd been a mentor to him as a child. Henry knew all the old legends, including the ones that gave Lake Wingra such a bad reputation, but he hadn't answered his phone.

Now Kyle pulled off his shirt and stepped out of his shoes. Mosquitoes drawn to his exposed skin darkened the air around him. He looked around, but the woods were empty of other people—not unusual on a Tuesday afternoon. He pulled down his jeans and underwear and, naked, stepped into the water. The relief as he did so overwhelmed him.

GARRETT BLOOM ANSWERED his cellphone before Bono got through the first chorus of "I Still Haven't Found What I'm Looking For" on the ringtone. He recognized the number at once.

"It's been three days," he snapped without preliminaries. "I expected to hear from you sooner."

He paused to listen, then said, "I know. We haven't found him, either, but he hasn't made any additional statements to the media. Maybe I was wrong about it being a conspiracy to discredit the project or me. Maybe he was just drunk."

He listened some more, watching his own reflection in the window. *Damn,* he thought, *I do look good for a man my age.* Then he said, "What do you want me to say? It worked out. Sometimes things just do. So we go on to the next step."

He closed the phone with a snap before the caller could say more, then paced to the window and looked out at the sunset. The staff was gone for the day, including Rebecca, whose mooning was beginning to worry him. He'd let some lines blur between them that should have stayed firm. He'd have to reestablish them.

There was a firm knock on the outer office door. He strode past Rebecca's desk and unlocked it, anticipating one of the cleaning people. Instead it was a tall woman with dark hair.

He blinked in surprise. "Can I help you?"

"Yes," she said.

After a silent moment, he prompted impatiently, "How?"

"By coming with me," she said. "To the park by the old mental hospital."

"And why should I do that?"

"Because Kyle Stillwater will meet us there. He wants to explain why he was so weird at the ceremony."

"Unless the reason is drugs or alcohol, I don't want to know. And even then, I don't care. He blew it, and that's the last of it."

"I think you'll change your mind when you hear what he has to say."

Bloom paused, intrigued, despite himself. "I'll drive myself there."

She shrugged. "As you wish."

RACHEL LOOKED OUT at Lake Mendota. The water was black and still. There was no night wind, and the moonless sky above her was clear. The inert air was still humid, and the unseasonable heat had not abated. Except for the few fireflies in the bushes, nothing moved.

She stood naked on the rocks at the water's edge. Her torso gleamed with perspiration. She wiped the sweat from her neck and beneath her breasts, feeling it trickle down her skin. She felt damp all over, but it was not her usual pleasant wetness. Rather, it was rancid, like the perspiration itself had somehow gone sour.

She glanced back up the hill. The park had been deserted when she arrived, but she'd still waited in the shadows for nearly half an hour, crouched and uncomfortable, to make sure no one appeared. And by "no one," she meant Kyle Stillwater.

The ring of stones by the effigy mound's head had not been disturbed, and they bothered her. The urge to scatter them was overwhelming, yet when she started to do so, she felt a stab of real terror. So she left them alone but felt their presence in the darkness like accusing eyes.

Tiny wavelets lapped at the lake's edge, and she tried to recall the way it felt when they did the same thing to her body. The memory came easily, but the feelings

that usually accompanied it—anticipation, arousal—
were nowhere to be found.

Still, the thought of the lake's cool water against her
bare skin was undeniably pleasant. She rubbed her
palms along her thighs and extended one foot into the
water.

A voice from the darkness froze her in place, saying
softly, "Hello, Lady of the Lakes."

She jumped into the bushes, her hands flying to protect her modesty. "Who's there?" she hissed, then
added hopefully, "Ethan?" Because if it *was* Ethan,
she'd cry with relief and joy, and not even worry how
he'd found out about her online identity.

Instead, a figure emerged from the water, rising
higher with each step. She recognized him at once.

Kyle Stillwater.

When he spoke, his voice sent tremors through
places no mere words had ever touched before. It was
as soft as a whisper yet reverberated like a call to arms.
"No, I am not Ethan. But I *am* what you seek tonight."

Her mouth went dry, as if the moisture was needed
elsewhere. What was happening to her? She grabbed
her clothes and held the bundle in front of her. "Look,
I don't know what you think—"

She could see him clearly now. The streetlights highlighted the strong planes of his face. His broad chest
was damp and glistening. He was completely naked,
and what the loincloth had covered on Saturday was
now revealed. It was as impressive as the rest of him,
and stood ready. Three days and nights of fantasizing
and desperation returned in force, immobilizing her.

He said softly, "I know you have been thinking of me. I am not here to threaten you."

She nodded at his erection. She was not a woman who dwelled on size, but he was big enough to both give her pause and make her tingle with anticipation. "I'm not sure I believe you."

He ignored her irony and continued. "I don't mean the thoughts of the past three days. For *years* you have wished for one of us to come forth from the waters and into *your* world. You were content to be the Lady of the Lakes in our reality, but you ached for the same fulfillment here, in yours."

She could barely breathe. Something cold and cruel and irresistible shone from his eyes. Yet his voice was soothing, comforting, hypnotic, and his words struck her with physical force. Still, she fought to maintain control, because whatever the hell was happening to her, he was wrong about one thing. It wasn't something she sought in real life. Or was it? Parts of her certainly seemed to, but . . .

"I am here to answer that wish," he concluded. "Come to me, Lady of the Lakes, and be fulfilled, as you've always wanted."

The blatant proposition broke the spell. *Why, you stuck-up bastard,* she thought. He was just another guy trying to get in her pants—at least metaphorically, since she wasn't wearing any at the moment. "I don't go around getting 'fulfilled' with total strangers, no matter how handsome they are. We'll just consider this a case of crossed signals, okay? Good night, Mr. Stillwater."

He moved closer. He seemed to be struggling with

something, and when he spoke again his voice was different—softer and almost pleading. "Please, I can't . . .
I *need* you. You're so kind, so gentle. I promise we'll be
gentle, too. You'll enjoy it . . ."

She hadn't expected to feel sudden pity for him, and
it confused her. She said, "I think a man like you can
probably find someone a little more willing without
too much trouble."

Then his uncertainty vanished and the arrogance returned. His voice rumbled from his chest and set up a
distracting buzz in her ears. Her thoughts grew fuzzy,
and the bundle in her arms felt suddenly heavy. What
was she doing?

"But I am here only for you," he said. "For you, I
have left my world and come into yours, seeking only
your touch, your caress. . . ."

He brushed her cheek with the back of one hand. At
the sudden contact, a weakness she recognized washed
over her, and her clothes fell from her slack fingers. It
was the same leaden lethargy that had kept her in her
bed the night before. Now it took all her will to even
stay upright. She was wetter inside than she could ever
recall, and her breasts felt heavy behind her tight
nipples.

"That's it," he whispered encouragingly. "Feel your
desire for me."

She tried to raise her hands to cover herself, but
her knees began to give way, and she grabbed at Stillwater for support. She sagged against him, every inch
of her skin aching for his touch.

"Please," she began, intending to follow with,
There's no way I'm letting you do this. But the rest of

the words wouldn't come—only a soft, drawn-out moan.

He put one hand on the small of her back, his fingertips brushing the cleft of her buttocks. His erection was pinned between them, hot and hard against her bare stomach. She couldn't see, couldn't think, but knew to raise her chin to his face. His lips came down on hers.

The kiss eliminated any thoughts of resisting.

His tongue danced inside her mouth. His grip on her rear tightened and was all that kept her on her feet. Her arms slid around his neck. When he broke the kiss, she thought she'd pass out. "Oh, God," she whimpered, "please don't stop now."

Again his supreme confidence had vanished, replaced by uncertainty and even fear. "I'm sorry." He sighed. "I wish this *could* stop, but it can't, and I . . ."

"I don't want you to stop," she breathed. "I want this."

Her knees did give way then, and he guided her slowly down to the mud, where he eased her onto her back. His hand slid between her thighs, and she struggled to endure the sensations racking her. He reclined beside her, withdrew his hand and trailed its wetness up her belly, between her breasts and to her lips. She licked his fingers hungrily.

His face was in shadow above her.

"You're really one of them?" she whispered, wanting to believe it. It felt as if the space inside her had grown so large, its edges so sensitive, that it might swallow her whole in an implosion of unbearable lust.

His only answer was a smile.

———

"SO HERE WE are," Garrett Bloom said to the woman. He'd followed her car to Olbrich Park, and now they stood together in the darkness below the old hospital, the light from the street barely reaching them. He had his hands in his pockets and sighed impatiently. "Where's the man of the hour?"

The woman sat on an old picnic table and rummaged through her purse. "He'll be along."

"Good, because I don't have all night."

The woman smiled. "I thought a man as powerful as you made his own schedule."

Bloom scowled at her. He wasn't terribly worried about his safety, even out here alone with this stranger. He carried a small .38 revolver in an ankle holster, and regular practice at the shooting range had improved both his aim and his confidence. "I *do* make my schedule, and that's why I hate wasting time."

"Tell me, why do you want to build this here?"

"Because it will benefit the neighborhoods, and—"

"No, I mean why *here*? Why not somewhere else? Why this spot?"

He grinned. "Are you trying to trick me?"

"Why would I do that?"

"Look at this place," he said, gesturing toward the water sparkling in the night. "This is a beautiful spot, a place where people can feel the peace and tranquility of the water. I've lived around these lakes all my life, and I love them. I want people who can't afford lakeside homes to be able to experience it."

"Peace and tranquility," the woman repeated. "Do you have any idea what truly lives in these waters?"

"What does that mean?"

She smiled. "Nothing. I guess I'm just a little tired."

"Well, me too. If your friend doesn't show up soon—"

"Here he comes now," she said.

KYLE STILLWATER POSITIONED himself between Rachel's thighs, his whipcord arms holding his upper body just above her. She put her hands on his chest and felt his muscles move beneath his skin. The head of his cock bobbed against her, taunting but not possessing.

He bent his lips to one breast and took the taut nipple into his mouth. She grabbed his buttocks, arching to take him inside. But he was so strong she might as well have tried to move a statue; his erection stayed just out of reach.

His lips left her breast and brushed her ear again. His deep voice ran through her like flame. "Whatever happens next, remember that you said you wanted it. Just as you've always wanted *them*."

"Yes, I do want it; I want *you*," she said, her voice trembling. She no longer worried about accommodating his size.

Then, at the moment he started to penetrate her, he suddenly stopped. His body froze in mid-stroke, and he looked around into the dark.

She grunted in desperation and repeatedly slapped the ground. *So close, so close . . .*

———

BLOOM TURNED TO look. "I don't see anything."

"I know," she said from behind him.

He didn't see the knife coming either. *But Artemak was right,* she thought. *There are uses for your heart, Garrett Bloom.* And she was about to invoke one of them. Artemak would know, would *sense,* this moment of sacrifice. Then, when she presented this gift to Artemak, he in turn would help her. He *had* to.

RACHEL COULD NO longer see his face in the darkness, or even the reflection from his eyes. He stared back over his shoulder at the lake. "Another is here," he said.

"'Another'?" She gasped, struggling to get him inside her despite this sudden threat of being watched. But he wasn't talking to her.

He shook his head as if to clear it, and when he looked down it was again the soft, human face. "Oh my God," he whispered, stroked her cheek with the back of his fingers, and ran his thumb across her lips. "You're so beautiful." He bent to kiss her.

"Don't kiss me," she wailed. *"Fuck me!"*

Her intensity seemed to momentarily frighten him. Then the arrogance returned. "I'm sorry, but something unexpected has come up. I will claim you another time."

And then he was gone.

CHAPTER TWELVE

ETHAN TOOK SEVERAL deep breaths and rolled his shoulders like he used to do before rushing from cover into a firefight. Then, with knots in his belly tighter than anything the Iraq War ever caused, he hit the call button and saw the word "dialing" appear beneath Rachel Matre's phone number.

It rang five times before her voice mail picked up.

He snapped the phone shut and put it in his pocket, as if somehow hiding the device would also hide his use of it.

He looked at the clock. Five minutes after one in the morning. What was he *thinking,* calling at this hour? Then again, who *didn't* answer their phone at this time of night? It could be only a wrong number or an emergency, and no responsible adult ignored the latter possibility.

"Dammit," he hissed, and looked around his living room. He saw his reflection in the patio door, and he scowled: unshaven, in T-shirt and boxers, and visibly

aroused. It was the way he'd spent every night since
seeing Rachel at the park. He couldn't keep going
this way.

In the desert he'd simply strode into the thick of battle. *One way or the other,* he'd thought back then, *it's
time to resolve this.* He'd never forget the smell of bul-
lets cooking the air as they passed near enough to singe
his skin. But he also always walked away the victor.

"One way or the other," he said to his mirror image.
A firefly flickered outside, its pale glow superimposed
on his reflection's heart. "It is *definitely* time to resolve
this."

Fifteen minutes later he was parked in the empty lot
outside Rachel's diner. He'd done this once before, and
Rachel had called the cops on him. Would she do the
same thing now?

No lights showed in her apartment above the diner,
and the blinds were all closed. He saw a shape inside
on one window ledge: Tainter, the most blasé cat he'd
ever met. Was Rachel in there asleep? Was she out with
someone else? Or was she down at the lake, consorting
with her spirit lovers?

He dialed her number again. In the dead silence, he
thought he heard it ringing faintly inside the apartment. It stopped when the voice mail again picked up.

*She'll see that I've called twice in the middle of the
night,* Ethan thought. *That should tell her something.*
He started his truck again and put it in gear. For a moment he considered turning left, toward Hudson Park
and the lake where they'd made love. But if she was
there, she might not appreciate him interrupting. He

knew he was already edging into stalker territory with this behavior, and he had no desire to frighten her.

So he turned right instead, toward home. The next move was hers.

RACHEL HAD NO idea how long she'd lain whimpering on the grass. The comedown from the maddeningly close encounter seemed to take forever, and when she could finally think straight again, she began to cry— not out of shame but from confusion. What the hell had she been doing? This wasn't like her!

She rolled onto her side and curled into a ball. *I want this,* she'd told Stillwater, and at the time it had been true. And why not? He was beautiful, hard and masculine, and clearly a master at these games. But something had happened that changed it from merely an impulsive quickie to . . . what?

Her clothes still lay where she'd dropped them. She should get dressed and go home, but she couldn't let *this* be the end. It was a level of frustration she'd never dreamed she could feel.

She got shakily to her hands and knees, crawled to the nearest tree, and used it to stand upright. A car passed on the street, and she ducked out of sight as the headlights raked the spot she'd occupied a moment before. When it was again safe, she took a deep breath and stumbled down the hill to the lake.

Her head went woozy, and she fell with a loud splash. She tasted water and felt it burn inside her nose, but she had no strength to swim or even stand. *I'm going to drown in three feet of water,* she thought in a panic, and tried to kick herself back to the surface. But instead she sank to the rocks and soft silt along the bottom. She put her hands flat against the silt and tried to push herself up, but even with the water's natural lift, she failed. She felt her last breath bubble out of her mouth as she tried to retain it.

Goddammit, I'm not dying like this! she bellowed in her mind. With every last bit of strength she shoved down, got her knees under her, and lunged upright from the water.

She opened her eyes into bright sunlight.

She stood knee-deep in the water near the edge of the lake. It was day, and the park loomed before her. Then she realized she was still nude, and crouched down to cover herself. But an unfamiliar voice said, "It's a little late for modesty."

On the hill above her stood an old woman with white hair and deep creases in her face. A blanket covered her shoulders, and beneath that she wore a dress that appeared to be made of deerskin.

Rachel looked around. It was Lake Mendota, all right, but there was no sign of civilization anywhere. No houses, no cars, nothing. The only sounds were birds, waves, and wind.

"What the hell?" she breathed.

"Not hell," the old woman said. "Come out of the water, where we can talk."

Rachel forced her hands to her sides and walked, chin up, from the lake. The air was cooler than it had been before, and she gratefully wrapped the offered blanket around her. The woman gestured for Rachel to sit down, but she was too dumbstruck by the view.

The lakeside houses, the streets and sidewalks—the whole neighborhood around Hudson Park—were gone. In their place stood trees of enormous girth, thick with leaves and alive with squirrels, birds, and insects.

And the effigy mound was covered with stones chosen by weight and color to add detail to the reptilian form. It was no panther or other mammal; it was a water dragon done in a style she'd never seen before.

Rachel sank to her knees on the grass. "Okay, this may sound a little out there, but I have to ask. Am I in the past?"

"Not for me," the woman said.

"You speak English."

"And you speak Lo-Stahzi. The important thing is that we communicate, not *how* we do it, because this will be our one chance. The spirits who succored you are now in danger—and at the hands of the man you just let touch you."

"You mean Kyle Stillwater?"

"I mean the thing *inside* him. And it is all your fault."

"*My* fault?" Rachel felt abruptly outraged. "I didn't go *looking* for him, you know. He just showed up. How could it possibly be my fault?"

"I don't mean *that*. I mean that you made a request of your spirits, to aid a friend. A generous gesture—but they chose to fulfill it by going to her in the form of a human male. This was not easy. In fact, it left them dangerously weakened. But for you, they would try to move the sun and moon."

Rachel felt a sudden surge of dread as the woman

gestured toward the lake. "The spirits were once humans like yourself," she continued. "Brilliant men and women in touch with the universe on a level even I can barely grasp. When their physical forms died, their spirits joined the waters. But not all brilliant men are also good men. Some were evil. Those spirits gathered in the lake you call Wingra, and they, too, can reach forth from the waters. The good spirits normally hold them in check, but when they were weakened following your request, the evil ones saw their chance. They summoned an avatar of their own."

"Kyle Stillwater," Rachel said.

The old woman nodded. "He has severed their connection to you. And had he been successful in coupling with you, you would have died. Soon he will be able to trap and destroy the spirits, and his brethren will spread into those waters. The only reason he has not yet done so is that he must learn to fully dominate the personality in the body he has chosen." She pointed a gnarled finger. "And he will not merely harm you but your human lover. Your spirit sister. They will suffer as surely as you will."

"How?"

"I do not know his methods, but he's wily. His kind thrives on dissent, on sowing suspicion and doubt. They can be defeated only with unity and love."

Rachel sighed with annoyance. "I'm not a hippie, you know; I have no interest in buying the world a Coke and keeping it company. Tell me what I have to do."

"I am not your mother. I don't know what's happening in your world at any given time. I can see only through the narrow door that brought you here. *You* must defeat them, because only you can walk between the water and the land. You are now the sole hope for this world—and the next."

Rachel started to speak again, but suddenly she was splashing in water, gurgling and choking as she struggled to get her feet beneath her. She found herself standing in the lake again, this time in the present, her head filled with the vividness of the information she'd just received.

She spun and looked out into the darkness. The water sparkled and shimmered, but she felt no draw from it, and no watery hands coaxed her forward.

"What the *fuck*?" she whispered.

Slowly she left the lake and dressed, and was about to climb the hill again when she spotted a shadowy figure on the sidewalk by the street. She immediately dropped flat onto the grassy slope, raising her head enough to see over the tops of the clipped grass.

It wasn't Stillwater. It was clearly a woman, but otherwise Rachel could tell nothing. She held her breath, wondering if she'd been spotted. At least she was fully dressed and doing nothing wrong, but something about the woman's appearance seemed as off-kilter as everything else. Had she been there all along?

Before Rachel reached any conclusion, the woman turned and walked away. Her footsteps faded almost as soon as her dark silhouette merged with the shadows.

Overwhelmed and confused, Rachel made her way back home. Running on her wobbly legs was out of the question, yet with each step, her emotions seeped back, pushing through the numbness. And the old woman's words rang in her ears: *"You are now the sole hope for this world—and the next."*

She fell asleep without a shower, and without checking her phone.

CHAPTER THIRTEEN

THE NEXT MORNING dawned hazy, with a low fog off the lakes that blanketed the isthmus like especially thick cotton candy. Cars drove slowly with their lights on, except for a few who never altered their driving habits in any weather.

Ethan Walker's foreman, Luis Alazar, arrived early at the Olbrich Park construction site, but not from any professional impulse. He had come straight from his mistress's apartment and lacked the stamina to face his wife's fury if he went home to shower and change. He kept a set of work clothes at the other woman's place for just such an emergency, and he would deal with Francesca that evening, after bracing himself with a few shots of vodka.

He parked on the street beside the old hospital's driveway entrance, now blocked with sawhorses. The grounds were enclosed by a chain-link fence topped with razor wire, to protect the equipment that was too big to cart away each evening. Already the Walker

Construction sign had been gang-tagged, and the pad-
lock on one of the gates showed marks where someone
had tried to break in.

Luis sat in his truck and ate his fast-food breakfast
while listening to the news on the Spanish-language
talk-radio station. Still half asleep, he watched the rising sun grow hotter and more vivid through the fog,
burning the mist from the air. He felt good. But then,
he wasn't the sort of man to dwell on the moral aspects
of his behavior.

Until he saw something that made him freeze in
mid-chew.

Just outside one of the fence gates was an old picnic
table mounted in a buried slab of concrete. Luis
blinked, squinted, and leaned forward until his forehead touched the windshield.

Something covered the table. At first he thought it
was just a sack of garbage—an opinion reinforced by
the half-dozen large black crows that stood along the
table's edge and pecked at it. But as the fog lifted, its
contours grew disturbing.

He got out of the truck and walked three steps
down the hill before the shape resolved into something
he could identify.

Then he threw up.

MARTY WALKER LOOKED down at the remains of
Garrett Bloom with professional neutrality. He would
react to it later, in private, when no one (except possibly his long-term partner, Chuck) was around. It played

into the cliché of the inscrutable Oriental, but that made it no less effective. And he was good at it.

At least he thought he was. But this kind of brutality tested his resolve.

Bloom was tied by the ankles and neck to the picnic table. He wore dark dress slacks and a blue shirt, and was gagged with his own tie. His shirt was torn open, exposing the ragged hole cut crudely through his sternum and ribs. The crows, still awaiting their chance to return, had pecked pieces out of the wound's edge, but they had not been the ones to remove both his heart and his right hand.

His hand was nailed through the palm to a nearby tree. Whoever removed his heart had taken it with them.

Marty lowered the plastic sheet over the body. Flies and ants, more circumspect than the crows, made their pilgrimages with slow, steady effort. The photographers had finished, and the forensics team. It was unlikely he would notice anything they had missed, but he had wanted to take one last look. Now he motioned for the paramedics to come and take the body away.

Ethan came down the hill with them. He was dressed casually, in the jeans and the Badger T-shirt he'd grabbed following Marty's call. "Holy shit" was all he could say.

"That's accurate," Marty agreed.

Ethan nodded toward Luis, seated in an open police car, his head on his knees. "You're not arresting him, are you?"

"No, but he's a wreck. His priest is on the way."

Two paramedics loaded the covered body onto a

stretcher. A third one began the delicate task of removing the impaled hand from the tree trunk. "What the hell was Bloom doing here in the middle of the night?" Ethan said.

"I have no idea," Marty said. "I've got to inform his wife, so maybe that will give me a lead."

"I don't envy you that."

Marty shrugged. He used to dread those confrontations, but experience taught him that when one spouse died, the other was usually involved. He now saw the task of delivering the bad news as just another step in the investigation.

Ethan stared at the blocked-off area. A small finch tried to land on the yellow tape, found it too unsteady, and flitted away. "So what does this mean for me?"

"What were you planning to do today?"

"Getting the last stuff out of the interior so we can knock down the walls of the old building."

"Trucks going in and out over there, on the far side?"

"Yeah."

Marty nodded. "Go ahead, then. We've looked around inside, and there's no sign anyone got through the fence. If you *do* find anything unusual, though, let me know."

ETHAN CLIMBED BACK up the hill. His crew huddled in a group, smoking and gossiping. No doubt they'd solved the murder a dozen different ways by now. They wore hard hats and steel-toed boots, but their eyes betrayed their worry. They dreaded what Ethan was about to tell them; they got paid only when they worked, and it seemed likely they'd be sent home.

"Good news, guys," Ethan said. "They're not going to shut us down. If you see anything out of place or unusual, stop immediately and call me, then the cops. Otherwise, let's get back to work."

The relief on their faces was almost religious. Ethan felt a small surge of pride as they quickly gathered their individual tools from their vehicles. In this economy, he was glad to be able to provide jobs to hardworking people.

He stopped one of the men and held him back while the others got to work. "Marcus," he said quietly, "Luis is a little shaken up, so I'm sending him home. I want you to be acting foreman today, okay?"

Marcus's eyes narrowed suspiciously. "Is that union?"

"No. But I'm still going to pay Luis as if he was here, so officially he's still the foreman. I just want people to have someone to come to if they find anything."

He nodded. "Okay, then. But I accept no real responsibility, you understand?"

"I'm all for doing that whenever you can get away with it," Ethan agreed.

"Hey, Ethan!" someone shouted from the back of the building. "There's something weird here."

RACHEL BLINKED AND shook her head a little. "I'm sorry, could you repeat that?"

The man at the counter scowled. He was a new customer, possibly a first-timer, and she was not making a good impression. "I *said* I'd like a Texas omelet with an order of hash browns cooked extra-crispy." He overenunciated each word as if talking to an idiot.

"Got it," Rachel said, and turned to go.

"Can I get a drink?" the man snapped.

"Of course," she said, forcing a smile. The man had every right to be annoyed.

"Orange juice. Without the pulp, if you've got it."

"We do."

"Thanks," he said with no sincerity.

She put the ticket on the carousel and spun it for Jimmy. She knew Helena watched her with concern, but she deliberately avoided any eye contact. Then she did something she seldom did: She left the diner and went upstairs to her apartment, leaving Helena alone with the end of the breakfast rush.

When the door closed, she did not open any blinds or turn on the lights. She sank onto her couch and took several deep breaths. She could not put into words how she felt, except to say that it was somehow, fundamentally, *wrong*.

It had begun with her dreams during the fitful couple of hours she managed to sleep after returning from the lake. In them she was being sexually taken multiple times, in ways similar to the spirits' approach to their trysts. Only she wasn't in the water, and while she couldn't quite make out the faces of the men, she sensed that they were all somehow Kyle Stillwater.

And then they all stopped just when she was about to reach climax. They would withdraw from her, laugh cruelly, and pass her to the next one. She seemed to be unable to resist them, caught in that insidious dream weakness that kept her immobilized except for involuntary grunts and thrusts.

She had showered repeatedly that morning, unable to feel completely clean. Her skin still felt damp and clammy, as if the mud from her encounter with Kyle Stillwater still clung to it. What had she been *thinking*? She wasn't some drunken sorority girl at a frat party.

And that didn't even begin to cover the strange near-death experience with the old woman. Had it really happened? Or was it just her brain firing randomly from lack of oxygen?

It *felt* real. Unlike conversations in real dreams, this one hadn't faded with wakefulness. If anything, it was even more vivid.

Tainter jumped on the cushion beside her and snuggled down against her thigh. She idly scratched the base of his skull and murmured, "Kitty, your mama made a bad decision last night."

A soft knock came from the door. "Come in," Rachel called, expecting Helena or Jimmy.

Instead Becky opened it, peered into the gloom, and said, "Rachel?"

"Light switch is by the door," Rachel said, getting to her feet wearily.

Becky turned on the light, then closed the door behind her. Rachel stood uncertainly, never knowing what the correct greeting was. She waited as Becky looked at the ceiling, the floor, the furniture—anywhere but at her sister.

"I think I did something terrible last night," Becky said at last as she ran a finger idly around the framed Frida Kahlo print beside the door.

Rachel said nothing.

"You know I've been working for Garrett Bloom, right?"

"Yes."

"Well . . . I'm also . . . um . . . I'm in love with him."

"With Garrett Bloom?" Rachel asked dubiously.

Becky's head snapped around. "What, you don't think a man like that could find me attractive?"

"That's not what I meant. I thought he was married."

"His wife is a dried-up old harpy who he won't divorce because he loves his kids too much. If that's any of your business."

"It isn't," Rachel agreed.

"And for your information, he's wonderful. He's kind and gentle."

"Does he know how you feel?"

"He does now. I called him last night and left a voice mail telling him all about it. I was a bit tipsy."

Rachel shook her head. She had no patience for this. "Becky, you're a goddamned idiot."

Becky's eyebrows rose. She started to speak, then turned and walked out, slamming the door behind her. Her footsteps echoed on the stairs.

Rachel knew better than to follow. A scene with Becky in the parking lot or, worse, in the diner would do no one any good. Besides, she was really in no position to claim the moral high ground.

And dammit! There it was again, that sense that she had done something wrong. *Becky* was in love with a married man, not her.

She went to the bathroom and splashed cold water on her face. She wished she had time for another shower, although she doubted what she wanted to wash away was susceptible to soap and water. Instead, she returned to the diner and worked very hard to keep her mind on her job.

CHAPTER FOURTEEN

LATER THAT MORNING, a battered white Jeep parked at the curb behind the two police cruisers. The door opened, and a petite woman with straight black hair tied in a haphazard bun climbed out. She put on sunglasses and looked around the area.

Then she raised the yellow police tape at the perimeter and ducked under it. She called out to one of the workers. "Hi! I'm supposed to ask for a Mr. Walker, or a Detective Walker. Is it the same guy?"

The nearest man removed his hard hat and shook his head. "No, ma'am. They're brothers."

"Really?" she asked.

He gestured with the hat. "That's Marty. He's the cop."

She turned as Marty Walker emerged from a door in one of the standing walls, then extended her hand to him and smiled. "Hi. I'm Amy Vannoy from the State Archaeological Commission. Lannie Boyd got called away at the last minute and asked me to come down in his place. Something about some artifacts discovered here?"

"Yes. Let's find my brother, and he'll show you what we found."

"Wait, you *found* something?"

"Just a little while ago. Aren't you here because of that?"

"No, I'm here to confirm there was nothing *to* find."

As they crossed the grass toward the remains of the building, Amy nodded toward the picnic table, where technicians continued to look for clues. "What happened there?"

"A homicide," Marty said simply. "A man was killed."

"How?"

"Unpleasantly."

"I'm sure. But I'm a scientist, not a squeamish housewife. You can share the gory details."

"The victim was tied to that picnic table, his chest was cut open, and somebody cut out his heart. They also cut off his right hand."

Before Amy could inquire further, Ethan emerged from the building. He held out his hand and said, "I'm Ethan Walker, the contractor doing the renovation. And you are . . . ?"

"Amy Vannoy," she said to Ethan as they shook hands. "Lannie Boyd sent me down here to check out your site. But I think I can also help you. Pinning the right hand of a sacrifice to a tree is a very specific bit of ritual from the stories of the Lo-Stahzi."

"Really?" Marty was suddenly interested. "Can you tell me more?"

"May I take a closer look at the crime scene?"

Marty raised the yellow tape around the table so Amy could duck under it. She looked at the table, then at the tree, and said, "Was he cut here, just under his ribs?"

"Yes."

"And his heart was removed that way?"

"So it appears."

She looked at the table again. "Which end was his head on?"

"This one."

"Ah. That's wrong."

"What do you mean?"

"The Lo-Stahzi always sacrificed their victims with the heads toward the water, so the souls could run downhill into the lake. They believed the water was a conduit to the afterlife."

"Is that a fairly obscure bit of trivia?" Marty asked.

"That's what you get with the Lo-Stahzi," Amy said. "They're an extinct tribe, so there's no one to ask. There's lots of bits and pieces, but many of them contradict each other. I'm probably the leading expert, and what I know with certainty wouldn't fill one sheet of a legal pad. There's only one real book on the subject, and most of it is nonsense. But my guesses are more educated than anyone else's." She turned to Ethan. "Lannie said you hadn't found anything, but when I got here they said you had."

"Yes, just this morning," Ethan said. "It's a little suspicious, since no one remembers it being there before, but I want to make sure it's okay before we keep working."

"Show me."

Ethan led her to one end of the excavated foundation. Four workers stood in a circle around a shallow hole. They stepped aside for Amy, and when she crouched to examine the hole, they stared at the top of the pink thong that showed above the waistband of her slacks.

She picked up some dirt and filtered it through her fingers. "Why were you digging here?"

"Looking for an old sewer line," Ethan said.

"Have you been digging here today?"

"No, not since yesterday. We were about to start again when we found those." He pointed to two small stone arrowheads and pieces of what appeared to be broken pottery protruding from the soil.

She stood, wiped her hands on her pants, and said, "Fail."

Ethan and Marty looked at each other, then at her. "What do you mean?" Marty said.

"This dirt isn't native. Somebody dumped it here, along with these beauties." She picked up one of the arrowheads, spit on it, and rubbed it clean. "I have no doubt this is a genuine artifact, but it's not a rare one, and it sure as hell wasn't originally buried here."

Marty looked at her skeptically. "You can tell that without any lab testing or microscopic analysis or anything?"

"Dirt is a huge part of archaeology, and I can tell that *this* dirt did not come from this sediment. Besides, look at the fence. You can see some of the dirt stuck to the razor wire where they dumped it over."

"So whoever did this was in a hurry," Marty said.

"Probably. If it was the same person that killed the guy, I could see why he wouldn't want to dally."

Marty nodded thoughtfully. "Thank you, Ms. Vannoy. If you'll excuse me, I need to call our forensics people about this." He went outside the gate and down the hill for privacy.

"So is there any reason we can't continue working?" Ethan asked her.

"Nah. I'll take these pieces with me and see if I can figure out where they came from. Do you have a card? I'll let you know what I find." And she walked back up the hill toward her waiting Jeep.

CHAPTER FIFTEEN

KYLE STILLWATER STAGGERED out of his apartment into the sun, leaving the patio door open behind him. He squinted into the light and stumbled over his rusted hibachi grill. He wore a T-shirt with a motorcycle on it and jeans that were split at the knee.

"Hey, bro," his neighbor Darius said. The middle-aged black man sipped coffee in his bathrobe and slippers. "You all right?"

"Huh?" Kyle turned and saw his friend. "Oh, hi, Darius. Just a little out of it."

Darius shook his head. "On a weeknight, even. You kids have no sense of responsibility, do you?"

"No, it's not like that. I'm just . . . I feel like crap. I think I'm getting sick, you know?"

"Yeah, I know. Eighty-proof sick. You know, if you ever need to talk instead of sitting in that apartment by yourself, you come on over. I'll grill us some burgers, and we can hash out the world's problems."

Kyle smiled. Darius was on disability from his

diabetes and always reached out to his troubled neighbors. If only everyone in the world was so kind. "Thanks, man. I may take you up on that."

Kyle's truck started after he raised the hood and wiggled the ignition wire. He always promised himself that after he got his big break, he would send that truck off the nearest cliff. He headed north out of Madison, toward the little farm owned by Henry Hawes.

He stopped at a convenience store and left the engine running while he gassed up. The news on TV that morning had rattled him. Garrett Bloom had been murdered in the same park where everyone said he, Kyle, had shown up on Saturday. Yet he hadn't. He had been hired to, but he'd somehow slept through it. Hadn't he? No one had any pictures, and the guy they described was older, with white hair. Was it just some coincidence that he called himself "Kyle Stillwater"?

His dreams this past night were just as troubling. He was making love to a beautiful white woman on the grass in the dark, and he could smell the water nearby. His memories of touching her were as vivid as any real sexual experience, yet the words he heard himself say came only partly from his own head. Someone else seemed to be speaking through him—someone whose personality was filled with hate and anger, and who delighted in causing pain.

The final straw had been finding the policewoman's business card on his refrigerator. He had no memory of talking to the cops, but surely they wouldn't have burst in while he was sleeping, only to leave a card where he could find it. He knew he needed help—the kind only Henry could provide.

He tried Henry on the store's pay phone. He'd lost his own cellphone sometime in the last couple of days. Once again neither Henry nor his wife answered, but the old man seldom left the farm. Kyle would find him there.

He *had* to.

PATTY PATILIA THREW open the diner's door so hard it almost knocked the little bell from its mount. "Have you *heard*?"

Rachel looked up from filling ketchup bottles. She realized she had no idea how long she'd been doing that; her thoughts were thin and scattershot. "Heard what?"

Patty's face shone with sweat and eagerness, and she was so out of breath she could barely enunciate. "Someone was killed over at Olbrich Park. *Murdered*. Where they're building that new community center."

The few post-lunch diners all turned to listen. Even Jimmy poked his head out of the kitchen.

"Who?" Helena asked as she stood beside Rachel.

"Garrett Bloom," Patty said. "You know, the guy who hired me to sing? We went to the ground-breaking on Saturday."

A girl with tattoos on both arms said, "Was that the hottie in the loincloth? I saw him. That'd be a real shame."

"No, it wasn't him. Mr. Bloom personally sought me out for the show. He said he wanted a local artist of my caliber to set the tone for the day." This seemed to affect her anew, and she paused. "Wow. He was alive then. Now he's dead."

"Who killed him?" asked Mrs. Boswell, one of the regular customers.

"I don't know. I just heard about it from one of the boys who plays Frisbee golf at Olbrich Park every morning. It's been on the news, but there's nothing on the *Lady of the Lakes*."

Her blog's name sent a jolt through Rachel. She put down the ketchup bottles and said, "Well, I'm sure it'll be all over the Internet by tonight."

Patty was still lost in her reverie. "I've never known anybody who was *murdered* before," she said, essentially to herself. "I didn't really know Ling Hu, and Korbus didn't *mean* to kill her. Gosh, I barely know anyone who's *died*. Even most of my childhood pets are still alive."

"You live in a blessed state, child," Mrs. Boswell said seriously.

Rachel's foggy consciousness tried to process this information. Whatever was wrong with her was not going away but seemed to be growing in intensity, putting distance between her and the world with every passing moment. It was almost as if Sylvia Plath's symbolic bell jar had been lowered around her, smeared and stained and impenetrable, reducing the rest of the world to vague, almost unrecognizable shapes.

And inside the jar, she could think of only one thing: *him*.

"So where was he killed?" Rachel finally asked.

"I told you already, at the park, where they had the

big ceremony," Patty said. "They found his body on one of the picnic tables."

Okay, focus, she told herself. The park. Where the old building was being torn down to make way for the new one. And both tasks were the responsibility of Ethan Walker. "Did you happen to hear anything about him?"

"Him who?"

Kyle, she almost said without thinking, but she caught herself. "Ethan Walker."

"Ethan? No. Why? Oh—right. But no, nobody mentioned him."

Rachel nodded. The others continued to discuss the murder while she took the full ketchup bottles and put them back in the refrigerator. The cold air seemed to penetrate the haze for a moment, and she realized how serious this was. Garrett Bloom was a mover and shaker; his death, especially by foul play, would send ripples in every direction.

She opened the freezer and pressed an ice cube to the hollow of her throat. What was *wrong* with her?

ETHAN CLIMBED THE hill to the curb without looking at the crime scene. It was blazingly hot, and he was starving. He'd had no breakfast or lunch, and wanted food, a shower, and a nap. His truck would be like a kiln, but he was glad it didn't have vinyl seats like his first two cars.

He unlocked the door just as another vehicle parked behind him. Julie Schutes emerged, dressed in a short skirt and summer blouse, her smooth flesh displayed to great advantage. She tossed her golden hair and said, "Well, hello there. Just the man I was after."

"Your timing sucks, then. I'm on my way home right now, so—"

"Five minutes for old times' sake," she said, and threaded her arm through his before he could move away. "Walk me down to the scene of the crime."

"Marty's still down there. You can talk to him."

"Ethan," she said in almost a purr. Julie was a wild-cat in bed, and when they dated that was the same tone she used to let him know she was in the mood.

"Julie—" he protested, and pulled away.

"C'mon, just walk down the hill with me."

"Why? Can't you find the bottom on your own?"

"What, are you afraid you can't restrain yourself?"

The heat made him quick to anger, but he controlled it. He would go along just to shut her up. Once she started talking to Marty, he should be able to get away. "All right," he agreed.

As they started down the slope, Julie said, "So, Mr. Walker, how does it feel to have another of your projects involved in a capital crime, like with the Arlin Korbus kidnappings?"

"I'm not going on the record with you, Julie, so just turn off the tape recorder."

"You know I don't record things. I do it the old-fashioned way."

"You make it up?"

"Ouch. Why are you in such a bad mood?"

"Because I'm *tired*. First my condo project was de-layed because of that kidnapping, and now the guy who hired me for *this* job is found dead on the site."

She nodded toward the men in hard hats going about their tasks. "Doesn't look like you've stopped this time."

"No. Not today, at any rate. I don't know what will happen tomorrow."

They reached the yellow tape around the bloody picnic table. She pointed to a figure down by the lake, staring out at the water. "What's Marty doing?"

"You know how he is. He likes to think, to make sure he doesn't overlook any details." Ethan recalled how furious Marty had been after he realized the crucial clue in the kidnappings of five local women had been right in front of him all along.

"Well, at least he's got a prime suspect in this one," Julie said.

"He does?"

"That guy who disrupted the ground-breaking ceremony. Kyle Stillwater. Everyone heard him threatening Bloom."

"I have no comment on that. Or about anything else. Now, if you'll excuse me . . ." He pulled his arm free of her grasp and turned to leave.

"Why are you so angry with me, Ethan? Is it because I went to see your girlfriend in the hospital?"

He stopped and faced her. "She's not my girlfriend. And yes, actually, that still kind of pisses me off."

"Do you know what we talked about? I'll tell you. We talked about how she wasn't good enough for you."

"And *you* are?"

"I don't know, but I'm better than her. I'm not some glorified fry cook."

"She owns her own business, Julie."

"She owns a cheap diner frequented by college students. I've seen it."

"Whatever. That has nothing to do with anything now."

"Then what about you and me?"

"There is no 'you and me.'"

"Can I quote you on that?" And when he glared at her she added, "Oh, come on. I'm just teasing."

"Well, I'm not laughing."

She met his angry glare with her own. "I know she dumped you. And while I'm not saying I'll take you back, I am saying I'm willing to talk about it. We make a good pair: the war hero businessman with the arm candy–worthy reporter by his side. Great for both our images."

"That's not my definition of great."

"Okay, forget it. I'll go talk to Marty. And don't feel obligated to wait around and walk me to my car."

"I don't."

She strode across the park, and he was delighted to realize that such an excellent backside no longer entranced him.

THE DINER DOOR slammed open again. Startled, Helena gasped and dropped a lunch special on the floor. Rachel whirled toward the interloper, ready to lay into him. Then she froze.

Becky Matre stood in the doorway. She leaned heavily on the frame, sobbing so hard she could barely stand. "Rachel," she forced out.

Rachel darted around the counter and caught her just as she was about to fall. Becky was shaking as if she'd just come in from a blizzard. "Becky, are you hurt?"

Becky shook her head. "No, I . . . It's . . . Garrett's dead!"

Rachel held her close and stroked her hair. "I know, sweetie, I heard." She *had* heard, yet her hazy mind had completely forgotten this morning's visit, when Becky confessed her love for the dead man. Then she realized the whole place was silent as everyone stared at them.

Becky curled in on herself. "I didn't know where else to go."

"*Shh*, honey, it's all right," Rachel said. "Let's go upstairs so you can lie down."

Patty came over to help, but Becky angrily shrugged her off. Rachel gave her an apologetic look as she and her sister went up the narrow stairs to her apartment.

EVERYONE IN THE diner stared after them in silence until they heard the door open, then close. Becky's sobs were still audible through the ceiling.

"I just wanted to help," Patty said. The hatred she'd seen in Becky Matre's eyes made her want to cry.

"Don't take it personally," Helena said as she cleaned up the dropped order. "Becky's a handful on a good day. She always has been."

"Why does Rachel put up with it?"

Helena shrugged. "She's family. You know?"

"No. I'm an only child."

"Really? Well, like Mrs. Boswell said, you live in a

blessed state. Be thankful." Helena turned to the others. "Okay, show's over. Don't be rude and ask about it either. Who wants more coffee?"

BECKY COLLAPSED ONTO the couch and continued to cry in long, keening sobs. Rachel poured a glass of wine and held it to her sister's lips. Becky took several small sips between gulps of air.

Rachel hadn't seen Becky this upset since they were children. "Okay, honey, calm down and tell me what happened."

She expected a defensive bit of sarcasm, but evidently Becky was too shaken even for that. "Like I told you, I left Garrett a message, telling him how I feel about him. I know he heard it, he checks his voice mail every five minutes. And now . . . now he's *dead*!" She began to wail again.

"Where were you?"

She sniffled, then looked up in surprise. "Me?"

"When it happened?"

"I was at home—where do you think?" Through the tears, her eyes blazed with familiar fury. "Why would you ask me that?"

"Honey, I just wondered."

She pushed Rachel away to the end of the couch. "You think I had something to do with it?"

"No!"

Becky jumped to her feet, fists clenched. "You do, don't you?" Then her anger changed to fear, and she collapsed on the couch again. "Oh my God, if *you* do, then the police will, too, won't they? When they hear that message . . . Maybe he deleted it? Can they get it back if he erased it?"

Rachel reached for her hand. "I don't think you had anything to do with it."

Becky looked at her desperately. "I didn't! I swear! I can't go to jail, I just can't, I couldn't bear it, I—"

Rachel took her by the shoulders. "Rebecca, *stop* it. Take a deep breath."

Becky did her best to comply. Rachel brushed her sister's hair back and asked, "Are you on any medication these days?"

"Oh, now you think I'm a murderer *and* crazy too?"

"No, because I was going to offer you a Xanax!" Rachel shouted. She forced herself to calm down. "I still have some from when I was in the hospital. I thought you might like one."

Becky started to snap out a reply, but she didn't have the resolve. Instead she just collapsed inward, sinking into the couch and cradling her head.

There was a soft knock on the door. It opened slightly, and Patty peeked in. Her voice shook with nervousness. "I don't mean to interrupt, but I wondered if I could do anything to help."

"No, she's just upset," Rachel said. "She got some terrible news."

Becky suddenly jumped up and pointed at Patty. "You wish *she* was your sister instead of me, don't you? Well, you just get her out of here, you hear me? This is *family,* and it has nothing to do with her!"

Patty stared, clearly shocked by this outburst. Rachel gently pushed Becky back onto the couch and said, "I'll be down in a bit, Patty. Thanks for checking on us."

"Okay," Patty said, her lower lip trembling.

Rachel closed the door and whirled on Becky. She was hazy no longer. "If you *ever* talk like that to one of my friends again, especially in my own home, I'll knock you across the room. There's *no* excuse for that!"

Becky slid from the couch to the floor, keening like an old woman. Rachel rolled her eyes, then helped her sister into the bedroom, onto the bed, and under the comforter. Becky curled up like a child, still whimpering, and Rachel drew the blinds and turned off the lights.

"I'm going downstairs to make you something to eat," she said from the door. "Just try to relax and rest. I'll be right back."

"I loved him, Rachel," she said between sobs.

Rachel sighed. Despite it all, Becky's ability to love with her whole being was something she envied. "I know, sweetie. I'm so sorry."

When she got downstairs, Michael Bublé blared from the CD player. Helena met her in the kitchen. "What the *hell* was that?" she hissed. "We could hear the shouting down here. I had to turn up the music."

Rachel turned down the volume as Patty emerged from the bathroom, her eyes red from crying. Rachel wrapped her in a hug. "I'm so sorry, Patty," she said. "She's just upset."

"No, it's okay. I was intruding," Patty said. She pulled away and managed a smile. "Look, I'm going to go. If you need me, call. Otherwise I'll see you tomorrow, maybe." She quickly departed.

"So will Becky be staying with you for a while?" Helena asked.

"I don't know. She's not in very good shape."

"And how is that anything new?"

Rachel looked over sharply, but Helena just met her gaze. Helena had known Rebecca long enough to be able to make statements like that. "It's not new," Rachel said at last. "It's just family."

CHAPTER SIXTEEN

KYLE PARKED IN front of the small wooden house at the end of the dirt driveway. Laundry fluttered on the clothesline, and a pair of chickens skittered off when he opened the truck's door. A thin woman with black hair opened the front door and pointed silently toward the barn. Kyle nodded.

In the barn, Henry Hawes had some two-by-fours stretched across sawhorses and was cutting them to the same length. Henry was sixty years old, wide-shouldered, and short-haired. His Native American ancestry showed up mainly in his cheekbones and dark eyes. A big flop-eared mongrel licked himself at the man's feet. Henry looked up, saw Kyle, and rocked back slightly on his heels.

"You could answer your phone," Kyle said.

"Wouldn't matter. I'd just tell you to come see me anyway," Henry said. He narrowed his eyes and studied the younger man. "What the hell have you gotten yourself into, boy?"

Kyle quickly ran down the events of the past few days—especially the things that he'd apparently done without knowing it. Henry listened until he finished, then slowly and deliberately rolled a cigarette.

Kyle tried not to show his frustration. Henry was one of the few Native Americans who had supported his desire to become an actor, and Henry had interceded with Kyle's parents on his behalf. Besides, rushing a man like Henry was like urging a glacier to hurry. The shaman took as long as he took.

"You swam in Lake Wingra," Henry said at last. "You know the stories about that place, right?"

"I know lots of stories," Kyle said defensively. "I don't base my life around them."

"I do," Henry said simply as he lit the cigarette. "There's *things* in that lake. They were sent there long before we came along, for being evil and spiteful. They're not happy about being there, but they can't leave unless somebody carries them out."

"Carries how?"

Henry touched his heart. "Inside."

"What, like demon possession?"

"Exactly."

Kyle laughed—even though he instinctively knew this was true. "You're telling me I'm possessed by a demon from Lake Wingra?"

"Not a demon like the Christians describe but a spirit that's evil because it *wants* to be. Because it likes it. It's using you to cause pain, misery, confusion, and maybe even death."

Kyle stuck his hands in his pockets and looked out the barn door toward the house. The laundry was very colorful, very bright. "So you think I killed Garrett Bloom?"

"Not you. The spirit. Using your hands."

"I don't think the cops will appreciate that distinction."

"Or maybe it wasn't you. It could've been something in the man's life coming home to roost."

"So what do I do, Henry?"

"I don't know. I can see it around you, though, like a faint shadow. It's growing stronger. And it's learning its way around. Soon it won't need you at all."

"So it'll kill me too?"

Again Henry touched his chest. "Not the way you mean. It'll kill you *here*. Then it will walk the world with your face."

With that, the old man turned on the saw and applied it to the plank. And the shriek of metal cutting wood echoed the scream of despair in Kyle's head.

ETHAN'S STOMACH RUMBLED as he drove down East Washington toward home. He passed Rachel's diner, but the sun's glare made it impossible for him to see inside. She hadn't returned either of his calls from the previous night, and she must've seen them by now. It was plain that she simply wasn't interested. The combined ache of his stomach and his heart made him doubly sad as he drove on.

He reached his office after a sandwich, a quick shower, and a change of clothes. Ambika stood the moment he walked in. "You might want to take a deep breath," she said.

He looked around. Nothing seemed out of place. "Why?"

She nodded toward his inner office. "You have company."

"Who?"

She pursed her lips, as if the name itself was unpleasant. "Vincent Anspach."

Ethan's eyebrows rose. "Really?"

"Yes. He wants to change the purpose of your current building and make it into a shopping center. With his principal opponent out of the way, he figures it's an ideal time."

"And he told you all this?"

"No, he told me nothing. And he called me 'sweetheart.' But he's been in there on his cellphone since he got here, and his voice carries."

As if on cue, a deep male voice said, "Harold, that's great. Send it out as a news tip and see who bites. I'll be available for comment tomorrow. Can't make it too easy for them, can we?"

"Oh God." Ethan sighed.

"Shall I bring you coffee?"

"Bring me crack," he said wryly. Then he opened his office door. "Mr. Anspach. Good to see you again."

Vincent Anspach turned and offered his hand. He was a big, rugged man, potbellied and sun-blasted. His shirt was open enough to show his salt-and-pepper chest hair. "Terrible thing about Garrett Bloom," he said in a voice better suited to calling football plays. "Just awful. First those poor girls got kidnapped, and now this. I tell you, Madison's just not safe anymore."

"I thought you and Bloom didn't get along."

"Oh, I couldn't stand the self-righteous little bastard, but I enjoyed having him around. He made things interesting."

Ethan looked to see what might've been moved. All the paper on his desk had been shifted slightly. Luckily he'd thought to lock his computer, or all his files might be on a zip drive in Anspach's pocket. The man had that sort of reputation. "What can I do for you?"

Anspach stepped close. "Ethan, I think we have a golden opportunity here. I know you're charging ahead on that community center project, and that's all well and good. But I think that property would better serve its neighborhood if it was developed *commercially,* don't you?"

"I don't have an opinion either way. I'll keep building what I've contracted for until I'm told differently. But it's not zoned for commercial use, I do know that much."

"Zoning issues are a problem, yes, but not an insurmountable one. But tell me—how far along would you have to be before changing it from a community center into, say, a shopping center would be more trouble than it's worth?"

"Garrett Bloom's not even cold yet, Vincent," Ethan said. "Maybe you should wait awhile to pounce."

"Come on, Ethan, you know how the world works. If somebody doesn't step in, then those Indians'll raise such a stink that the land will just go to waste. I heard they found arrowheads or wampum beads or something there. If it falls apart now, you get nothing. Is that what you want in this economy?" When Ethan didn't answer he continued, "So how much time to repurpose what you're doing?"

"There's a lot of variables to consider," Ethan said evasively. Anspach had a valid point, but Ethan wouldn't be hemmed in so easily.

"Oh, I know, I know. There always are. But just roughly."

"It would have to be pretty soon. And I'd need new plans and permits, and that zoning issue would have to be addressed."

Anspach smiled and patted Ethan's shoulder. "That's fine. And would you have any problem with that on, say . . . moral grounds?"

"I have no problem with *honest* work of any sort."

"It would be honest, I assure you. And profitable. I'll be in touch about this, okay?"

After Anspach left, Ethan sat down and considered what was underfoot. If the project changed direction, it wouldn't really affect him; he could build a strip mall as easily as a community center. But it would certainly change the public's perception of his company, since being associated with Anspach would attract a shadier kind of attention than he liked. The question was, did it matter? Work was work, and with things as they were, if he could get it, he should. Shouldn't he?

He stared out the window at the capitol and pondered this. Then he picked up the phone. The lone sandwich had not subdued his hunger, and he felt the need for company that didn't make him feel like he needed to wash his hands afterward.

———

"REBECCA WAS PRETTY upset," Helena said as she wiped down the tables after closing. She and Rachel were alone in the diner, the late-afternoon sun making them both sweat profusely. The air conditioner ran only when there were customers, and then only when it was absolutely necessary. The old building was about as well insulated as a colander.

"Yeah," Rachel agreed. She assumed Becky was asleep; she certainly hoped she was. "She was in love with the guy who got killed."

"I gathered that. He was married, wasn't he?"

Rachel shrugged. "It doesn't matter now."

"Do you think Becky had anything to do with—"

"No!" Rachel snapped. "For God's sake, Becky used to campaign to keep rabid dogs from being euthanized. She couldn't kill anything."

After a long moment of silent work, Helena said, "So do you want to talk about what's bothering *you*?"

Rachel propped the mop against the counter. Helena was her best friend, and her sole female confidant. If she couldn't share something as basic as an ill-advised tryst, how deep could their friendship truly be? "Man troubles, too, I'm afraid."

Helena blew a strand of hair from her face. "Still debating whether to call Ethan Walker?"

"No, that's not it." Rachel looked up at the ceiling and let out a long breath. "I got caught up in the moment last night, and did something I shouldn't have."

"Was this with someone we both know?"

"No. And it doesn't matter who, anyway."

"Maybe not in the grand scheme of things, but I'm going to obsess over it until I find out. Do you really want me to wonder if every man who comes in the diner might be the one?"

Rachel smiled. "Fair enough. It was . . . Kyle Still-water."

Helena's eyes opened wide. "The loincloth guy? The one Michelle can't stop talking about?"

"Yeah."

"When did *that* happen?"

"Last night."

"Was he here?"

"No, I ran into him while I was out . . . jogging."

"And you went back to his place?"

Rachel looked down now, at the scuffed toe of her sneaker. Her head throbbed with the effort of remembering the details, as though her brain was trying to eliminate them before she could express them. "That's what's trashy about it. We just did it in a park. On the ground. And we didn't go all the way. We got interrupted. But I sure would have." *Even if it meant dying, like the old woman said,* she thought. *I wanted it that badly.*

Helena's eyes stayed wide open. "Wow. *Wow.* That doesn't sound like you at all."

"I know."

"And he hasn't called you today?"

Rachel blinked at the question. She hadn't even thought to check her cellphone. She pulled it from her pocket and, like a spear through her heart, saw the name of the person who *had* called last night, while she was writhing under Kyle Stillwater.

Ethan.

Helena saw her face. "So he *did* call?"

"What? No, he didn't."

Before she could close the phone, Helena snatched it away. "Then let's see who *did* make your jaw hit the floor."

Rachel grabbed for it. "Give me that!"

Helena fended her off and looked up in mock surprise. "Why, *Ethan Walker* called you. Twice."

Rachel grabbed the phone, snapped it shut, and stuffed it into her pocket.

The two women stood in silence for a long moment. At last Helena said quietly, "Rache, I saw how worried Ethan was when you disappeared. He's a good man."

Rachel said nothing.

Helena leaned close so their shoulders touched. "Well, you've been pretty levelheaded your whole life. I suppose you're entitled to one episode of sluttiness."

"So you think it *was* slutty?"

"I can't say. You can have sex with whoever you want. Only you know if the reasons were slutty."

Rachel pushed her slightly with her shoulder, and Helena responded in kind.

Rachel thought about Helena's observation. It *wasn't* slutty, she decided. It was . . . compulsory. She could no more have stopped herself than an addict like Jimmy could've walked away from a full needle of heroin.

Still, that knowledge did nothing to ease her mind. Or other areas that were growing more insistent as the day wore on.

MARTY WALKER LOOKED around Garrett Bloom's office in the dim illumination filtering through closed blinds. It looked standard: desk, filing cabinet, bookshelf, photos on the wall. The only sign of anything unusual was the yellow police tape across the door.

"Didn't you guys do this already?" a wiry young man said from the outer office. His name was Knox; he had curly hair and a scraggly beard, and crossed his arms nervously.

"We did," Marty said, "but I want to dig a little deeper."

"I wish Rebecca was here," Knox said. "She knows where everything is. I hardly ever got to come in Mr. Bloom's office."

Marty stood in the middle of the office, making a methodical circuit with his eyes. He hoped anything out of place would catch his attention. "Rebecca's his secretary?"

"Assistant. If you call her a secretary she'll either hit you or cry."

"What's her last name?"

"Matre. M-A-T-R-E."

Marty did not visibly react. He ate breakfast at the diner often and had heard Rachel mention her sister, Becky. And it had also come up earlier that day, during the routine questioning that went with any investigation.

Marty turned on the light. The added illumination showed the remains of fingerprint powder on every smooth surface, but no fresh clues jumped out. "Did he have a day planner or an appointment book?"

"I don't know," Knox said. "Do you want me to see if I can find Rebecca's phone number?"

"No," Marty said. "Just stay there for a minute while I look around."

"Shouldn't you have a warrant?"

Marty patted his jacket pocket. "You've been so helpful I haven't had to wave it around."

He pulled on rubber gloves and went behind the desk. He picked up the photograph of Bloom with a woman in a sundress: Mrs. Bloom, with essentially the same expression she'd had after learning of her husband's demise. Was she sour enough to cut out her husband's heart and nail his hand to a tree?

A calendar book was open to a date two days ago. Marty made note of all the appointments, knowing he'd have to call each person and find out what the meeting involved. Then he flipped ahead to the next day and wrote down all those appointments too.

"Was he working on anything pressing that you know of?" he asked Knox.

"That community center. Everything seemed to revolve around that lately."

Marty looked at what Bloom had written. "This says 'tribal council meeting' for tonight."

"Really?" Knox said, with what seemed to be genuine surprise. "That's actually kind of odd. He never said anything about that."

"So you don't know which tribe?"

"I'd assume the local Karlamiks. You know, the ones who run the bingo hall just outside town."

Marty made another note. The Karlamiks were a thoroughly modern band of Native Americans who employed top-notch PR in their quest to enter the lucrative gaming market. So far the state had refused permission to build casinos in Dane County, saying it was too near the capital, but that hadn't stopped the Karlamiks from opening an elaborate bingo parlor that had all the bells and whistles of a casino.

He put his notebook away. "There'll be some men here shortly to box up all these papers. Can you give them a hand?"

"Everything?" Knox said dubiously.

"We're looking for a murderer."

"I know, it's just . . ." He looked away and scratched his unshaven neck.

Marty's eyes narrowed. "There's something Bloom keeps secret, isn't there?"

Knox said nothing, but he pointed to the picture of Bloom and his wife. Marty picked it up, looked more closely, and found the CD stuffed into the frame between the picture and the backing board.

MARTY CLOSED THE folder on his desk, leaned back in his chair, and stared up at the ceiling.

Garrett Bloom, the great social activist, was a *fraud*.

The notes and correspondence he'd printed from the hidden CD proved beyond a doubt that Bloom's whole drive to build a community center was built on a deliberate deception. First the community center would be finished, with the surprise blessing of someone hired to represent the long-departed Lo-Stahzi. A ready-made story describing how they were actually the ancestors of the modern-day Karlamiks was already prepared, conveniently ignoring the utter lack of evidence for it. Then just before the center was to open, ancient artifacts would be discovered. This would cause the building to be classified as on tribal land, and the resurrected Lo-Stahzi would use the existing Karlamik PR organization to gain public sympathy for this once-forgotten tribe. Once that happened, a lawsuit would be filed, and the settlement proposed. Then the building would be retrofitted into a tribal casino located smack-dab in the middle of Madison.

And Garrett Bloom, in the center of this web, would reap profits at every turn—first as the savior of the local neighborhood, then as the "evil" developer trying to hang on to land that rightfully belonged to the Lo-Stahzi, before finally coming around and supporting the casino settlement. It was a reversal worthy of professional wrestling.

So what had gone wrong?

Kyle Stillwater, the Native American actor hired to pose as a Lo-Stahzi, was supposed to bless the project, not dispute it. Yet the man who showed up did not match the description of the actor, even taking makeup or special effects into account. Had Bloom been double-crossed by his coconspirators, represented in the notes by numerical codes?

Marty had no answers. And at the moment it didn't matter, because the trail to Bloom's apparent murderer led in a completely different direction. Yes, Kyle Stillwater threatened him, but so did someone else. Someone with a much more mundane motive and plenty of opportunity.

He locked up the files, then prepared to meet Ethan for dinner.

———

IT WAS ALMOST time for Martyn Park to close, so Patty tried to stay out of sight behind a tree. She often wondered how the city thought it could close a wide-open park with no fences or other ways to separate it from the rest of the world. Would an alarm go off if you stepped on the grass after eleven o'clock?

She felt like a spy, or a ninja. She wore a black T-shirt and black sweatpants, and wore her dark hair down around her face. There was probably no need for such an elaborate getup, but it added to the fun.

Not that her day had been much fun so far. After the scene with Rachel and her sister, Patty had gone home and cried herself to sleep. Then she woke up, wrote a few lines of a new song, and sat in the bathtub as the sun went down.

Rachel doesn't need that kind of psychodrama, she thought as she soaked. *No one does, but especially not someone like Rachel. She deserves a sister who cares about her, and supports her, and is there for Rachel—and not just when* she *needs something.*

She needs a sister, Patty thought with sudden realization, *like me.*

Then she remembered the lake spirits.

So now she stood in the darkness, looking down at the water lapping and smacking against the erosion-blocking rocks. The wind was strong, and the waves more violent than they'd been earlier. Patty knew the water was barely knee-deep here, but in the dark it looked bottomless and empty, a void waiting to swallow the unwary.

She peeked around the tree. The park was deserted, and a police car drove slowly down Yahara Street. *Where were they when I was being kidnapped?* Patty thought. *They've fixed the barn door after the horse has been rescued.*

When the car was safely out of sight, she kicked off her shoes, pushed up her pants legs, and sat down on one of the rocks, her feet dangling in the water. Once again, the smell reminded her of Dewey, and she smiled as she recalled their night together.

Then she closed her eyes and cleared her mind as much as possible. "I want to meet Rachel's spirits," she said aloud, since spoken intent carried more power.

Then she waited.

Until a shadow cast by one of the streetlamps fell over her.

CHAPTER SEVENTEEN

POSTED BY THE Lady to the *Lady of the Lakes* blog:

> The Lady needs your help. I want to find the rather, ahem, attractive gentleman who disrupted the ceremony at Olbrich Park over the weekend. I promise confidentiality, but I'd like to interview him for this blog. I know my readers, at least the female ones who appreciate a fine specimen of manhood, would love to know more about him. So if you're out there reading this, Kyle Stillwater, drop me a line. You have my word it'll go no further.

"THERE IS NO record anywhere of a Kyle Stillwater who matches the description of the man we saw," Marty said. "There's an actor with the same name, but he doesn't look like our man. We interviewed him, and it wasn't him."

Ethan and his brother sat in the Irish restaurant on the south side of the square. It was early evening on a weeknight, so they had the place mostly to themselves. Their server—a college boy with dyed-black hair— watched them from the bar in case they needed anything. They were his only customers.

"If he's an actor, maybe he was using makeup or wigs or something."

"You were there. Did he look like he had on makeup?"

"No," Ethan had to admit.

"It was probably an alias he got out of the phone book, or somewhere online. He needed a Native American–sounding name."

"And nobody has *any* photographs of him?"

"Not one that clearly shows his face. A lot of the people we talked to said their cameras or cellphones fritzed out on them. Even the newspeople didn't get anything substantial."

Ethan frowned. "That's weird."

"Yeah."

"And he's your prime suspect?"

"He's one of them. Everyone is until they're weeded out. Stillwater claimed to be a Lo-Stahzi, and Bloom was killed in imitation of a Lo-Stahzi sacrifice, so that puts him high on the list, if you're looking for something blatant."

"And are you?"

Marty shrugged. "Experience has taught me to look a little closer to home."

Ethan took a sip of beer. "How about Vincent Anspach? Is he on your list?"

"Sure."

"How high?"

Marty put down his utensils and narrowed his eyes. "Not very. He and Bloom didn't get along, but they're in politics, so *nobody* gets along. Why?"

Ethan told him about the meeting. When he finished, Marty said, "Well, that moves him up a few notches, for sure. But if he *was* involved, I doubt he was the triggerman. Or knife man, in this case. He's a backroom negotiator all the way."

"Maybe he hired a hit man."

Marty chuckled. "A hit man? Have you been watching cop shows again? Next thing, you'll want me to 'put the word on the street.'"

Marty's teasing annoyed Ethan. "He's already trying to horn in on the project, and Bloom's not even in the ground yet. I just wanted to pass on the info, smart-ass."

"Sure. And thanks." Marty reached over and took a swallow of Ethan's beer.

"Hey!" Ethan protested.

Marty burped slightly. "I'll have to work all this off in the gym tonight. By the way, have you talked to Rachel?"

"I tried. I called her twice. She didn't answer."

"And you're going to leave it at that?"

"Yes."

"Why?"

"Because I said I would. I shouldn't have even tried to call her."

Marty nodded. "I still eat breakfast at her diner, you know."

"I know."

"She looks very sad these days. Not in an unhealthy way, but just . . . lonely. I think she'd like to hear from you."

"I *tried*, Marty. She didn't call me back. There's only so much I can do."

Marty shrugged. "Well, be that as it may, I want to warn you about something. We have a prime suspect in the Bloom killing, and it's not that Stillwater guy."

"Really?"

Marty nodded. "There was a message in Bloom's voice mail left the night he died but before the time of death. It was . . . I don't want to get into specifics, but there was a veiled but clear threat."

"Isn't 'veiled but clear' a contradiction?"

"I believe the message said, 'Romeo and Juliet are together in eternity, and I want that for us, and I'll do whatever it takes to make it happen.'"

Ethan laughed. "You don't recognize that line? It's from a song. 'Don't Fear the Reaper.'"

"I know that. It's part of the 'veiled but clear' bit. And if Bloom wasn't lying in a morgue, I probably wouldn't think anything about it. But he is, and before it happened someone said they wanted to die with him. That's a clue."

"Maybe. It's thin."

"It's what we've got. And the person who left the message has no alibi. Since it's such a public crime, I *have* to make an arrest based on it, no matter how thin it is. That way we'll at least *look* like we're making progress. Hopefully the suspect will get a good lawyer, because the charges really shouldn't stick." He shook his head, disgusted with his own words.

"Why warn me?" Ethan asked.

"Because of who it is."

RACHEL WENT UPSTAIRS to her apartment after balancing the cash register and opened the door as quietly as possible. Becky didn't wake up well on good days, and if she was still asleep, Rachel would just as soon she stayed that way.

She heard the shower, though, as soon as she closed the door behind her. She went into the bedroom and saw Becky's clothes neatly arranged on the bed. Her purse stood open as well, and the temptation to snoop through it was strong. But Rachel ignored it. She went into the kitchen instead and got a beer.

By the time she finished her drink, Becky emerged from the bathroom. She wore a towel tucked under her arms, and her hair hung straight, parted in the middle. Her eyes were swollen from crying. She saw Rachel through the bedroom door and said weakly, "Hi."

"Hi," Rachel said, and held up the empty bottle. "Want a beer?"

Becky shook her head. Her voice was subdued and lacked its usual defensiveness. "No, thanks. I hope you don't mind me using your shower."

"No problem." Rachel came into the bedroom and sat on the foot of the bed. "Feel like talking?"

Becky dropped the towel and began dressing. "No. I should probably go down to the office. It'll be a madhouse, and I may be the only person who knows where everything is."

"It's late."

She shrugged. "We never kept set hours. Garrett wanted to be available when people needed him."

Rachel nodded. "I'm sorry about him."

"Me too," Becky muttered.

Rachel idly watched her sister put on her clothes.

"Rachel," Becky said abruptly, "can I ask you something?"

"Sure."

"Do you remember how Daddy used to watch the news and say, 'Some people just need killing'?"

"Yeah."

"Do you think that's true?"

"Yeah. The problem is, who gets to pick?"

Becky considered that as she buttoned her blouse. Finally Rachel said, "Do you want to stay here tonight? So you won't be alone?" It would mean Rachel could not slip away to the lakes, but for the first time in months she didn't mind.

But Becky shook her head. "No. If no one's at the office I'll go home. I want people to be able to reach me. I feel bad that I freaked out earlier."

She adjusted her clothes, smoothed down her hair, and managed a smile. Rachel stood and reached to hug her, but Becky put up her hands and stepped back. "Don't, Rachel. I'm barely holding it together as it is."

"Okay," Rachel said. She was silent as Becky gathered her belongings and went to the door.

Becky paused there but did not look back or say anything. Then she was gone, her footsteps fading as she descended the stairs. In the silence the back door opened, then closed with a loud click as the lock slid back in place.

Rachel picked up the discarded towel and went into the bathroom. As usual, Becky had left it a mess, and she spent several minutes cleaning and straightening. When she finished, she got another beer and sat on her couch.

Tainter emerged from under it. He'd known Becky his whole feline life and understood that it was best to be scarce when she was around. Rachel often wished she had that option as well.

She scratched the cat behind his ears while he stretched and raked his claws lightly over the couch's fabric. It was unlike her to have a second beer, but she felt so odd and off-kilter inside, she figured it wouldn't matter. By the third sip she was yawning, and she stretched out to sleep away the rest of the evening.

JAMES RED BIRD reclined on his bed in the Best Western across from the state capitol. He wore only boxers emblazoned with an American eagle, and his long hair was loose around his shoulders. He watched the local news, which was rife with coverage of Garrett Bloom's murder. They talked to everyone who ever met him, it seemed, including James Red Bird; he was watching to see if his comments would be used.

The bathroom door opened and a blond girl emerged. She wore a towel around her hair, and nothing else. She was intimately clean-shaven, and had a Native American design tattooed across the small of her back.

Red Bird glanced at her, then turned back to the TV. Her name was Stacy. She was one of those middle-class white girls with just enough enlightenment to feel culturally guilty for what her people had done to his, and he was happy to show her ways to make reparations. She'd spent the evening doing just that, convinced she was helping him through a difficult time.

That made Red Bird smile. Providing a way to get this beautiful girl on her back was the best thing Garrett Bloom had ever done for him. Too bad it was also the last.

"Are they still talking about your friend?" Stacy asked as she began to brush her hair.

"They took time out for the weather and the score from last night's Mallards game," Red Bird said. "Now they're doing a bio on him."

She stretched out beside him and fingered his hair. "Will this be coming off?"

Red Bird frowned. "What?"

"Don't your people cut their hair to express their grief?"

"Yes, when family dies. Garrett Bloom wasn't family."

"You said he was like a brother to you."

Red Bird shrugged. "It's hard to talk about."

She kissed his bare chest. "Okay."

As her kisses proceeded down his torso, his mind turned to what he would tell the police when he met with them tomorrow. It was important that most of what he told them be the truth; complex lies were too difficult to track.

By now Stacy had reached her destination, and her expert caresses were stirring him back to life. He laced his fingers behind his head and said pitifully, "Stacy, I don't know, I'm just so upset about Garrett. . . ."

She renewed her efforts, and they had the expected result. He reached down and ruffled her blond hair, still wet from the shower, the way he might pet a dog. "You deserve this, Jim," she said huskily, and returned to her activity.

He smiled at the ceiling, and at the certainty that she was, in fact, dead right.

CHAPTER EIGHTEEN

RACHEL STOOD OUTSIDE the diner's back door in her running shorts and T-shirt. It was past midnight, and the air was hazy with humidity. Insects swarmed the security light, and she knew that if she didn't get moving, the ones drawn to blood would then swarm to *her*. But she couldn't quite make herself move yet.

She put her hands on her hips and closed her eyes. The old woman from her . . . dream, vision, *whatever,* had said: *"He has severed their connection to you."* And the spirits had avoided her when she sought them after her tryst with Stillwater. But surely they were strong enough that they could still come to her if they wanted.

Her head still buzzed from the beer, and the off-kilter feeling had grown. What did she truly hope to find at the park? Her lake spirits, Ethan Walker, or Kyle Stillwater?

She knew what her *body* wanted to find. Despite

everything, the thought of how Stillwater had felt beside her filled her with an unexpected longing. Not even Ethan inspired this. But there was no tenderness to it, no sense of love, only pure lust of the most degenerate kind. He'd been a millimeter away from possessing her intimately, and her body desperately wanted to close that gap.

And that's what held her in place. Shouldn't she be craving the comfort and tenderness of Ethan, the man who'd risked his own life to save hers? Shouldn't she fucking *call him back*? Why couldn't she?

She sighed and set out down the street. Maybe nonsexual physical exercise would help clear her head. A lone taxicab passed her, and the driver waved lazily. She recognized him but couldn't dredge up his name.

Her joints felt stiff and awkward, and she wished she'd stretched more beforehand. But she forced herself through the discomfort, and soon her muscles were sliding with their usual smoothness beneath her damp skin.

"Soon he will be able to trap and destroy the spirits," the woman had said.

Rachel felt a tingle of warning as she approached Hudson Park and stopped a block away. She drew deep breaths as she took in the familiar view: the streetlamps swarming with insects, the grass glittering with dew, and the shape of the lake-spirit effigy mound, the weeds and grass atop it uncut out of respect.

Bad things had happened to her here before, of course. Arlin Korbus had kidnapped her, for one thing. She could've chosen a different spot for her nightly swim after that, since the spirits waited for her wherever she entered the lake. But Hudson Park was *her* sacred space, and she refused to be chased away.

Still, she ducked into the shadow of a tree and peeked around it, studying the small park in more detail. Nothing moved. All was silent, except for the expected noises. *You're paranoid,* she scolded herself.

Then she heard something else. It was too soft to identify at first, and then it grew louder. Someone in the park was *laughing*. A woman.

Rachel clutched the tree trunk so hard that one of her fingernails bent.

Faint but clear, the chuckles came out of the humid night like the echoing call of a ghost. The contempt and triumph in the sound made Rachel grit her teeth.

At last a female silhouette came up the hill from the water's edge. At first Rachel couldn't say what was odd about it, and then she realized: The woman was wet from swimming, and *nude*. Her skin glistened the way Rachel's always did, sparkling as the droplets ran down. She clutched something like a small football in one hand.

The stranger picked up a robe from the ground, pulled it on, and cinched it tight. Rachel gasped. Now she recognized her silhouette. It was the woman who'd spied on her following her tryst with Stillwater.

The woman paused by the effigy mound's head. She paused at the circle of stones. "Thank you for holding them for me, Artemak," she said. "It made catching them so much easier."

Rachel recalled the strange word from the ceremony at the park. Was this the woman she'd also glimpsed that day?

Still chuckling to herself, the woman walked to a small car parked in the darkness beneath a tree. She drove two blocks before turning on her lights, then disappeared around a corner.

Rachel stayed in the shadows. Her stomach was knotted not with the usual sensual anticipation but with an uncertainty so strong it paralyzed her. She felt absolutely no tug toward the water. She watched the surface of the lake sparkle in the night, but nothing happened within her. Her clothes did not grow uncomfortable, and her body did not tingle with slow arousal. She took several deep breaths and tried to force the feeling that had sustained her for so many years, but nothing happened.

With a sigh of resignation she turned and started home. Every few steps she glanced back, hoping to see—or was it dreading to see?—Kyle Stillwater loom out of the night and beckon her into his embrace. She imagined running to him, crushing herself against his hard body, falling to her knees before him to worship him with her mouth. My God, she wanted that, and the realization filled her with self-loathing and loneliness. But he didn't appear, and eventually she turned the corner and lost sight of the park.

KYLE STILLWATER SAT in his bathtub as his shower rained weakly down on him. The water was no longer hot, but he did not move. Henry Hawes had told him he was possessed, and Henry knew about such things. There was something inside Kyle now that delighted in causing others to suffer.

Kyle looked at his hand. The tiny scar on one knuckle was still there. He'd gotten it as a child riding his bike, and his mother had bandaged it with a piece of paper towel and some duct tape, since they couldn't afford real Band-Aids. *My sweet little boy,* she'd said to him, and held him while he cried. Could a man with that memory of kindness really be possessed by something evil?

At last he stood up and turned off the water. He toweled off his hair and body, ignoring the body spray he usually wore. Then he stepped out of the tub and grabbed the edge of the sink as a wave of nausea hit him.

When he looked up and saw his face in the mirror, he screamed.

It was him, and yet it *wasn't* him. Instead of his own light blue eyes, there were round black orbs bigger than they should have been. His strong nose had elongated to a sharp point, as had his chin. He would've looked, in fact, like the Christian devil if his skin wasn't suddenly bone-white.

His upstairs neighbor stomped on the floor. "Shut up!"

He turned away from the mirror, his heart thundering in his chest. He closed his eyes, took a deep breath, and looked back.

His face was normal. But now his *hair* was snowy white.

He pulled a strand in front of his face. It wasn't a hallucination or mistake. What the *hell*?

And then he blacked out.

DARIUS DID A double take as his neighbor came outside. The older man slept only in short bursts, and since he couldn't afford to run the air conditioner, he sat out on his patio even in the middle of the night. He knew the young Indian was trying to be an actor, but he'd never seen him in costume before. "Whoa, that's quite a look. What's up with that?"

Kyle turned and gazed at the older black man. "What do you mean?"

"That white hair. You going to an audition or something? Gonna play an old man?"

Kyle smiled, and the look made Darius nervous. "No," Kyle said. "I'm going . . . for a swim."

"At this time of night?"

"Oh, yes. And I don't think I'll be back."

"Before morning?"

The smile widened. It made Darius think of the wolves he'd seen on the Discovery Channel. "Ever," Kyle said, and strode away down the street.

CHAPTER NINETEEN

R ACHEL?" HELENA SAID a second time.

Rachel looked up. She was alone in the diner's tiny, genderless restroom; Helena's voice had come through the door from outside. Rachel said, "Huh? What?"

Helena was obviously trying to mask her concern. "Just wondered if you were about done in there. We're getting a line."

"Yes, I'm sorry." Rachel turned off the tap and dried her hands. Her fingertips had pruned; how long had the water been running?

She dried her hands and caught sight of herself in the mirror. She saw something different in her face but couldn't identify it. Did she look older somehow? More worried and stressed? Were there lines on her face that hadn't been there before?

She opened the door. Almost before she could get out, a slender college girl slithered past her. Her sigh of relief was audible through the door.

Helena tried to meet her eyes, but Rachel ignored her. She also ignored Patty, seated at the counter, watching with blatant concern. She went into the kitchen, where Jimmy was finishing an order of hash browns. His sleeves were long today, pushed halfway up his forearms. That meant he either had fresh needle tracks to hide or needed to do laundry because all his short-sleeved shirts were dirty. Rachel didn't have the energy to determine which. If he was using again, she'd have to fire him.

Jimmy saw her and volunteered, "It's laundry night tonight."

She smiled weakly. "You don't have to prove anything to me, Jimmy."

"I know. I just don't want you thinking badly of me when there's no reason."

Helena touched Rachel's arm and said quietly, "You're sure spacing out today. Are you getting sick?"

"No, I'm just a little out of sorts."

"Why don't you go upstairs and lie down? I can handle this until the lunch crowd starts. I'll call in one of the other girls. Hell, Patty can help out, after all the free coffee we've given her."

"No, don't be silly. It'll pass."

When she returned to the dining room, Patty waved her over. "I really need to talk to you," the girl said eagerly.

"What about?"

Patty looked around, then leaned close. She whispered, "It happened again."

"What did?"

Still whispering, she said, "Remember that boy

Dewey Raintree? Well, I don't think he was . . . I mean, I know he was *real,* but I don't think he was . . . *human.*"

"I don't understand," Rachel said.

"I think your lake spirits sent him."

"Why do you think that?"

"Because of the way he smelled. I know how it sounds, but he smelled like lake water. Not like he'd been swimming in it, but like . . . he was made of it."

Rachel put all her energy into focusing on this. "Okay, but . . . you said it happened again. Did he come back?"

"Not him," she said with a blushing giggle. "Someone else. Someone else so perfect, he just *has* to be from them."

Rachel felt a chill at what this could mean. The old woman had said Rachel's "spirit sister" was also in danger; had Stillwater also come to Patty? And if so . . . "Who was it?" Rachel asked.

Before Patty could answer, the bell over the door rang. A tall woman with unruly jet-black hair entered, looked around, and took a seat at the counter. Her dark hair and eyes made her look like a Gypsy. She had a theatrical quality that drew every eye.

Patty stood, bouncing with excitement. "I have to go. We'll talk about it later, okay?" Before Rachel could protest, the girl was out the door, almost dancing away down the sidewalk.

On her way out of the kitchen with a tray full of orders, Helena said, "Can you get that woman that just came in? I've got my hands full right now."

"Sure," Rachel said, still gazing after Patty. She

would have to pursue this, but for now, she had a customer. Rachel took silverware and a glass of water to her and said, "Hi. Welcome to Rachel's. You've got about five minutes left on breakfast, or you can go ahead and order from the lunch menu."

The woman looked at her closely, with a kind of scrutiny that made Rachel nervous. The woman wasn't trying to place her but seemed to be looking for something in her face.

"Just coffee for the moment," she said at last. Her voice was deep and throaty. She rested her hands flat on the counter. The nails were bare and ragged, and what looked like pinpoints of paint stained her dark skin. "You're Rachel, aren't you?"

"I am."

"I'm Betty McNally," she said, and offered her hand. "It's a pleasure to meet you."

They shook. Betty's hand was long-fingered, heavy-veined, and warm. When their skin touched, Rachel felt a strange, almost erotic, tingle. She pulled away as quickly as possible.

"Is there something I can help you with, besides coffee?" Rachel asked.

"I think you and I may have something in common."

"Really? What's that?"

She put a business card facedown on the counter. "It's something we should discuss in private. Can you come by my place this evening?"

"I don't know, I'm awfully busy tonight," Rachel demurred. She had to talk to Patty, and Betty was giving her the creeps.

Betty leaned over the counter and said quietly, "It has to do with the lakes."

Rachel's mouth went dry. As casually as she could manage, she said, "What about them?"

"What lives in them," Betty said. Then, so quiet even Rachel could barely hear, she added, "What they do to you."

Helena appeared beside Rachel with a cup on a saucer. "I heard you say you'd like some coffee," she said brightly. "Would you like cream with that?"

"No, thank you," Betty said to Helena, although she continued to look at Rachel.

Helena said nothing but waited to get Rachel's attention. The two women seemed to be locked in a staring contest, and when another customer called, Helena sighed in exasperation and left.

Betty said, "Like I said, we have something in common, and I have information you need to know."

It took Rachel three tries to pick up the card with her trembling fingers. It advertised Art Waves, a gallery and tarot salon. It was no stretch to imagine Betty laying out cards and peering into a crystal ball. "I'll try," Rachel said.

"It would be in your best interest to talk to me."

The haze cleared for a moment. "Is that a threat?" Rachel asked.

Betty smiled. "No, honey. It's a warning." She kissed the tips of her first two fingers and touched them to Rachel's lips. "I hope to see you soon."

She stood, put a five-dollar bill down beside the untouched coffee, then left. Rachel stared after her until Helena said, "Who was *that*?"

Rachel handed the card to Helena. "She owns an art gallery, apparently."

Helena looked at it. "Never heard of it. Or her."

Rachel tucked the card into her jeans pocket, went back to work, and tried unsuccessfully to put the woman out of her mind.

ETHAN WEARILY CLOSED the door to his inner office. Ambika was busily shutting down her computer and filing things in appropriate cabinets. He reached the office door, stopped, and leaned forward until his head rested against the wood. "Damn," he muttered.

Ambika looked around. "Forget something?"

"No." He tossed his briefcase contemptuously onto the guest couch. "I'm just disgusted with life at the moment."

She crossed her arms, displaying her immaculate white nails. "How so?"

"I just want to build things, you know? Houses, apartment buildings, whatever anyone wants. I don't need to be rich, and I'm not using this as a stepping-stone to politics. So why do I feel like everyone I talk to is trying to put something over on me?"

"Because most of them are."

"I know. I just wish it didn't have to be so complicated." He sighed as he retrieved his briefcase. "Wouldn't it be a great world if people just said what they meant?"

Ambika smiled wryly. "That world doesn't exist. People are so invested in their own realities that they'll protect them at any expense. The truth, to them, is a threat."

He laughed. "Are you a philosopher too?"

"Goodness, no. I'm simply amused by what I see around me."

"Is it different in India?"

"The details are different. The underlying motivations are the same."

He smiled, patted her arm, and left the office. On his way down the stairs, the urge to call Rachel was so overwhelming it was like physical hunger.

CHAPTER TWENTY

ART WAVES OCCUPIED a building not unlike the one that housed Rachel's diner. It was a free-standing two-story brick structure with the business on the ground floor and what looked like living quarters above. Nestled among the tiny houses along Atwood Avenue, it looked more like a spooky fortune-teller's grotto than anything. The windows were heavily curtained, and shelves between the fabric and the glass displayed odd, vaguely unsettling objets d'art.

Rachel stood indecisively on the sidewalk, debating whether or not to go through with this. The street was completely deserted; it wasn't yet dark, but none of the houses—mostly old ones divided into student apartments—showed any signs of life. She'd brought an umbrella, since the weatherman predicted the occasional thunderstorm, but the sky was clear at the moment. The sunset cast a red glow over everything.

There was a Closed sign tucked in one corner of the

front window. But she was expected, so she took a deep breath and tried the door. It opened.

Cool air hit her, and a little chime sounded somewhere in the back. It took a moment for her eyes to adjust to the dim interior. Finally she began to make out shelves and tables of elaborate pieces, as well as huge canvases covering the walls.

She yelped as light flooded the room. Track lighting carefully illuminated each painting, and the first thing that registered was an enormous oil canvas directly in front of her. Its colors were primarily blue, green, and black, with hints of yellow for texture. This limited palette made it hard to decipher, but she picked out a human form emerging from what appeared to be a whirlpool. The figure was clearly male. *Uncomfortably* male, Rachel noticed, and tried not to blush.

A voice behind her said, "Charismatic, isn't he?"

Rachel again jumped in surprise. Betty McNally chuckled and said, "I'm sorry. I didn't mean to be dramatic."

This almost made Rachel laugh. Betty wore a strapless sundress with little, if anything, beneath it. Around her neck was a choker with a drop in a shape that was familiar but that Rachel couldn't quite place.

Betty stood with her hands on her hips. The pose was provocative yet at the same time defensive. She added, "That's a self-portrait. If I were a man."

Rachel's eyebrows rose. "Interesting."

Betty gestured to herself. "I'm quite voluptuous as a woman. If I were a man, how would the same level of masculinity manifest?"

"That's one way," Rachel agreed, increasingly questioning her decision to come here.

Betty moved closer, invading Rachel's personal space. The air between them seemed to quiver. "So you came," she said firmly. "You want to know what *I* know about . . . *them*."

"I'm curious as to what you meant, yes."

Betty smiled. "I'll be blunt, then. I meant that I know about the spirits that live in the lakes, who fuck you when you swim with them and keep you tied to them with sexual bondage."

"I'm not tied to anything," Rachel said, and took a step back.

Betty smiled knowingly. "How many human men have made you come, eh? You don't have to hide the truth from me."

Rachel glanced at the door, wondering if she could get to it and escape before Betty did . . . what? Besides, Rachel was here to find out what Betty knew, and playing dumb would just prolong things. She chewed her lip thoughtfully, then said, "Okay, yeah."

"I'm right?"

"Yeah. You're right. They . . ."

"Own you?"

"I prefer to think we have an arrangement."

Betty nodded, then went behind the counter and produced a bottle. She poured red wine into two waiting glasses. "Then that makes us sisters."

"How so?" Rachel said.

Betty laughed and handed her a glass. "I've been taken by the spirits too. Do you recognize this?" She held out the necklace that had looked so familiar.

Rachel leaned close, then caught herself staring not at the drop but at the woman's neck. There was an odd tension between them. It wasn't *sexual,* the way women occasionally hit on Rachel when she was out with Helena. But it spoke of skin, and sweat, and things done urgently in the dark. And it gave Rachel a serious case of the creeps. "No," she said at last. "I don't recognize it."

"It's one of the lakes," Betty said.

Wingra, Rachel suddenly realized. It was the outline of tiny Lake Wingra, the smallest of the three lakes inside the city limits. A lake that she avoided, that always gave her the willies, and that seemed to carry an evil reputation. "You swam in Lake Wingra, then?"

Betty laughed. "'Swam'? No, honey, I took off my clothes and let the spirits in the lake wring me out, just like you do. I fought and struggled and screamed, and they just wouldn't stop. Each time I swore I'd never go back, but when it's the only way you can have an orgasm, 'never' doesn't last too long."

"It's different for me," Rachel said, recalling the gentle caresses, the supple manipulations, and above all, the kindness shown even during the wildest moments.

Betty shrugged. "I'm sure it is. But my spirits haven't touched me in years. And do you know why?"

Rachel shook her head.

"Because of *him.* That man who came from the lake that day in the park. He came to me as well, many years ago. He looked exactly the same too. He seduced me, then left me alone. After that, my spirits wouldn't have me."

Something nagged at Rachel's memory. In her vision, the Lo-Stahzi medicine woman had claimed that Kyle Stillwater was possessed by a Wingra spirit. Yet that couldn't be right if Betty was telling the truth. . . .

Betty's voice grew distant as she continued. "I've thought about it over the years, and I don't think it was because I made love to him. I think it was because I *wanted* him in the first place. The lake spirits are jealous."

Rachel could barely breathe. "But . . . what does that have to do with me?"

Betty stepped close, and again there was that weird moment of connection. "He'll come to you, Rachel. He'll say what you want to hear, and you'll respond. But you *can't give in.* You can't *want* him. The moment you do, your spirits will no longer want *you*."

Rachel couldn't breathe. "That's crazy."

Betty shrugged. "So is having lake spirits as your lover. But we both know that happens."

Rachel licked her lips. "If . . . If I do . . . give in to him . . . how can I fix it?"

Betty looked at her. "You can't. I've already tried everything. I've begged, pleaded, made sacrifices, and cast spells. I've tried to reclaim my sexuality. Men, women, singles, groups, devices . . . I tried them all. Each time I got close, the feeling just . . . stayed. Hovering there, just out of reach. I even spent time in a mental hospital, for God's sake. They diagnosed me as 'sexually maladjusted, likely due to childhood trauma.' They thought I'd been molested and blocked it out—the whole 'repressed memory' thing."

Rachel turned away but found herself facing the

huge painting of Betty McNally as a man. Her knees wobbled, and she had to lean on the wall.

"I've come to believe only one thing can end my torment, and the torment of anyone else unfortunate enough to fall victim to the same thing," Betty continued.

"What?" Rachel said, eyes closed, trying not to pass out.

"We must summon Kyle Stillwater on our own terms. And make him do our bidding."

MARTY WALKER HAD parked on the street outside the police building instead of in the garage. He was tired, and his head hurt. He did not relish the arrest he'd have to make tomorrow, but the district attorney insisted the voice mail was an indictable threat. Marty's instincts told him differently, but those carried no weight with the D.A. He was about to open his car door when a voice said, "Fancy running into you here."

He turned to confront the speaker and stopped dead. Amy Vannoy, in a tight black dress cut low in front and high on her thigh, stood with a cardboard box under one bare arm. Her black hair was done up formally, and she wore restrained but perfect makeup.

"I'm speechless," he said honestly.

She held out the box. "I have something here I want to show you. I called ahead and asked the desk sergeant if you were around. Looks like I got here just in time."

"Did you dress up to come see me?"

She laughed. "No, I was at a faculty dinner when I had a brainstorm. I slipped out between speeches."

Marty took the box, and they went back into the station. The desk sergeant stared as Amy passed, and she rewarded him with a wink as the elevator doors closed.

At Marty's desk, Amy opened the box and pulled out a small clay bowl. Clearly of Native American design, it was missing a large section of its lip. "We had this in the museum on campus."

"What is it?"

"A Karlamik bowl. Probably four hundred years old."

"Should you be toting it around?"

"I'm being careful. But I want to show you something. Like I said, I was at this faculty function in the museum and saw this on display. It made me think of the fragments from the construction site. I still had them in my Jeep." She held up a plastic bag. "I suspected from the moment I saw these that they were the same type of pottery. But there's something more to it."

She took out an irregular fragment and matched it to the missing part of the pot. The edges fit perfectly.

"It's not just from the same culture, it's from the exact same pot. Now that's either a coincidence or a clue."

Marty frowned. "I'll say. What does it mean?"

"I did some checking on this pot's provenance. Everything that's tied to a Native American tribe nowadays is scrutinized very carefully, to make sure it wasn't stolen. This wasn't; it was donated."

"By whom?"

"A Mr. James Red Bird of the Karlamik tribe."

Marty's eyes widened. "Aha."

"You know him?"

"His name has come up."

She carefully returned the pot to the box. "Then I helped?"

"Definitely. Thank you."

She picked up the box, but he put his hand on it. "I'm afraid this now counts as evidence."

She looked appalled. "But I can't leave this here. I'm not even supposed to *have* it. I could lose my job."

"And a murderer might go free if I lose this."

"Oh, come on, detective, seriously. It's in a locked case at the museum, and only a few people have a key."

"That's a few too many." But when he saw how distraught she was, he smiled. "All right, I'll tell you what. Is your party still going on?"

She checked her watch. "Probably."

"Then let's you and I go back to the museum now, and I'll pretend to make a brilliant deduction. That way you're off the hook, I have my evidence, and the bad guys don't get away."

She looked so relieved he almost laughed. "*Thank you, officer.*"

"Please, call me Marty."

"Thank you, Marty."

IT WAS FULLY dark by the time Rachel returned home. The wind brought distant rumbles of thunder as a storm approached from the west. She numbly let herself into the closed diner, ascended the stairs to her apartment, and then locked the door behind her. She leaned back against it, and only then did she begin to shake. Her breathing accelerated, and she found herself on the verge of hyperventilating.

At last she regained control and went into the kitchen. She poured herself a glass of wine, drank it quickly, then topped off her glass and drank even more. By the time her face began to tingle from the alcohol, she saw that her fingers no longer trembled.

Ethan. I have to suck it up and call Ethan. He's the only one who'll understand.

She went to her cellphone and opened it. She had told Ethan she would contact him when she'd worked through the trauma of her abduction, when she could see him without also seeing the sweaty, scowling face of Arlin Korbus. She hadn't done that. It was time to grow up and face her fears.

She found his number in her missed-calls list. He'd tried to reach her in the middle of the night, just as she was falling under Kyle Stillwater's spell. Cosmic coincidence, or her spirits trying to keep her from making a horrible mistake? And why hadn't she called him back, *really*? What in the sonofabitching goddamned hell *was* she afraid of?

She hit the dial button. It felt like calling the first boy she ever had a crush on. The line rang several times. Then his voice said, "Hi, you've reached Ethan Walker of Walker Construction. I can't take your call right now. . . ."

She closed her phone. She understood now why he

hadn't left a message. What kind of message could either of them possibly leave?

She drank some more wine. First things first. There was only one way to know the truth of Betty McNally's warning. And it was too early in the evening for that yet.

Big raindrops splattered against the window.

"YOU AGAIN," A female voice said.

Ethan looked up from the weight bench, where he lay on his back with seventy-five pounds across his chest. A smiling redhead with freckles on every inch of exposed skin looked down at him.

"Cindy," he said, instantly recalling her name.

"Very good," she replied.

He pushed the bar up and away from his chest, trying to make it look easy despite the protest in his shoulder. He was used to heavier weights, but the change in the weather had made his weakened shoulder ache, and he'd learned the hard way to give it a break at times like this. "Did you have another late meeting?" he asked as he sat up.

She tossed him one of the small white towels the gym provided. "Actually, yes. And it was about to start raining, so I knew that if I didn't work out now, I'd talk myself out of it."

He wiped his face and neck. He'd first met Cindy just before the whole Rachel Matre experience, and while she was definitely a stunner as well as being quick-witted, he'd brushed her off as politely as possible.

Now, though, he'd accepted that Rachel would never call.

He noticed that she was sweaty as well. "Are you finished, then?"

"I could be," she said.

He stood. "Then let's get cleaned up and go have a drink."

JAMES RED BIRD listened as his lawyer, Maurice Langkamp, spoke quickly and earnestly. "I was at a function at the campus museum, and a cop came in, looking at the pottery collection. He confiscated one of the pieces you donated."

Red Bird's stomach plummeted. He kept nothing from his lawyer. "How in God's name did he *know*?"

"I don't know, but he did, and you better act fast. Come to my home right now and we'll figure out our next step."

Red Bird snapped his phone shut, tucked it back in his pants pocket, and turned to his wife. "I have to go out for a while."

She looked up from the couch, where she was reading *Us* magazine. "Will you be late?" she asked flatly.

"I'll try not to be gone too long."

"It's raining," she said. "Take an umbrella."

"Thanks."

He looked away, unable to bear the steady, laser-hot scrutiny of his wife's gaze. Their marriage existed on a bed of unspoken knowledge with edges that blurred if looked at too closely. She knew he was unfaithful, but he was careful to keep the details out of public sight.

And if she, too, had lovers—something he found impossible to imagine—she kept that to herself. To the public they were a successful married couple, and an example to all Native Americans, not just other Karlamiks. They both understood the importance of that role.

He backed out of the garage and into a deluge. The wipers barely kept pace as he headed down the highway toward Madison.

"I KNOW I keep harping on it, but this just isn't ethical," Maurice Langkamp said.

Marty Walker laughed. "Ethics and lawyers. That's like military intelligence, isn't it?" He looked around in disgust at the palatial lakeside home.

"You have no cause to talk to me like that. And besides, if you know who killed Garrett Bloom—"

"I'm going to make an arrest. That's not the same thing as knowing who did it. And I'm doing your client a favor, Maurice, so don't push it. I've got enough evidence to have him very publicly hauled in for questioning as an accessory. I'm betting it won't help his fund-raising if the label 'person of interest' gets attached to him."

Langkamp sighed. "I can't always pick and choose my clients, Marty. And if I take one on, I'm obligated to do the best I can."

Marty was saved the need to reply by a soft knock at the study door. James Red Bird opened it slightly and said, "Maurice? Antoinette said you were in here."

"Come on in, Jim," Langkamp said. "And close the door."

Red Bird stopped suddenly when he saw Marty. "Who's this?" he asked suspiciously.

"Detective Martin Walker, Madison police," Marty said formally. He did not offer to shake hands.

Red Bird's eyes cut between the two men. "What's this about?"

"About the murder of Garrett Bloom, Mr. Red Bird," Marty said. "I have evidence that places you at the scene the night of the killing."

Red Bird began to sweat, but his voice was steady when he asked Langkamp, "Am I under arrest?"

"If you were," Marty said, "I'd have read you your rights by now. Truthfully, I don't think you had anything to do with it, because Bloom's death put the kibosh on your plans to open a casino on the isthmus."

"To do *what*?" Red Bird said, eyes wide with the perfect level of confusion. "Garrett Bloom was a great man, and—"

"And he kept copious notes," Marty said. "He wasn't about to get caught with only his neck on the block. But that's not what really interests me right now. I want to know what you saw that night. If you tell me now, I'll keep my source to myself if I possibly can, which keeps you out of the news."

"I was nowhere near Garrett Bloom when he died," Red Bird said formally.

Langkamp sighed. "Jim, please. He's doing you a favor."

"You were seeding the site of the new community center so that it would be classified as Indian land,"

Marty said. "I can positively link you to the pottery shards you used. I can prove you were in league with Bloom on the casino plot."

The study was silent. Finally Red Bird said, "Maurice?"

Langkamp ran a hand through his thinning hair. "My advice is to answer his questions now in private, instead of later on the record. This is off the record, right, Marty?"

Marty did not reply but continued to stare evenly at Red Bird. A flash of lightning lit the room, followed by a window-rattling thunderclap.

"Apparently the Great Spirit wants me to answer your questions too," Red Bird said wryly. "All right. Yes, I seeded the site. I'm not admitting to any reason for it, but I did it."

"What time?" Marty asked.

"Just after midnight."

"Did Garrett Bloom know you were going to do it?"

"Yes. He didn't know when, though. Plausible deniability and all that."

Marty nodded. "Did you see him that night?"

"No."

"What *did* you see?"

"Nothing. I was in and out in ten minutes. I didn't expect the gate to be locked, so I had to throw the stuff over the fence. I'm not a very good petty criminal."

"Did you see anyone else in the park?"

"No."

"On the street?"

"No, I said. Look, really, if I did, I'd tell you. Garrett was my friend. Whatever else you may think about me, I swear to you that much is true. I liked him, we'd known each other for years, and we had plans for the future. If I knew anything that would help, I'd tell you."

Marty nodded. "All right. I believe that'll be all, Mr. Red Bird. *If* you've told me the truth."

"I've answered your questions."

Marty smiled. "And we both know that's not the same thing."

Again Red Bird looked from Langkamp to Marty. "So I'm off the hook?"

"As long as you had nothing to do with his murder, you're off *my* hook," Marty said. "I can't speak to what other government agencies might do."

"But somebody would have to tip them off first, wouldn't they?" he said.

Marty shrugged. "They might, if you try to hone your petty-crime skills. If you don't, I have no reason to ever discuss you with anyone. And truthfully, that makes me very happy."

Red Bird nodded, turned toward the door, then stopped again. "In the spirit of full disclosure, then . . . there's one more thing."

CHAPTER TWENTY-ONE

RACHEL STOOD NAKED, ankle-deep in the water. The rain had stopped, and now everything glistened with moisture. The night air was heavy with the promise of more precipitation, and even the mosquitoes seemed intimidated by it. Or perhaps the fear radiating from her repelled them.

More tentatively than she'd done in years, she stepped out into the water. It rose up her legs as it always did, but this time it felt unnatural, warm and slick with pollution and algae. When she was waist-deep, she waited for the first caress—the initial foreplay that signaled her lovers' presence—but nothing happened.

She stood very still. The water, turbulent from the wind, began to slap her more roughly. Beneath the surface things would be different, and it wasn't until a surge struck her in the face that she worked up the nerve.

She slid down under the water and let herself drift, waiting for the spirits to announce themselves. Above her the water still swirled and fought the wind, and she found it hard to keep herself oriented. She surfaced for a quick breath and instead got a face full of wind and water, which choked her and sent her into a momentary panic.

She managed to get some air and slid beneath the water again. It was black, and the noise sounded like a train muffled by layers of blankets. She kicked and tried to stay in place, awaiting the steadying caress of water-formed fingers.

She held out until her lungs burned. The spirits couldn't abandon her, she thought desperately—not like this, not without warning. She gulped a new breath and sank three more times. But nothing happened.

The spirits did not come to her.

Were they ignoring her, as Betty McNally had said? Or were they weakened and nearly destroyed, as the old Lo-Stahzi woman had told her? She felt panic rise, along with the desperate need to take another breath.

Old woman, she cried mentally, *tell me what to do! There must be a way!* She burst above the surface, praying she'd see the untouched shoreline and the Lo-Stahzi medicine woman, but it was still night, and she was still in her own time.

She stumbled from the water as the storm hit, pelting her bare skin with needle-sharp droplets. Her tears were lost in the rain, and she struggled to pull on her soaked clothes as thunder crashed above her.

Suddenly there was a crash so loud that it tore through her ears like an ice pick, and a bright blue light illuminated the area. With a rifle-shot crack, a tree limb crashed down through lower branches and landed jagged end first in the midsection of the effigy mound. If the mound had been a living animal, this would've pierced its heart.

And Rachel screamed as if it had pierced her own.

ETHAN DROVE HOME slowly through the rain, wondering what the hell had just happened to him.

He and Cindy had watched the storm from a booth at Pedro's, his favorite Mexican restaurant. They had discussed many things, none of them serious. When he started to feel the Dos Equis, he rose to take his leave, but she suggested they go to her townhouse for a nightcap.

He knew what she meant. He also knew he wasn't in love with her, and that he never would be. But he followed her car through the rain anyway.

When they got to her place she kissed him the moment the door closed behind them. Squirming against him and making little whimpers of delight, she began unbuttoning his shirt before their lips parted.

He kept his hands demurely on her waist. "Whoa, wait. Shouldn't we talk a little first?" he asked when she let him breathe.

She laughed. "No. I want you right now, Ethan. On the floor, even. How do you like that?"

Part of him liked it a lot. She wormed out of her jeans, revealing firm freckled thighs and a lime-green thong. "When I first met you, I fantasized about you for a week," she said as she pulled off her T-shirt. "I mean, what are the chances of knocking you down on the street, and then seeing you at the gym?"

"Pretty slim," he agreed. She wore a matching green bra, which quickly joined her other garments on the floor.

"So you'll forgive me if I don't need a lot of foreplay the first time out," she said breathlessly, with a smile that promised things he no longer thought existed.

She took his hand and pulled him toward the stairs. For a long moment he resisted, but the way she stood against the rail, breasts swaying, every inch of freckled skin calling out to him, finally overcame his resolve. Only they never made it to the top step.

"I'm sorry," Ethan said. "I just . . . I can't."

She frowned at him. "Oh, come on. You don't mean—"

"No, it's . . . I won't."

"'Won't'?" she repeated in annoyance.

"There's someone else," he said.

ETHAN PARKED IN his garage, turned off the engine, and sat in the dark. Okay, he'd wanted to sleep with another woman. That was fine, actually; he had no ties to anyone, and had not broken his word. But at the last moment, all he could think about was Rachel. Until that wasn't true, he couldn't just fuck someone for fun.

He was too wide-awake to sleep, so he started the truck again and backed out of the garage. The rain had stopped, but the streets were still wet, and he drove around for twenty minutes before heading back home, using a route that would take him by the construction site for the new community center.

As he approached, he noticed a car parked at the

curb. It was a BMW, which seemed odd enough in this neighborhood. And the emergency flashers were not on, which he'd expect if it had broken down.

He drove past it, then parked around the corner. He strolled back toward the park, not hiding but not making himself obvious. Down the hill, he saw the unmistakable glow of a small flashlight.

Ethan reached for his cellphone, then remembered he'd left it in the truck, inside his gym bag. He debated going back for it but decided not to. There was probably no need for the police. It was likely just kids out for a cruise in Daddy's car, messing around with petty vandalism, and he could easily scare them away with his drill sergeant's voice.

He crept down the hill, almost losing his balance on the wet grass. By the time he reached the fence, the light was gone. The gate had been bent enough to allow someone fairly small to wriggle through. Ethan silently unlocked it, slipped inside, and fastened it behind him.

The flashlight reappeared over near the corner where the new sewer pipe would be laid. Ethan moved silently through the shadows, edging closer. When he was twenty feet away, he saw that it was a lone man holding the light in his teeth as he scooped things from the ground and dropped them into a small cardboard box.

Ethan crossed the distance between them so fast that even though the man heard the approach, he had no time to respond. Ethan grabbed him by the back of his collar, yanked him to his feet, and slammed him face-first into the fence.

"Don't fucking move," Ethan growled. Still holding

the man against the wall, he bent to pick up the dropped flashlight. The man tried to make a break for it, but Ethan tripped him. He landed face-first in the fresh mud and skidded a few feet.

Ethan yanked him to his feet and shone the light on his face. The mud hid his identity. "Wipe your face off. And if you try any more shit with me, you'll be eating creamed corn from now on."

The man used his shirt sleeve to wipe his mouth and lower face. "What does that even *mean*?"

"It means I'll knock your teeth down your throat."

"Oh! I've always wondered. Thanks for clearing that up."

Ethan shone the light again, and this time he was momentarily speechless. "Red Bird, right? John—"

"Call me Jim," James Red Bird said sheepishly.

Ethan grabbed Red Bird by the arm and dragged him over to the box. He shone the light into it and saw several pieces of broken pottery, as well as what looked like a stone ax head. "Holy shit, you were seeding the site?"

"No," Red Bird said. "I was *un*seeding it. I seeded it for the second time earlier tonight. Sorry about your gate; I could throw stuff over the fence, but I had to actually get inside to pick it up." He shrugged as if he'd merely spilled something on the couch.

Ethan bit his lip as he tried to decide the best thing to do. "You have a cellphone? Give it here."

Red Bird dug his phone from his pants pocket. "It's not what you think, really."

Ethan looked at him. "Uh-huh." He dialed Marty's number.

Red Bird said, "If you're calling the police, ask for Detective Martin Walker."

Ethan stared at him in surprise just as Marty sleepily answered, "Hello?"

"Marty," Ethan said.

"Are you all right?" Marty said at once, his voice instantly clear. "Where are you calling from? I don't recognize the number."

"I'm down at the new community center site. I caught somebody putting out more artifacts."

"Is it James Red Bird?"

Ethan looked from the phone to Red Bird in confusion. At last he said, "I'm way out of the loop on this, aren't I?"

"Yes," Red Bird said.

"He's not planting them, he's picking them up," Marty said wearily. "Or at least that's what he'd better be doing."

Ethan looked at Red Bird. "Tell me what you were doing here. Seriously."

"I put these here earlier tonight; I was picking them up before someone found them."

"That's what he says," Ethan told Marty. "Do you want me to hold on to him?"

"No, let him go. But make sure he gets everything first. It's sort of a plea bargain."

"Uh-huh. You could've told me."

"I didn't expect you to be prowling around at two in the morning. Just let him go. I know where he lives, and I know what he's been up to. I'll tell you about it tomorrow."

"It's already tomorrow."

"You know what I mean. Good night, Ethan."

Ethan closed the phone and handed it back to Red Bird. "He said to make sure you finish and then let you go."

Red Bird stood with as much dignity as the situation could give him. "Thanks."

"Hold on, I'll get a floodlight. It'll make it easier."

"Thanks," Red Bird said again. And for the next half-hour, Ethan held the light while James Red Bird retrieved dozens of pieces of pottery, arrowheads, and beads.

WHEN HE HUNG up, Marty sat on the edge of the bed for a long time. His partner, Chuck, rubbed Marty's back and said sleepily, "You okay?"

Marty stood. "Yeah. Can't sleep. I'm going downstairs to watch TV."

"Do you need to talk?"

"Nah, it's just work stuff."

"Okay," Chuck said, and rolled over. Marty got a glass of milk and settled in to watch infomercials.

In a few hours he would have to arrest Rebecca Matre for the murder of Garrett Bloom. Officers were watching her, and if she tried to run they'd nab her; otherwise, he would make the collar right after the news media were surreptitiously notified. He hated that, but it was the way the world worked.

And then he prayed the real killer would make a mistake. For Rebecca Matre's sake, and his own.

CHAPTER TWENTY-TWO

RACHEL SAT AWAKE all night, curled up on the couch. The TV played infomercials about some exercise program that used enormous rubber balls.

There was nothing she could do. She had been abandoned. The lake spirits that had nurtured her, that had helped her in return for her help, were no longer interested.

But why? She had two mutually exclusive explanations—one of which might've very well come from her own subconscious. She had no way of knowing if her conversation with the old Lo-Stahzi woman was real or not. And at least Betty McNally's story came from a real, if dotty, human being who'd shared some of the same experiences.

And Betty also had a plan, sort of. *Kyle Stillwater must be made to do our bidding.*

She hugged the pillow to her chest. It smelled of cat hair. Tainter lay at her feet, looking up expectantly.

Occasionally he meowed softly, as if to remind her that he was here for her.

Fine, she thought. *Kyle Stillwater must be made to do our bidding. I know what I want him to do, God forgive me.* But Kyle Stillwater first had to be found, and she had no idea where—

Patty.

Patty had tried to tell her about "someone else." In her selfishness, she'd completely forgotten about that. Kyle had come after Rachel first, as the avatar of the good spirits he opposed, so Patty would be a logical next step, the woman those same spirits called their "treasure."

In the bedroom, her alarm went off. Tainter stood, arched his back, and stretched his claws against the area rug. Rachel sat, listening to the harsh sound, before its meaning got through. It was time to start another day at the diner.

She went into the bedroom and turned off the alarm. The sudden thought of routine, of tasks known and understood, appealed to her more than she could say. She put aside the supernatural worries, started her shower, and picked out clothes for work.

PATTY DIDN'T SHOW up for breakfast that morning. She also didn't answer her phone when Rachel called.

The ringtone Rachel had programmed for Becky was "The Real Me" by The Who. It was a harsh song, and it always got Rachel's attention. But she was so out of it that she missed the call, grabbing her phone just an instant too late. She tried Patty again while her phone was open, but there was still no answer.

She tried calling Becky back at once but got her voice mail. She hung up without leaving a message. It seemed to be the thing to do these days. Then she tried Patty again, but there was still no answer.

"Was that Becky calling?" Helena said. She knew the song's significance as well.

"Apparently," Rachel said. Jimmy hit the bell to announce that an order was ready, and Rachel carried it to the table. She heard the chime that meant she had a voice mail, but the diner was so busy that it was twenty minutes later before she had a chance to check it.

There were harsh voices in the background, and the sound of heavy doors slamming shut. Rebecca sounded like she was in tears. "Rachel? This is Becky. I'm at . . . I've been arrested. For Garrett's murder."

THE CITY JAIL smelled like bleach and urine. It was cold, and the officer who led Rachel down the bright corridor was wide enough that her hips could've easily bumped from wall to wall with every step. Her expression was so devoid of compassion or any other human emotion that Rachel wondered if she might be mentally impaired. But when she growled, "Ten minutes," Rachel understood that she was simply a woman who didn't care about anyone unless they wore a blue uniform.

The room looked exactly like she expected from all those television shows: blank concrete walls and a single table with a metal folding chair on either side.

Rebecca was already seated there, watched over by another female officer as overweight, bored, and contemptuous as the one who'd shown Rachel to the room.

The orange jumpsuit highlighted Becky's red, splotchy face. Her hair was unbrushed and tied back; she wore no makeup or jewelry. The urge to hug her was overpowering, but Rachel had been warned not to attempt any physical contact. She pulled out the other chair and sat down.

"So where were you when I called?" Becky snapped.

"Working," Rachel said. "I just missed it."

Becky shrugged. "Yeah, well . . . it doesn't matter. I have nothing to worry about, they tell me. I'll get either a public defender or one of the attorneys who does pro bono work for PBN. It shouldn't be hard to prove I didn't kill Garrett, because I didn't."

"Why do they think you did?"

"That phone message I left. I mentioned Romeo and Juliet, and since they both died, apparently that counts as a threat."

"You can't be serious."

"That's what they told me. I might've sounded a little . . . unbalanced when I left it too. That probably didn't help." She sniffled and seemed like she was about to cry again.

Rachel was silent for a moment. Then she said, "So have you been officially arraigned?"

"No, they have to do DNA tests and fingerprints and all that CSI crap. But until then I have to sit in here."

"What's your bail?"

"Bail? Haven't you been paying attention? I haven't

been arraigned yet, and even when I have, I've been arrested for murder. There *is* no bail."

"Is that what your lawyer told you?"

"I don't have a lawyer yet."

Then you don't know, do you? Rachel thought. *Just
like always.* But she said, "Then I'll see what I can do."

"You do that," Becky said, crossed her arms, and
looked away. She'd spent her whole life in variations of
that pose, it seemed to Rachel.

Rachel stood. "I *will* try to help you, Becky. I
promise."

Becky said nothing and did not move, but Rachel
saw the tears roll down her cheeks. *She must be so
afraid,* Rachel thought; she did her best to avoid con-
sequences, and now there was no denying them.

"Be strong, baby," Rachel said softly, again fighting
the urge to hug her sister. Then she turned to the door
and knocked to be let out before Becky could say
something else crass and change her mind. The cruel-
mouthed matron waddled to comply.

MARTY SAW HIS brother emerge from the elevator.
Ethan was dressed for work in a pressed shirt and
khakis, but his eyes were red and he'd shaved haphaz-
ardly. When he reached Marty's desk he said, "I know,
I look like crap."

"You do."

Ethan lowered himself gratefully into the visitor's
chair. "I saw on the news that you arrested Rachel's
sister."

"Yep."

"Did she give you any trouble?"

"No." *Except for screaming, collapsing, and having to be transported to jail in an ambulance,* he thought.

"Did she tell you what she did with his heart?"

"She says she's innocent. We're still looking."

"Has she got a lawyer?"

"Not yet. She'll be appointed one if Bloom's office doesn't make its own arrangements. I get the feeling that no one there wants to step in and be in charge."

"And everyone's happy with this?"

Marty shrugged. "The chief's happy. The mayor's happy. The D.A.'s happy. They're the only ones who matter to me."

"What about your friend Mr. Red Bird?"

"James Red Bird is *not* my friend," Marty said with certainty, "but I made a deal, and I'll stick to it. Sometimes you have to pick your battles. He lost his; the whole casino scam is off. So I'm satisfied with that for now."

"Yeah, well, I still think I should've beaten some decency into him instead of helping him pick up his toys." Ethan yawned and shook his head.

"It's probably better that you didn't," Marty said.

"So does Rachel know about Becky yet?"

"I have no idea. We don't generally inform the next of kin of suspects. Has she called you?"

"No."

"And of course you haven't called her."

Ethan scowled and stood. "I have a meeting to get to. I'll talk to you later."

"*You* could tell her."

He laughed humorlessly. "I'm not paid to do your dirty work."

"It would give you an excuse to talk to her."

"You're like a broken record, Marty."

Marty said nothing as Ethan walked to the elevator. His brother looked like he'd lost everything. His big shoulders were slumped, and he radiated a weariness that was more than just physical.

As Ethan stepped into one elevator, the doors of the other one opened and Rachel Matre exited. Neither saw the other, and Marty fought the urge to laugh at this *Doctor Zhivago* moment. But when he saw the look on Rachel's face, he was glad he'd kept silent.

"Rachel," he said formally when she reached his desk. He stood and gestured toward the guest chair.

"I suppose you know why I'm here," she said as she took the offered seat.

"Yes," he said.

"Becky didn't kill Garrett Bloom."

"I believe you, actually."

She blinked in surprise. "You *do*?"

"Yes. But at the same time, I also believe the evidence we have linking her to the crime."

"The phone call?"

"I can't really talk about it. But let's just say that some people higher up than me heard a distinct threat in it. And the timing made it suspicious. So orders were sent down."

"What about bail?"

"That's up to the district attorney's office. This was a heinous crime of particular brutality. I don't see him letting her out."

She nodded. "I could give her an alibi."

"That's perjury."

"Only if it isn't true."

"But it wouldn't be, would it?"

She sighed. "No. But have you considered that guy who showed up at the ground-breaking ceremony? He certainly seemed to have a bone to pick with Bloom."

"Kyle Stillwater? We haven't been able to find a trace of him. I suspect . . ." He stopped when he realized he was about to disclose confidential information.

"What?" Rachel prompted.

"It's official. I shouldn't talk about it."

"Please, Marty. I won't tell anyone. Especially not Becky."

"All right. We found out Bloom was running a con. The whole community center project was a fraud, to get a casino here in town."

"What? How could he do that?"

"It's complicated. But it might've worked."

Rachel said nothing.

"Anyway," Marty continued, "if my instincts are right, the real killer now thinks he's gotten away with it. Maybe he'll slip up."

"And until then, Becky rots in jail?"

"She won't *rot,* Rachel. It's not a country club, but it's not a gulag. She'll be fine. And safe."

She stood. "Thanks, Marty. And . . . you really have no idea where Kyle Stillwater is?"

"No. None at all. I'm sure it was an alias. It's almost like he doesn't exist."

"Oh, he exists," Rachel said enigmatically. Then she left.

———

AN INDIGNANT HORN interrupted Ethan's yawn to inform him the light was now green. He resisted the urge to flip off the driver behind him, a young man with a tuft of hair on his chin and a Bluetooth in his ear. The little car zoomed around Ethan's truck at the first opportunity, only to get stopped at the next red light. As he came up behind it, Ethan smiled.

If he hadn't been so tired, his own frustration might be wound as tight as Mr. Bluetooth's. There was only one way to deal with it, really, and that was to simply march into Rachel's diner and demand that the woman speak with him. The problem was, he wasn't sure he trusted himself in her presence. He didn't worry about his temper; it was all the other emotions, the ones he kept private and hidden. If *they* burst out, he might never get them back in their box.

At the next light, Mr. Bluetooth was in the lane beside him. He leaned forward over his steering wheel and stared at the light as if he could will it to turn green. His hands impatiently opened and closed around the steering wheel.

Ethan laughed again and turned on the radio. An army recruiting commercial was in mid-spiel, urging young men to become "an army of one." Usually this amused Ethan, but this time it was different. He felt his spine straighten, his shoulders go back, and his jaw firmly set. *By God, I am an army of one,* he thought. *And it's okay to be scared to face the enemy, as long as you still suck it up and do it.*

When the light changed, he gunned the engine and

switched lanes in front of Mr. Bluetooth. Then he stayed there until he turned in to the parking lot of Rachel's diner.

IN HER CAR, Rachel turned on the air conditioner and took several deep breaths. These damned crying jags had to stop; people were depending on her, for God's sake. She looked at herself in the mirror and winced at her red, puffy eyes. She'd have a hard time blaming them on allergies, that was certain.

Worse was the rippling, tingling desire that always hovered just at the edge of her consciousness. She would have to try the lake again tonight. Maybe the spirits were just annoyed and now missed her as much as she did them. She refused to think about Betty's warning and the possibility of a lifetime of feeling this way. One problem at a time.

She took a drink of water from the bottle in the cup holder. At least now the quest wasn't just personal. If she could find Kyle Stillwater, she could help both Becky *and* herself. Stillwater had to be behind Bloom's murder; his ties to the Lo-Stahzi were too great to ignore. He had to be found and brought in for questioning. But how?

There was one other source of information she could try, although she'd almost rather eat her way across a table of broken glass. Yet Becky was depending on her, and it was silly to stand on pride.

Yes, that was it. It was all for Rebecca.

CHAPTER TWENTY-THREE

E THAN LOOKED DOWN at his feet moving along the sidewalk outside the diner. He recalled watching his boots in Iraq the same way, only then it was to check the ground for IED triggers or other booby traps buried in the sand. Here the IEDs were entirely in his heart, and he was going to trigger them deliberately.

He took a deep breath and pushed open the door.

There were a half-dozen customers, all seated along the counter. He saw Rachel's friend Helena and another waitress he didn't recognize. In the kitchen, the scruffy cook worked intently over the griddle. The air smelled of eggs, coffee, and air-conditioning, while smooth jazz came from the radio. There was no sign of Rachel.

He took a stool at the end of the counter—the same one he'd chosen the first time he came here.

The waitress he didn't know came to greet him. Her name tag said "Clara." "Hi. Welcome to Rachel's. First time here?"

"First time in a while," he said.

"Would you like to start with some coffee?"

"Please," he said, then added before she turned away, "Is Rachel around?"

"No, she had some family emergency. Do you know her?"

"We're acquaintances."

"Well, I'll be right back with your drink. Today's specials are on the wall."

Ethan's heart sank, and he berated himself. Of course, her sister was arrested this morning; she was dealing with that. How self-centered he'd been not to think of it. He picked up the menu and stared at it until he sensed the waitress's return.

When he looked up again, it wasn't Clara. Helena stood before him, smiling crookedly. "You have great timing. Or was this on purpose?"

Ethan put down the menu. "No, I actually *did* hope to find her here. I just didn't think about what happened with her sister."

"Then you know? Oh, of course; Marty told you, didn't he?"

"Yeah."

She looked around to make sure no one was listening, then said quietly, "I know it's none of my business, but you've been a total wuss about this whole thing. Yeah, I know, you promised and gave your word and blah-blah-blah, but you really need to man up here, and I don't mean that macho bullshit they teach you in the army. I mean see what needs to be done and *do* it. If you're waiting for her to make the first move, it'll never happen."

A little offended, Ethan began, "I don't think—"

"Yes, you do. You're a man," Helena shot back. "All you *do* is think. But if you want Rachel, you're going to have to learn to *feel*. You have to feel how much she needs you."

"I'm sure she can handle—"

"Dammit!" Helena exclaimed, and a few people looked their way. She leaned over the counter. "I'm not talking about this stuff with Becky. I'm talking about when there's *not* a crisis or an emergency to distract her. I'm talking about the quiet times. That's when she needs you, tough guy. Good God, you could feel that she needed you when she was locked in a basement in the middle of nowhere, and you can't feel *this*?"

Before Ethan could answer, she turned and stormed off into the kitchen, passing Clara on her way. Clara put down the coffee and said, "Do you know Helena too?"

"Not as well as she knows me, apparently," Ethan said.

The door opened again, and an older woman with dark, curly hair entered. She looked around, then asked Clara, "Is Rachel here?"

"Everybody wants the boss today," Clara said. "No, she's not here. I don't know when she'll be back."

The woman held out an envelope. "Please make sure she gets this. Can I trust you?"

"Sure," Clara said.

Ethan glanced up and caught the woman staring at him. He smiled, but she didn't look away. That inner sense he'd developed in Iraq, where danger could be hidden in plain sight, sent warning tingles up the back of his neck. "Do we know each other?"

"No," the woman said. "We don't. I'm Betty."

"Ethan," he said but did not offer his hand.

Betty smiled. "You're here looking for Rachel too."

"I am?"

"You are. I have a sense about these things."

"Well . . . she's not here, so I guess I'll be leaving." He stood, which forced Betty to step back. He tossed some bills on the counter, then turned, only to find the woman in his path.

He clenched his fists. Whoever she was, she affected him not like an attractive woman but like another man who meant him harm.

"It was a pleasure meeting you, Ethan," she said without breaking his gaze. "I'm sure we'll see each other again."

"Uh-huh. Good day, ma'am." He went around her as quickly as he could without being rude.

JULIE SCHUTES'S GORGEOUS blue eyes opened wide with surprise. "Ms. Matre," she said after a moment, then stood as a man might do. *As Ethan did on our first date,* Rachel recalled vividly.

She wondered about Julie's first date with Ethan as she admired the woman's taut body and impeccable style. Did they have sex that night, and if so, in his house (which she still hadn't seen) or hers? Had she dressed for it, in slinky underthings that she peeled off sensually and slowly, or had the connection been a surprise to them both?

She managed a neutral smile. "Have you got a moment?" she asked, hoping her voice didn't shake.

Julie nodded. She was taller than Rachel—model tall, in fact—but that might just be the shoes. "Of course. Please sit down."

Rachel did so, keeping her back straight and her hands formally in her lap. She was about to speak when she noticed a manila folder on Julie's desk labeled "Lady of the Lakes." She hid her true reaction, nodded at the folder, and said casually, "So are *you* the Lady of the Lakes?"

"Hardly," Julie said as she sat and smoothed her skirt, "but I intend to find out who is. And what they're up to."

"'Up to'?"

"There has to be an agenda. And where there's an agenda, there's money. Eventually I'll find the money trail, and then I'll unmask this so-called Lady." She smiled coldly. "But that's not why you're here."

"No." Rachel looked down at her fingers. "I'm sure you know my sister's been arrested for the murder of Garrett Bloom."

"I wrote the story," Julie confirmed.

She managed to gloat in a way that Rachel could not react to without seeming paranoid. "I don't believe she's guilty, which is probably not a surprise either."

"Most families have a hard time accepting that. I once covered a trial where the mother of the suspect threw a Bible at the trial judge. Knocked a hole in the drywall right beside his head."

Rachel waited, then said, "I believe I know who *did*

kill Garrett Bloom. I thought you might like to know as well."

"Of course. Who?"

"Kyle Stillwater."

Julie's forehead creased in surprise. "The Indi— I'm sorry, I mean the Native American activist who crashed the ground-breaking ceremony?"

"Yes. If he really is an activist. Or Native American. Have you found any trace of him?"

"I haven't really tried. The police established that he used the name of a local actor, so there's very little to go on. Besides, they seem very sure they've got their culprit."

"They could be wrong. Stillwater threatened Bloom in front of an awful lot of people."

"Even more reason to doubt he's the actual killer."

"Unless he's crazy."

"All killers are crazy. They have to be, to do what they do." She paused. "I'm sorry. That was glib and thoughtless."

"Yes, it was."

Julie tapped her pen against her lips thoughtfully. "Still . . . you might be right. Even if he wasn't the killer, there's something not quite right about the whole Stillwater thing. Where did he come from that day? And where did he go? And why hasn't anyone seen him since?"

"It sounds like a story to me," Rachel said. She wished the woman would stop saying the name Stillwater, since each time she did, it sent an intimate jolt through her. *My God,* she thought in horror, *it's only been days. How can I survive years of this if I end up like Betty McNally?*

Julie's eyes narrowed, and the bitchiness returned. "Yes, it does. And one that might help get your sister off the hook, if it pans out. If it doesn't, then it's just my time wasted."

"What's your point?"

Julie sat back and crossed her arms. "I usually get paid for my time, Ms. Matre. That's what a reporter brings to the table: time, expertise, connections. If you want me to use them . . ."

"Are you saying I should *hire* you?"

"Good Lord, no. I wasn't talking about money. I was thinking more of . . . a trade. I do something for you, you do something for me."

Rachel felt herself flush red with fury. "Let me guess. You want me to stay away from Ethan?" she asked calmly.

"Forever," Julie hissed, suddenly so cold and vicious it made Rachel start. "I don't ever want you to come near him or contact him again as long as you live."

Rachel had to swallow hard in the face of this blatant rage. Icily she said, "What if he contacts me first?"

Julie flicked her hand as if swatting a fly. "Then you send him away. You work as a waitress in a dump of a diner; you know how to give men the brush-off."

Rachel's rage swelled to a degree she'd seldom experienced. Through clenched teeth she said, "And what kind of guarantee do you give me that you'll genuinely try to help?"

Julie leaned back, smug and triumphant. "That would be *my* promise. You and I may not like each other, but ask around: I keep my word. You stay away from Ethan, and I find out the truth about Kyle Stillwater."

Rachel wanted to scream, as the name had its usual effect. "Fine," she said tightly.

Julie turned back to her computer screen. "Then you can go. We have nothing else to discuss."

Rachel got to her feet and turned to leave, then paused. "I'll be in touch, you know. A lot."

"Oh, you can call *me* whenever you want," Julie said, already typing. "Just remember your promise. Stay away from Ethan Walker."

Rachel strode away. If she looked back and the bitch was smiling, she'd have to knock those perfect white teeth down her pale, slender throat.

JULIE WATCHED RACHEL leave. The woman *was* attractive, in a hippie sort of way, and she could imagine Ethan's desire to get his hands on that tight ass. Certainly he'd once had a hard time keeping them off her own, which she kept as firm as a high school senior's. And now that he'd overcome the performance issues caused by his stint in Iraq, she looked forward with renewed excitement to behaving like a cat in heat for him. He was strong enough, physically and otherwise, to make her do things she normally wouldn't consider, and she loved it when he gave in to that impulse to dominate her.

She picked up the phone and dialed his office. She wanted to strike while the iron of Rachel's promise was hot. She got his voice mail, but that was okay. This was the campaign's opening salvo, not its final battle.

"Ethan?" she said in her sweetest voice, careful not to lay it on too thick. "It's Julie. Oh, but I guess you know that. Anyway, I . . . Oh, hell, I just wanted to see you and talk to you. Why don't we meet for dinner tonight? Call me back and let me know. Oh, and you can tell me to go to hell again if you want, but really, I just miss spending time with you. I miss your company. That's all."

She hung up quickly before she tipped her hand. She was good at faking sincerity, and this wasn't even all faking. She *did* want to see him.

Ethan would do one of two things. He would call her back when he was sure he'd get her voice mail and tell her to leave him alone, or he'd grudgingly accept. Either response was fine, actually. What she mainly wanted to do was provoke him into calling Rachel, so that the little diner whore could break his heart. Then Julie could swoop in with the dustpan and the super-glue, and put it back together again her way.

But she hadn't lied when she said her word was honorable. The mystery of Kyle Stillwater, and the memory of his delectable body emerging from the lake, did actually intrigue her, so it wasn't a hard promise to keep.

CHAPTER TWENTY-FOUR

WHEN RACHEL GOT back to the diner she was twitchy and damp, and her clothing felt unbearable. She walked past the folks at the counter, completely missing Helena's wave from across the dining room. Instead, she climbed the stairs to her apartment, stripped naked, and flopped on her bed.

She was not aroused in any normal way; it was more like being stuck on a low-wattage setting where her body tingled and pulsed but never developed into any full-blown feelings. It was more upsetting, really, than being simply turned on with no outlet.

Worse, she felt she'd betrayed something fundamental about herself in her deal with Julie Schutes. Before, there had been hope that perhaps she and Ethan would again be together. Now she'd killed even that.

But that was the least of her problems, she thought, as she put her feet flat on the bed and idly rubbed her hands up and down her raised thighs. She had to help Becky. She had to help her lake spirits. And she had to survive whatever this feeling was that threatened to overwhelm her.

Tainter emerged from under the bed with a confused yowl. He jumped up on the covers beside her, then backed slowly away. He did not hiss, but clearly there was some change in his mistress, of which he did not approve.

Rachel took slow, measured breaths, trying to slow her skittery heartbeat. She flexed her fingers and toes, stretching them tight to give the energy somewhere to go. She had too much to do, too many responsibilities, to endure this right now. But her hands rose, almost of their own volition, to her breasts and squeezed them. Her nipples, already tight, seemed to tighten even more.

Slowly her back arched and her knees drew up. She squeezed her thighs together, sending demanding tingles up from the area where they met. In her mind, she saw Ethan above her—the muscles of his bare shoulders working as he rose, then fell, rose, then fell—his face drawn tight with the effort to reach his own completion. . . .

She sat up at the firm knock on the door.

JULIE SCHUTES PICKED her way around the back of Kyle Stillwater's apartment building and peered through the patio door. No lights were on inside, and from the detritus of fast food and soda cans, it was obvious that no one had cleaned it for a while. She was still looking when a voice said, "Looking for Kyle?"

She turned. An elderly black man in a robe and

slippers stood on the patio next door. His creased face was unreadable, but his eyes were suspicious.

Julie smiled. "If he's the actor Kyle Stillwater, then yes."

"He is. Are you a cop?"

"No, I'm a reporter. Julie Schutes, with the *Cap Jo*. And you are—"

The man sipped his coffee and said at last, "A neighbor."

"Have you seen Kyle lately?"

"You asking about that thing at the park?"

"Yes. I'd like to talk with him about it."

"Wasn't him. It was some guy using his name. The cops already cleared that up."

"I just want to ask him what he thinks about it."

He shrugged. "Too bad for you, then. People in hell want ice water too."

Julie kept the smile. "Does he live here by himself?"

"Far as I know. His last girlfriend moved out a month ago. Got tired of cleaning up after him."

She held out a card. "I left one of these in his mail slot, but could you pass this to him if you see him?"

The man looked at the card, then at Julie, then back at the card. "You for real, then, huh?"

"I am."

"I'm going to tell you something, then. You don't quote me on it, understand? But I'm going to tell you."

"Okay."

"There's something wrong with that boy. He walked out of here in the middle of the night with a long white wig on. Like the news says that fella at the park wore."

"So it *was* him, then?"

"I don't know. About half the time lately he ain't been himself. I think he might be on drugs or something."

Julie nodded encouragingly. "Did he say where he was going?"

"Naw. He said for a swim. And that he wasn't coming back."

Julie felt a chill. "Was he suicidal?"

"Seemed happy as a clam."

"Listen, please, if he does come back, please let me know. Maybe I can help." Which was a lie, but if it got her a story, it served its purpose.

THERE WAS ANOTHER firm knock at the door. *Hard, firm,* Rachel repeated in her head. *Ethan?*

"Hey, Rache?" Helena's voice called. "Are you all right?"

Rachel swallowed and got unsteadily to her feet. Her knees were weak, and her belly fluttered. She let Helena in and closed the door behind her.

It took a moment for Helena's wide-eyed expression to register. Rachel said, "What?"

"Um," Helena said, and gestured in her direction. "Your fly is open."

Rachel looked down at herself and softly laughed. She should have been embarrassed standing there stark naked, but instead it seemed like nothing to be concerned about. She had nothing Helena didn't also have, and they'd been like sisters for years. "Yeah," she muttered. "Just felt a little . . . overheated. Needed to cool off."

Helena continued to stare. At last she said, "That tattoo removal is impressive. I mean, your skin's not even red."

Rachel flushed. "I've always been a quick healer; you know that."

"Yeah. Well, anyway, someone left this for you." Helena held out a manila envelope with the name "Rachel" scrawled on it in big letters.

Rachel tossed the envelope on the couch without looking at it. "I guess I should come downstairs and help, huh?"

Helena continued to stare. "Not like that."

Rachel looked down at herself, and shame suddenly penetrated her hazy thoughts. She covered her breasts with her arms. What was she *doing*? "I'm sorry, I was about to take a quick shower," she said. "I've got a lot on my mind."

"I can see that," Helena said. She looked everywhere but directly at Rachel. "I'll just . . . go, then." She left quickly, and her footsteps pattered rapidly down the stairs.

Rachel shook her head. *What the hell?* Helena was her best friend, but she was also gay, and this little scene could've easily been taken the wrong way. Yet the burning embarrassment left almost as soon as it started, and the heavy, heated sense of her own arousal returned. She rather calmly thought, *Why not? We're adults, we're already friends. . . .*

As if he could read her thoughts, Tainter hissed from the bedroom doorway.

She slapped herself hard. *Stop it!* The fog in her brain cleared, and she quickly dressed for work.

AT THE BOTTOM of the stairs, Helena paused before going back into the diner. She took a few deep breaths and tried a mental calming exercise she'd learned at a seminar.

She'd seen Rachel nude before but never like that. It was as if, after all these years of friendship, Rachel was suddenly daring Helena to think of her sexually. It hadn't worked—and never would, Helena thought ironically—but it *had* rattled her. Rachel's ex-husband, Don, claimed Rachel had mental problems. Was he right after all? Had the whole Arlin Korbus thing brought them to the surface?

Helena looked back up the stairs toward the closed apartment door. She'd been so startled that she hadn't mentioned Ethan's visit, and she wasn't about to go back up there now. Maybe it was for the best. Ethan was a normal, decent guy who probably didn't deserve a crazy girlfriend.

And do I deserve a crazy best *friend?* Helena thought. But she had no answer.

"SO WHAT WAS in that envelope?" Roya asked later, as she and Rachel wiped down a table. She'd replaced Clara for the end of the shift so Clara could register for a fall class. Now they were cleaning the unoccupied areas to prepare for closing while Helena attended to the three remaining patrons.

"*Mm?*" Rachel said. "Oh . . . You know, I didn't even look. Did you see who left it?"

"No, I wasn't here then. Helena might know."

Rachel nodded and continued writing the next day's lunch special on the dry-erase wall. She caught Helena looking oddly at her from across the diner, but she turned away before Rachel could comment on it.

"I heard about your sister," Roya said quietly. "I'm very sorry. If there's anything I can do . . ."

Rachel smiled and shook her head. "Thanks. She didn't do it, so I'm sure it'll work out."

"I grew up in Milwaukee," Roya said, "I'm not prone to trust the police or the justice system."

"She'll also be getting a good lawyer."

"That's a start." Roya patted her on the shoulder, trying to show support across racial, economic, and generational divides. It was an awkward but heartfelt gesture.

Rachel's eyes fell on the counter stool at the end, where she'd first seen Ethan Walker. He'd come in at Marty's suggestion, ostensibly to try the breakfast menu. Instead he'd gotten in a confrontation with Caleb, a former regular who'd insisted on smoking despite the ordinance against it.

Rachel remembered the way his blue shirt had offset his eyes, his unruly bangs falling down on his forehead. Her body shuddered with desire as that thought led to the memory of clinging to him in the lake, his hard maleness inside her, firm and steady as she thrust back and forth. She had never had an orgasm with a man inside her before, and it was awe-inspiring, and terrifying, and wonderful, and . . .

"Rachel?" Helena said urgently.

Rachel blinked. Helena and Roya, along with regular Josh Charles and another male customer she didn't know, formed a circle of faces that looked down at her. She felt the cool tile on her legs below her shorts and realized that she lay on the floor.

She sat up, and they all reached down to help. "Should we call 911?" Roya asked. "You banged your head pretty good when you hit the ground."

"No, I'm fine," Rachel said. She tried to stand and was nearly knocked down again by everyone trying to aid her. She snapped, "Jeez, people, give me a little room here!"

She got to her feet and sat at the counter. She felt stranger than ever, as if a great emptiness had opened inside her belly, the edges fluttering and hypersensitive. She closed her eyes and took several deep breaths.

When she turned, all eyes were still on her. It was so comical she almost laughed. But she controlled herself and said, "I'm going upstairs to lie down for a while. I'll be back as soon as possible."

"Take as much time as you need," Helena said. "Roya and I can handle things."

AS SOON AS she closed her apartment door, Rachel whipped off her apron and stripped out of her clothes again. She stood with her hands on the wall, looking down at her bare feet, trying to get her thoughts in order.

And as always, Ethan Walker appeared in her mind's eye. She imagined watching the top of his head, hair sweaty and tousled, as his tongue worked its magic on her. She could see down the length of his bare back to the firmness of his buttocks as he buried his face in her. His moans, transmitted by his lips, rippled against her own nether region.

She screamed in utter, complete frustration and pounded her fists into the wall. *Not this. Please, not this. Not a lifetime of wanting and never having.*

She went into the bathroom, blew her nose, and washed her hands. In the mirror her face and neck were red, as were her eyes. She thought she looked older as well, the strain causing her mouth to grow tight and harsh, her forehead creasing in despair.

She walked back into the living room, and only then noticed the envelope she'd tossed on the couch. Grateful for any distraction, she opened it and removed a stack of photocopies. Tainter peeked out at her from under the couch, then approached and cautiously rubbed against her legs.

She sat at the kitchen table and began to peruse the pages with a growing mix of fascination and horror.

ROYA LOOKED UP at the ceiling. "Wow. What was Rachel hollering about?"

Helena shook her head. "I don't know."

"Should we check on her?" Roya asked.

The ceiling creaked as Rachel moved above them. "No, just . . . let her chill," Helena said.

"I need a napkin," Josh said. "It scared me so bad I spilled coffee all over myself."

Roya went to help him while Helena sat on one of

the empty stools. It was the point after the lunch rush when the staff usually ate, but Helena was not hungry. Instead she was confused in ways she never expected.

The Arlin Korbus affair was not that long ago, so it wasn't a surprise that Rachel might be experiencing some post-traumatic shock. Still, screaming and passing out seemed much more indicative of a physical problem than an emotional one. Besides, Rachel was smart. If she was truly having issues related to the kidnapping, she'd seek help.

So what if this was a sign of something unrelated, like a brain tumor? *Come on, that's a Lifetime movie, not real life,* Helena berated herself.

She got herself a glass of ice water and went to the window, where she could watch traffic zip past on East Washington. With all the chaos and weird behavior, Helena still hadn't told Rachel about Ethan's visit.

CHAPTER TWENTY-FIVE

ETHAN LOOKED ACROSS the bistro table at Julie. "I really don't think," he said carefully, "that this is a good idea."

She wore a sleeveless blouse that emphasized her bust, and tight slacks that did the same to everything below her waist. Her hair was loose, the way he always liked it, and she wore far less makeup than normal—also a concession to his opinion. He knew all this was entirely for his benefit, but it affected him despite his best efforts. He wasn't going to make it easy for her, though. He wore old jeans, a faded polo shirt, and his workout sneakers. He continued, "We have too much history to just reboot this relationship. We both said things we can't take back."

She stirred her drink with the swizzle stick. They sat on the outdoor patio at the university's Memorial Union, in shade made pleasant by the breeze off the lake. A bluegrass band, of all things, trilled away on a stage by the water, but it was far enough away that they could converse over the music.

She said carefully, "I can't deny I meant those things at the time, Ethan. But that was *then*. We're different people now."

He laughed despite himself. "After what, a year? Don't be silly. *I'm* not a different person."

She raised her eyes to his. "Maybe *I* am. I haven't had a serious relationship since we broke up, and I don't want one. I want *you*. On your terms."

"My terms?"

She nodded. "Anything you want. *Anything*."

The emphasis on that word sent a thrill up his spine at the possibilities. There had been certain things that were off-limits when they'd dated before. "I appreciate that, but it still seems like picking up the snake again after it's already bit you."

"I don't bite," she said. Then, with a devilish smile, she added, "*Hard*."

"Ha," he said flatly. "And I *have* had a serious relationship. One that isn't"—he searched for the right phrase—"done for certain yet."

"With that waitress?"

He sighed. "Yes. With Rachel. Who is *not* a waitress."

"I thought she told you to go away."

"She said she needed time. After what happened to her, I can understand that."

"Has she called you?"

"No."

"It's been two months. Nearly three."

He shrugged. "There's no timetable on these things."

"Call her, then. Settle it. If she wants you back, I'll step aside gracefully. If not . . . I promise I'll make you glad you gave me a second chance."

"I'll think about it. Now let's just listen to the music, okay?"

He turned toward the band, away from Julie, and got a little rush of satisfaction at her exasperated sigh.

IT WAS DARK by the time Rachel finished reading the papers from the envelope. Her heart thudded in her chest, and she wondered if any of it could possibly be for real. And if so . . . which parts?

The envelope had contained pages photocopied from an old book on Native Americans. A few pages of one chapter related tales about the Lo-Stahzi handed down through the Karlamiks and the other Plains tribes. The illustrations were crude woodcuts, done in a style popular two centuries earlier. She'd long ago consulted this same book in the campus library, attempting to understand her spirits. Little of it had seemed relevant then—and certainly not the tales of pagan bloodthirstiness attributed to the tribe.

Now, though, she had to reconsider. According to the text, the Lo-Stahzi worshipped the spirits in the lakes, even making human sacrifices to them in times of dire need. The spirits in turn guaranteed bountiful fishing, protection from other tribes that used the waters in attacks, and peaceful travel between this world and the next.

But the lakes were not all beneficent. *Things* lurked in them—things the spirits could use in any way they saw fit. And over some things, it was implied, the spirits had no influence at all.

So which was it? The old Lo-Stahzi woman in her vision had said the spirits were once human, but the book implied they were not. The book listed a half-dozen nonhuman spirits, such as the Geen-Po-Vis—a spirit of sickness that emerged in times of drought, when the water level dropped and fish began to die. That made sense, of course; lake shores lined with rotting fish would be a breeding ground for disease. It definitely wasn't supernatural.

And then there was the H'tik-jo-colph.

This spirit came from the water and laid claim to the young women of the tribe. Once he had taken them, no other man could ever wed them. He was not a rapist, like an incubus, but rather a cruel seducer. He placed them under a spell that took their "capacity for happiness"—a euphemism if she ever saw one. And the description perfectly fit Betty McNally's description of Kyle Stillwater.

So was Stillwater an evil human spirit, as the old woman said? Or was he a supernatural being who'd never been human, as Betty McNally's research proposed?

In order to make sense of it all, Rachel tried to put the events in a cause-and-effect order. First she had asked the spirits to help Patty, and they did. But doing so left them too weak to contain the spirits in Lake Wingra, according to the old woman. And according to Betty McNally, the evil ones then turned the tables and contained *them*.

But how? Did Garrett Bloom's murder have something to do with it?

The old woman said that the evil spirits must be defeated. Betty had said that Kyle Stillwater must be summoned to do their bidding. Whichever story was true, they seemed to agree on that: Someone must deal with the H'tik-jo-colph. But how do you kill a spirit?

She dug out Betty McNally's card and called the number on it. She got voice mail.

"This is Rachel Matre. I've looked over the information you sent. I need to know what to do now. Please call me so we can talk."

She waited an hour, but there was no return call. During that time she paced, took a cold shower, fought the urge to touch herself, and finally began to drink again. She stopped when her head grew fuzzy, and then she switched to black coffee.

Finally she sat on the edge of the bed, looked at Tainter, and said, "I can't do it. I know what I said, but I can't. I need help from someone I trust. And . . . dammit, I love him. Does that make me a bad person?"

Tainter purred and rubbed her bare ankle. She reached down to pet him.

"I'm going to blame it all on you, then," she teased. Then she got dressed.

IT WAS AFTER ten when Rachel stood in front of the house. She'd parked on the street and got no farther than the sidewalk before her stomach knotted in uncertainty.

She'd often wondered what sort of house Ethan

would live in, and the sheer normality of it took her by surprise. The windows were dark except for the blue light of a television leaking around the bay-window curtains. The shrubs along the sidewalk were neatly trimmed, and the lawn had a uniform look and texture that spoke of chemicals and seeds carefully applied. No stray dandelions or thistles marred its surface, just as only the faintest road film dulled the shine of the truck in the driveway.

She clenched her fists. It was late—probably too late, in every sense, for what she was doing. She was making herself a liar, a hypocrite, and worse: a weak-willed woman. She couldn't blame Tainter for that. Or was she doing the opposite and at last standing up for what she wanted and needed?

The reasons didn't matter. Only the need. Not the physical one this time, but the one that made her crave a safe place to let down her guard and be weak for a time.

Each step grew heavier and more difficult. The side-walk gave way to the driveway, which became the short walk to the porch. The two steps up seemed insurmountable, but she managed them and stood before the door. The bell had a faint light inside the button. She held her thumb lightly over it for what seemed like millennia before mustering the courage to push it.

The muted buzz was decidedly anticlimactic.

Seconds went by. Each felt like a year. Then she jumped as the porch light came on, and she felt the whoosh of air-conditioning as the door opened.

And there he was.

He wore running shorts and a tank top. His chin

was stubbly, and his hair was mussed. He looked beautiful.

"Rachel," Ethan Walker said blankly.

She tried to speak, but no words could do the moment justice. She stepped close and put one hand on his chest as if afraid he might vanish like a bubble.

He didn't move.

She swallowed the lump that rose in her throat. "I should say something profound, but nothing fits the moment."

"I love you," he blurted.

She looked up at him and saw the truth of his words in his eyes.

He laughed nervously, and the words tumbled out. "Sorry. I suppose I should say 'How are you?' first, but I've been wanting to say those words for so long they just jumped to the front of the line." Then he shrugged, bashful and adorable. "I hope *that* fits the moment."

She smiled. "I stand corrected."

The kiss made everything—every doubt and uncertainty—vanish. The weeks of loneliness were simply washed away. It was like she'd never been out of his arms, had never not been kissing him, had never been anything but rolling around with him on the foyer floor by the light of his aquarium. He kicked the door shut and, breaking the kiss as seldom as possible, they both undressed. They made love with an urgency verging on violence, but although he was stronger, she met him thrust for thrust, moan for moan, touch for touch. It wasn't about reaching orgasm for either of them, it was about making up for all the time they'd missed. And for the first time in weeks, Rachel no longer *cared* if she ever came again. As long as she could make *this* man happy, she was content.

When they finished, she lay beside him on the rug and said breathlessly, "I think we scared your fish."

"They'll forget it in thirty seconds or so," he said, his face sweaty and his hair even more mussed.

She rose on her elbows and traced a fingertip down the bridge of his strong nose. "I'm sorry."

"For what?"

She sighed. "Staying away. At least for so long."

He gazed into her eyes and touched her cheek with the back of his hand. She leaned into it and sighed. He said, "Is this a bad time to ask why?"

"Honey, it's the best time to ask for anything."

"Why, then?"

She licked her lips. They tasted salty. "I was just . . . afraid."

"Of what?"

The words came out as she formed them. "I just couldn't believe you'd really share me with . . . with *them*. I couldn't imagine any man being understanding enough to do that. In my experience, you're all territorial, controlling, and jealous. At least, the ones I usually pick are."

"I know a few women like that too."

She rolled onto her back. The foyer's light fixture had faint cobwebs that needed dusting. "I know that. I'm not saying it's rational. I mean, I couldn't even tell my ex-husband about them, so he thought I was just frigid."

He caressed her nearest breast. "I think it's safe to say you're not."

"But I was with him, because I knew he'd be insanely jealous if he knew the truth."

"I'm not him."

"I know you're not. I was just afraid that I hadn't looked closely enough at you, or that . . . you'd change."

She began to cry. They weren't tears of failure or weakness but of relief at finally understanding what had kept her from him for so long. She rolled against him, and his arms held her close. He kissed the top of her head.

"I can't predict the future," he said. "I *will* change, and so will you. But at the risk of quoting Whitney Houston, 'I will always love you.'"

She began to giggle through her tears. "And you'll share me?"

He nodded. "You didn't keep it a secret, and you didn't lie about it. I can't swear I'll always feel good about it, but I'll work through any problems that crop up."

Rachel wiped her eyes. "I told Julie Schutes I'd stay away from you forever, you know."

"You did? When?"

"This morning."

He smiled. "You did a terrible job of it, then."

She laughed. "I did, didn't I? Well, live and learn." She kissed him again, and if he'd been able to perform again so soon, she'd have done anything he asked. Instead she broke the kiss and said, "Think we could get a drink of water? I'm thirsty."

He stood and offered his hand. "Of course."

She got to her feet, looking up into his kind, strong

face. Then she stepped close, pressing her body against his. She was used to being nude, but this was the best kind of naked. Every part of her body that touched his skin felt warm, and when he put his arms around her it was like melting into safety.

"I love you," she said.

"I love you too."

She pulled away enough to look up at him. "And . . . I need your help. Something terrible has happened, and I may be the only one who can handle it. But I can't do it alone."

He smiled. "Anything at all."

As if on cue, the cellphone in her discarded purse began to ring.

CHAPTER TWENTY-SIX

ETHAN SQUINTED UP at the sign over the door. "Art Waves, huh?"

"She does a lot with water imagery," Rachel said. Betty had invited Rachel over immediately, apparently anxious to brainstorm a solution to their mutual problem, only no lights showed anywhere. Rachel used the brief time to tell Ethan about Kyle Stillwater, the old woman in her vision, and her missing lake spirits. He had listened calmly, and when she finished gave no sign he thought she was a lunatic. She loved him more than ever.

"It looks closed," Ethan said.

"I'm sure the door's open. She's expecting us." But Rachel made no move to try the handle. The darkness, the empty street, and the lifeless building made her nervous.

"And you think she can help you?"

"She understands what's happened to me. That makes us sisters, of a sort."

He put a hand on her arm. "I'll be here no matter what, you know."

She felt tenderness for him on a scale she never knew possible. She patted his huge, strong hand. "I know. But it's not just about me. My spirits must truly be in danger, because they'd never just abandon me like this. They wouldn't punish me for being tricked."

"Are you sure?"

"Yes. I can't explain why, but I am. It's . . . a feeling. So I have to help them if I can, just as they'd help me."

He nodded. "I've had to trust my feelings sometimes too. Even when there's no logical reason for it. It's saved my life."

"So I'd make a good soldier?"

"No. You're *already* a good warrior."

She stood on tiptoe to kiss him. Then she tried the door. Once again it was open, and she led him inside. She said loudly, "Betty? It's Rachel."

The track lighting came on, bathing the room in ambience and spotlighting the various artworks. Ethan stopped dead at the sight of the huge self-portrait.

"That makes me feel . . . inadequate," he said quietly.

"It would make Milton Berle feel inadequate," Rachel agreed.

"Where in your house would you even put that?" he asked.

"The game room, of course," Rachel shot back, trying not to giggle.

They stopped when another door opened somewhere and Betty emerged from the shadows at the back of the gallery. She wore a tank top and jeans, both of which could barely contain her curves.

She paused when she saw Ethan. "I didn't know you were bringing company."

"This is Ethan," Rachel said.

"We've met," he said curtly.

Rachel looked surprised. "You have?"

"Yes," Betty agreed. Then she turned to Rachel. "I should speak with you alone."

"Ethan can know—"

"Then you can tell him when we're done. But I'd feel more comfortable discussing this in private up in my apartment."

Rachel turned to him. "Would you mind waiting down here?"

"Try not to touch anything," Betty said, masking the snide words beneath a tone of extreme politeness.

Rachel gave Ethan a last look and what she hoped was a reassuring little smile before she followed Betty upstairs.

ALL THE DOORS to the other rooms in Betty's apartment were closed, so Rachel could see only the living room. It was enough.

It looked like some Asperger's sufferer's idea of sophisticated homoerotica: Garish nude men were everywhere, from strange statues to black-velvet paintings. She noticed that on the inside, the doorknob was even the head of a brass penis. She tried to find someplace to focus her eyes that didn't involve parts of the male anatomy.

"I got your notes," Rachel said, intently studying the couch. "What do we need to do?"

"It should've been clear," Betty said. "He killed that man Bloom and used the dead man's heart to trap the spirits of the lake. They were already weakened by you, after all."

Rachel flushed angrily. "Stop saying that. I didn't make them do anything. But I do want to help them."

"Why? So you can get off again, and then you can run home to your boyfriend? Is that all they mean to you?"

"No! They've been kind to me and helped me, and they do good for people. They don't deserve to be sent into limbo for all eternity. And if it's in my power to save them, I want to do it. You should want to as well. It might show them that you're worth helping too."

"Don't patronize me," Betty snapped. "You have no idea what I've gone through because of them. All right, so you want to help. It's pretty straightforward. We have to summon Kyle Stillwater and force him to give up the heart. Then we can release the spirits."

"Can we do it anywhere?"

"'It' what?"

"Release the spirits."

"No, it has to be in the water. If I'm right about what lives inside that man, he won't be far away from the water either."

"So how do we find him when no one else has?"

"No one else knows what they're looking for." Betty smiled. "And how do you catch something? With bait."

"What sort of bait?"

"You."

"Me?"

"He came to you once but didn't finish what he started, did he? He didn't really *have* that tight little body of yours, did he?" Betty tapped Rachel's behind, and Rachel reflexively slapped her hand away. She glared at the older woman, who shrugged and laughed. "He'll want to do that. He'll *need* to do that, to complete his dominion over his enemies. These spirits are as sex-mad as any man of flesh and blood, and the temptation of the one who got away will be too strong for him to resist."

Rachel hated the excitement that coursed through her at the thought of Stillwater touching her again. *It's not me,* she thought. *It's not really me.* "So how do I go about letting him know I'm available?"

Betty laughed. "You really are having a hard time thinking. Your mind's settling down to that one track, isn't it? The answer is obvious. Go for a swim."

"And he'll just show up at the park again?" Rachel said, annoyed at how easily this woman could read her.

Betty stepped close, into Rachel's personal space. It felt as weird as it had before, maybe even weirder. "I don't mean at *your* usual place. I mean at his. Lake Wingra."

AS SOON AS he heard the door close above him, Ethan petulantly touched about a dozen pieces of artwork. He knew it was childish, but it was late and the woman annoyed him. Then he wandered through the gallery, idly examining the other artwork. He knew enough to judge good art from bad, and most of this was mediocre at best. But the huge self-portrait kept drawing his eye, and he was glad no one was there to see him examine it minutely. Marty and Chuck had a single piece of homoerotic art—a small brass statue that was barely noticeable—in their home. Yet it had taken months before Ethan was able to stop concentrating on not looking at it, which of course amused Marty to no end.

Seeing Betty's face, her full lips and vaguely Asian eyes, above a nude male body with an erect penis the size of his own forearm puzzled Ethan. What sort of woman was this Betty McNally? She didn't really seem like a lesbian, and certainly she had the voluptuous form most men would relish. She could be bisexual, he supposed. Madison *was* a college town, after all. Yet when he'd met her at the diner, she'd looked him over like . . .

Like another guy, he thought suddenly. That was it. He *knew* that look, that belligerent chest-first pose, all too well. From junior high through his tour in Iraq, he saw it practically every day of his life. Betty's impressive breasts distracted him so he didn't recognize it at first, but now he did.

And that puzzled him even more. Was she a transsexual? It seemed unlikely, but whatever else she was, every instinct honed during the war warned him that she was trouble.

The ceiling squeaked as either Betty or Rachel moved around upstairs. He wished he could make out their murmuring voices more clearly.

_____

"SO WHEN DO we do this?" Rachel said.

"No time like the present. How about later tonight? Say, two a.m.? We'll meet where the spring comes out from beneath the tree. There's an observation deck there. Know where I mean?"

"The Arboretum's closed then."

"Come on. You skinny-dip in the middle of town, don't you?"

"So should we pick you up?"

Betty noticed Rachel staring, and smiled. "No, I'll meet you there. I have to gather some things to help us break the spell. You do understand that's what this is, right? A spell? You're under one, and we're going to use one to summon him."

"I'm not worried about the terminology, just that it works."

"Good."

"But my friend downstairs will be with me." At the outrage in Betty's eyes, Rachel said, "He knows all about me, and I want him there. It's not open to discussion."

"Then I won't waste my breath on it, except to say he may not like what he sees. Is he willing to watch you make love to another man—or at least something that _looks_ like another man—in order to save yourself?"

Rachel didn't answer. She hadn't thought of that. In the presence of Kyle Stillwater, how would she behave? Was it fair to Ethan to make him watch that?

Betty smiled. "That's what I thought."

"Yes," Rachel answered suddenly. "Yes, he is. If that's what I need to do."

Betty's smile widened. It was a cold, malicious smile, filled with contempt. "We'll see, won't we? In two hours, then."

RACHEL HELD ETHAN'S hand in silence as they left Betty's gallery. He followed her around to the driver's side and held the door open for her. "Since you're the passenger, shouldn't I do that for you?" she said.

"Next time," he said. Then he climbed into the other seat and buckled his seat belt. The drive to the diner took only a couple of minutes, and then he walked her to her door. As she unlocked it he said, "Now what?"

"Wait for two a.m., I suppose," she said. "Kill an hour and a half watching infomercials."

"Are you hungry?"

"Not really."

"You sound tired."

"Well, we did just exert ourselves before we left your place."

"That's true. Do you want to lie down and rest?"

She laughed. "I don't think that's possible right now."

"It's that bad?"

The humor left her voice. "It's all I can do not to scream, Ethan."

He nodded sympathetically. "I can go away, if it's what you want. I don't want my presence to make things any worse. I'll meet you back here a little before two."

He was so sincere, so utterly earnest in his solicitous care of her, that she wanted to cry. She put her arms around his neck and kissed him with unmistakable ardor, pressing her body against his. "No. Come upstairs with me."

"Can you—"

"I can do anything I want, Ethan Walker. And if I want to spend the evening as a slave to your every wish, no matter what, then I can do that. The question is, after what we already did, can *you*?"

She felt his manhood swell. "I think I can rise to the occasion, as James Bond would say. Is it what you want?"

"I want to do whatever you tell me to do. Nothing's off the table. Or the bed," she added with a little grin.

"Won't it make things worse?"

She smiled. "You let me worry about that. You worry about what you're going to make me do."

CHAPTER TWENTY-SEVEN

RACHEL AND ETHAN arrived at the gate to the Arboretum at one-thirty. It was closed, so they parked in the lot just outside it. They might get a ticket, but it was unlikely that Rachel's car would be towed before morning.

The huge preserve—1,200 acres of forest and carefully restored prairie in the middle of the city—was popular with hikers, joggers, and bicyclists. In the winter, the trails were given over to cross-country skiers. Ethan didn't know how often it was patrolled, but Marty had mentioned several times that the place needed a greater police presence. He hoped that meant they wouldn't get busted for trespassing.

Both of them were exhausted, running on adrenaline and tension. For Ethan it was the same uncertainty he'd experienced in the army, when he was unsure where the danger would come from, or what form it would take. His eyes adjusted to the darkness and scanned the shadows for movement—a task made more difficult by the wind that made everything in the darkness move. It also made the air cooler than it had been in weeks.

"Her car's not here," he observed.

"Maybe she parked somewhere else."

"There aren't that many places to park, and the other end of the Arboretum is much farther from the place we're supposed to meet. You think she stood us up?"

"She has as much reason to be here as I do," Rachel said.

"There's something weird about her, Rachel. I can't put my finger on it, but I don't trust her."

"Neither do I," she admitted, "but I have to see this through."

Ethan pulled Rachel's gun from the glove box. It was a short-barreled .45 revolver, and he spun the cylinder to make sure the action was clean. When Rachel had suggested bringing it, he insisted on being the one to use it. She protested, but he pointed out the obvious: He'd shot people before. She hadn't.

He stuck the gun in the waistband of his jeans and let his T-shirt hang over it. Then they went around the gate and followed the two-lane road through the preserve. City noises surrounded them, yet with the trees and wind it was impossible to see anything except the next pinkish streetlight ahead. Their footsteps were loud against the pavement.

Ethan looked back over his shoulder. He had the sense of being watched and followed—something he was unerringly accurate about. It had saved his life more than once, and he felt it now almost like a physical hand on his back. No one was on the road behind them, and nothing was visible in the thick woods. He knew that on the right was thick forest, while across the road to their left stretched a marshy area crisscrossed with walkways for tourists and nature lovers. Hiding would be a cinch; following them, either through the swamp or undergrowth, almost impossible. And yet he was certain someone was.

"We're being followed," he said softly to Rachel.

He was impressed that she didn't look around. "By whom?"

"I don't know. But I'm sure of it."

She sighed. "Not much to do about it, is there?"

"Not really."

THEY REACHED THE trail that led down to the observation deck where they were to meet Betty. The woods were dark and impenetrable—so thick that even the moonlight didn't penetrate.

"Spooky," he said quietly.

Rachel took his hand. They had made love for almost an hour back at her place. She'd teased him and held him back as long as possible. She never imagined she'd hear a man like him beg for anything, but he had, and at last she'd allowed it. He'd clung to her so tightly that she worried he was having a breakdown, but he'd merely been overwhelmed by the sensation. They both dissolved into laughter and kisses when it passed.

"Don't worry, big guy," she said now. "I'll protect you."

He grinned. "If anyone can, it's you."

Rachel picked her way down the trail. It was tricky

enough during the day, when you could see the mud and exposed roots that tried to trip the unwary. At night it was even more dangerous, and a turned ankle would leave her helpless in a way she definitely didn't want. A flashlight was out of the question, since technically they were trespassing. Her lithe runner's body was more suited to this than Ethan's bulkier form, so she led the way. His grip on her hand was firm but not crushing, and she sensed the trust in it.

She stopped. He did as well, remaining a step behind her. She heard water lapping at the shore ahead of them. There was a break in the trees, and beyond it they saw the waters of Lake Wingra. Its odor rode the wind, different in subtle ways from the friendlier lakes Monona and Mendota. She'd avoided this lake for most of her life; one swim in it had convinced her that it was fundamentally different from its fellows. It hadn't felt dangerous exactly, just disorienting and out of synch. Now she understood why.

"This place gives me the willies," Ethan whispered. "I can believe an evil spirit would come out of it."

I just hope we can put him back in *it,* Rachel thought.

They continued on until they saw a small concrete platform with a solid metal railing imbedded in it, looking out over a shallow channel. To one side rose a tall, ancient oak tree. Beneath it, as if emerging from it, a spring bubbled up and flowed down the channel to the lake.

Rachel leaned against the rail and looked out at the quietly churning water. She saw no sign of Betty. "What time is it?" she whispered.

Ethan checked his watch. "Exactly two o'clock."

"Don't worry, I'm here," Betty said.

Rachel jumped and let out an involuntary yelp. She felt Ethan start as well.

Betty emerged from the darkness dressed in a long black sundress and carrying a satchel. She clicked on a flashlight beneath her chin. It made her face look long and angular. "Boo," she said. Then she turned off the light.

Rachel fought to control her surge of anger at the woman's cavalier tone. "We're here. So what do we need to do now?"

Betty looked down at the water streaming from beneath the tree. "You know this is the spot, don't you? Where the spirits all originated? That's the spirit spring."

"I thought they were the spirits of good men and women granted immortality," Rachel said as casually as she could.

Betty frowned. "Now where did you hear that?"

"I think I read it somewhere."

Betty shrugged. "Anyway, let's get to work. Take off your clothes."

Rachel's eyebrows rose. "What, just . . . like that?"

"Are you shy all of a sudden? I assume he's seen you naked, and I'm another woman."

Who's also seen me naked, Rachel thought, *because you were spying on me.*

Betty continued, her tone mocking, "Plus, we all know Kyle Stillwater has seen you without your clothes on, right?"

"Why don't you just explain the overall strategy here?" Ethan said quietly.

"They won't come to her unless she's naked," Betty said in exasperation. To Rachel she added, "You know that as well as I do."

"It's okay," Rachel said to Ethan. She glanced back at him, but his face was hidden in the darkness. Taking a deep breath, she quickly undressed, leaving her clothes in a pile beside her. She felt a rush of embarrassment at her nudity, and shivered as the wind suddenly gusted over her skin. Goose bumps rose, and her nipples tightened painfully.

"Nice," Betty said admiringly. "Even by moonlight."

"Get on with it," Rachel said, crossing her arms.

Betty knelt by the satchel and opened it. There was a smell from it that Rachel couldn't identify, but it nauseated her, and she stepped back involuntarily. She winced as a twig poked into the sole of her bare foot.

Betty stood with a long feather in her hand. "We have to ritually cleanse you before you set out. It'll make your allure more powerful. Follow me," she said, and nodded for Rachel to step around the railing, down to the spring tree.

Rachel picked her way over the rocks, wincing when a sharp edge dug into her tender feet. In her lake everything was soft grass and gentle mud; even the stones were smooth and easy to traverse. It seemed like everything in Lake Wingra was out to inflict pain.

Betty impatiently waited for her beside the tangle of roots. The sound of the spring was loud, and the water looked like quicksilver in the moonlight filtering through the overhang.

"Hold up your hands," the woman said, and Rachel raised her arms as if she was being robbed. "Clear your mind of everything but what you want. What you *really* want."

Betty whispered something in a language Rachel didn't understand, then began to caress her with the feather. Its touch was so delicate and insubstantial that Rachel began to tremble. Betty started at Rachel's forehead, then moved down her cheeks and neck. The strokes touched the tips of her already erect nipples, the soft undersides of her breasts, the gentle slope of her belly. As it threatened to go lower she thought she might burst.

She felt rather than saw Betty's lascivious smile as the feather brushed her nether hair. "Oh," Rachel sighed. By the time the feather stroked her shins and the tops of her feet, she was weak-kneed with arousal.

"I think you're ready," Betty said.

Rachel glanced up at Ethan, standing silently at the railing. Did he know how she felt? Could he sense it on the wind still coming off Lake Wingra? Did he understand that this might be her life, caught at this feverish level of desire with no chance for either lessening or resolution?

WHAT IS IT about this woman? Ethan thought as Betty wafted the feather over Rachel. There was something erotic in the two women's actions but not in the usual way. Like most men, he didn't necessarily mind the idea of two women together, but Betty set off all his interior alarms.

The wind shifted a little, and he froze. A strange, vaguely familiar smell reached him, but he couldn't quite place it. He concentrated to find the source. It seemed to come from the satchel Betty had left on the concrete. He edged discreetly toward it, glad for the comfort of the gun tucked into his pants.

BETTY STOOD BEHIND Rachel, her hands on Rachel's shoulders. She could also feel the other woman's body against her own. It felt strange and uncomfortable. "Call him," Betty said softly, so close to her ear that Rachel jumped.

"Should I tell him to bring the heart?"

"What?"

"The dead man's heart, where the spirits are kept."

"Oh. No, that's for later. We have to get him here first."

Rachel had to lick her dry lips and swallow hard. "Kyle," she said.

Betty pushed her lightly forward. "Not that way, honey. He won't hear you. You have to be in the water."

Rachel turned and stepped down into the stream coming from beneath the tree. It was barely ankle-deep, but it would be enough. If the spirits wanted her, they could find her. The waters were all connected, especially here at the source.

She looked out at the lake. The dark waters of Wingra seemed more like a gulf that would pull her in than a welcoming place where spirits might dwell. She felt a rush of terror, and her physical exposure only added to it.

"Kyle," she said again. "Kyle Stillwater."

"Keep going," Betty said.

Rachel swallowed hard and continued out toward the open water. Each step across the rocky channel bottom seemed to grow more difficult.

When the water reached her waist and touched her intimately, she froze in fear and revulsion. The wind increased, and she hugged herself for warmth.

ETHAN SLOWLY KNELT beside the satchel, his eyes never leaving Betty. He knew how to move in silence and how to keep his movements slow and steady to avoid drawing attention from the corner of someone's eye. He seemed to still have the knack. She was oblivious to him, focused entirely on Rachel's form easing out into the darkness.

The wind gusted in the treetops. The weather said nothing about a storm, but the air seemed charged nonetheless.

Rachel was a slender, feminine silhouette moving down the channel toward open water. She looked small and vulnerable, her narrow waist and broad shoulders emphasizing her femininity. He felt all the intangible warnings of danger, and he wanted more than anything to scoop up Rachel and carry her to safety. But he also knew that a warrior had to fight his, or her, own battles. And in her way, Rachel was a formidable warrior.

The satchel was halfway unzipped, enough for his hand to slip inside. He went slowly, feeling for anything sharp; he didn't want to cut open a finger on a knife. First he encountered what felt like a plastic grocery bag. As he pressed harder, it crinkled, and he froze. But the wind masked the sound, and Betty had not noticed him.

Rachel, the water now to the middle of her back, was almost to the open lake. His heart thudded with anxiety.

He pushed harder. Whatever was inside the bag was solid yet spongy. His fingers slid over it, establishing its shape as vaguely round and about the size of his fist. He reached the bottom of the bag and felt something wet and sticky.

Suddenly the smell resolved in his mind. *Blood.* Not fresh but definitely blood. He continued to explore, working his hand into the bag and feeling the wet, tough, sticky object it contained. With a shock, he comprehended what was in the bag.

A human heart. Garrett Bloom's heart.

But Betty had said the evil spirit, Kyle Stillwater, killed Bloom and used his heart to trap Rachel's spirits. If that was true, then why did she have it?

And if it *wasn't* true . . .

RACHEL WAS CHIN-DEEP in the water now, and so scared tears ran freely down her cheeks. How could she have let this happen? Whatever lived in this lake, whatever she was approaching at her most open and vulnerable, it was not the kind, loving spirits she'd known in the other lakes. She felt them swirling around her, malicious and cruel, biding their time. But for what?

Then she froze. Hands touched her waist. A presence loomed up behind her, no spirit but flesh and blood. *Definitely* flesh and blood; she felt his erection press against the small of her back.

"Hello, Rachel," Kyle Stillwater said.

The words shot through her, and she would've fallen if he hadn't caught her under the arms and turned her to face him. She was weak with a surge of unwanted desire, limp in his hands, and the water lifted her feet from the bottom. Her legs drifted apart on their own, and she could hardly breathe.

She looked up at him, silhouetted against the starry sky overhead. She didn't want him rationally, but the primal need swelling in her with every second could not be controlled much longer. He was right there; all she had to do was guide him where she wanted him to be. . . .

She could not see his face, but his voice purred with confidence. "We never did finish what we started the other night, did we? Is that what you're here to do?"

Yes, she wanted to scream. *Yes, take me, fuck me, end this awful sense of hovering and send me over the edge!* She had to grit her teeth against the words.

"Just say it," he murmured. "Say what you want." She could feel him hard and ready, bobbing in the water. He lifted her slightly and eased her forward, ready to claim his prize.

And then Ethan's voice rang out from shore. "Rachel, don't! It's a *trap*!"

CHAPTER TWENTY-EIGHT

BETTY WHIRLED TOWARD Ethan. "Shut the fuck up!" she snarled, and began lobbing fist-sized rocks from the streambed. He tried to elude them in the darkness, but one hit him solidly in the temple and he fell, dazed.

By the time he shook off the stars, Betty stood over him with a stick she'd evidently snatched from the ground. It was a yard long, and the end above his head was jaggedly sharp. "You've just outlived your usefulness," she hissed, and drove the crude spear at Ethan's head.

He rolled aside, and it struck the concrete base of the little observation deck. Acting on instinct, he kicked her feet out from under her, and she fell hard on her back. He rolled on his own back beside her and drove his elbow hard into her sternum. She gasped in pain.

Then he straddled her, pinned her arms with his knees, and held her by the hair. "What the hell is going on?" he demanded. "Who the fuck are you?"

She glared up at him, her eyes jet-black in the darkness.

AT ETHAN'S WARNING, Rachel found the strength to wrench herself away from Stillwater. "No!" she managed to cry, before he claimed her and everything was lost. She fell into the water with a clumsy, loud splash.

Instantly she was disoriented, and when she tried to kick her way back toward the surface she encountered only more water. The dark currents changed chaotically, tumbling her until all sense of direction was useless.

Then watery hands began clutching roughly at her. They were similar to the ones formed by her lake spirits, but these were knobby, sharp-nailed, and groping. They touched her everywhere with no regard for gentleness, and she writhed uselessly to escape them.

The depleted air in her lungs burned, and she fought the urge to let it out, knowing that only dank Wingra water awaited her. She clenched her teeth against the bubbles, but they escaped, and that desire to take the next breath grew too powerful. *I'm going to drown!* she thought helplessly.

A new hand, solid and powerful, closed around her throat. Suddenly she was yanked from the water and found herself staring into Kyle Stillwater's face. But it wasn't the desperately handsome visage she'd seen before: This was a sharp-featured, black-eyed demon glaring at her with utter contempt.

She clutched at his forearm and kicked madly at the water. She still needed to breathe, but his iron fingers held her windpipe shut so tightly she could get only the slightest bit of air. He pulled her close against him, and she again felt his erection touch her.

"I'm going to take you so hard you won't survive it," he hissed. "I've locked your spirits away from you, and when I'm done with you, I'll use your heart to trap them forever. Any heart will hold them, but only yours will *torment* them. How does that sound? I'm going to love you to *death*."

Fury surged through her at the threat. "With what?" she croaked, and used both hands to bend his erection like a dry twig.

He screamed and released her. This time she hit the water swimming and headed back toward the inlet and the spring. With each stroke she expected the vile clawed hands to grab her and pull her down, but they didn't. When the water was shallow enough, she stood up and splashed through it, ignoring the pain in her bare feet. She looked back over her shoulder, but there was no sign of Stillwater.

She heard Ethan's voice demanding, "Who the fuck are you?" and then Betty's cold laugh. She climbed over the rail, soaking wet and shivering from the wind, and saw Ethan astride Betty.

"Wh-what happened?" she asked, rubbing her pebbled arms with her hands.

Ethan didn't look away from the woman he held. "*She* killed Garrett Bloom, not Kyle Stillwater."

"What?" Rachel gasped. She knelt by the open satchel and pulled out the plastic bag. The smell and weight confirmed what Ethan said: This was a human heart, Garrett Bloom's heart. *Any heart will hold them,* Stillwater had said.

Betty began to cry. "He's gone. . . ."

"Are they in here?" Rachel demanded. "Are my spirits inside this?"

Through her tears she snarled, "Of course. I sucked them in like minnows in a vacuum cleaner. They were so weak they couldn't even fight back, thanks to you."

Rachel's blush of shame was hidden by the darkness. "Let her go, Ethan. This is all we need."

"Yes, it is," Kyle Stillwater said from inches away.

Rachel jumped and backed into the rail, which was cold against her bare buttocks. Stillwater stood naked before her, feet wide, hands balled into fists. Water trickled from his sculpted body. He was no longer erect but still radiated danger. "Now give me the heart."

Rachel was trapped against the rail, and the wind grew more violent. The memory of his fingers at her throat made her tremble even more. "No," she said.

Behind Stillwater, Ethan rose like a dark, avenging shadow. "Let her alone and back away, pretty boy."

Stillwater did not look around. To Rachel he said, "I will snap him in half and then take my revenge on you. His death will at least be quick. Now *give me the heart.*"

In a small voice Betty said, "Artemak?"

Stillwater looked as if he'd heard a ghost. He turned away from Rachel as if she didn't exist and looked down at Betty. "I am Artemak. Who are you?"

"Teculor," Betty said, her voice trembling. She got to her feet, smoothing down her sundress. "I am Teculor. Look at what they've done to me."

Stillwater looked Betty over intently. He seemed to have forgotten Rachel and Ethan. "Teculor," he breathed in wonder.

"They have made me into a woman," Betty said hatefully. "A woman! My body is weak, and prone to disgusting things, and I can do nothing to stop it."

"Teculor, my brother," Stillwater said. His own voice shook now. "What is going on here?"

"I saw you the day you emerged at the park. I knew your presence meant that the sanctimonious nether-worlders who imprisoned you had been weakened enough for you to escape. So I made a sacrifice. It was so simple, Artemak. They flowed into the heart just as easily as they once flowed out. I could hear their screams." She nodded at Rachel. "Then tonight I used their avatar to summon you, to present you with this gift."

"I'm here, my brother. I locked our jailers into their lake at the first opportunity, but it took me some time to wrest full control of this form from the conscious-ness that inhabited it."

"I know. I had the same trouble with this one at first." They both giggled, siblings sharing an inside joke.

Ethan slipped around the two and stood beside Rachel, one hand across her shoulders. He took the heart from her and held it out of sight behind his back. Then he slowly eased them both down the rail-ing, trying to get in a position to make a run for it. Rachel slid her bare feet along the concrete.

Betty suddenly turned serious. "You must help me,

Artemak. I have lived in this form for years now, and I can bear it no longer."

"Anything, my brother," Stillwater said.

Betty's voice was so small that Rachel barely heard it. "Free me from this prison. Being a mere spirit is better than this soft, pliable flesh."

Stillwater sounded genuinely regretful. "I cannot. It would take all my power, and I will not allow myself to be that weak again. You must endure this until its normal span of time reaches its end."

"You must try!" Betty shrieked, simultaneously petulant and desperate. "You are my brother!"

Rachel and Ethan were almost in the clear. Ethan gave her the barest nod toward the trail. Rachel squeezed his hand in acknowledgment.

Stillwater took another step back from Betty. "I thank you for your help, my brother. Together we have defeated those who judged themselves superior to us. Now I will destroy them utterly. It will not be as poetic as I had planned, but it will be just as permanent."

Simultaneously Betty screamed, "No!" and Stillwater flung himself at Rachel and Ethan. Instinctively Ethan pushed Rachel aside and braced for the impact, but Stillwater was supernaturally nimble. He snatched the plastic bag from Ethan's hand and leaped over the rail. He landed in the shallow spring pool and kept going down into the water until he disappeared.

Rachel did not even pause to think. She jumped up, put one bare foot on the rail, and leaped in after him. Ethan was an instant behind her.

By the time Betty got to the rail, three people had vanished into a pool barely six inches deep. The surface rippled to show their passage, but otherwise there was no sign of them. Betty heaved herself onto the rail and jumped but landed with a painful thud in the shallow water. She sat there helplessly, knowing where they'd gone but unable to follow. Only willpower opened the channel between the worlds, and her will was imprisoned with her masculine spirit, both impotent inside her female form.

"No!" she screamed again, and slapped the water like an angry child. It shimmered in the moonlight.

CHAPTER TWENTY-NINE

RACHEL AND ETHAN burst from the water one after the other. They found themselves standing waist-deep off the shore of Lake Wingra, but it was no Wingra that Ethan had ever seen before. Just ahead was the same spring-fed channel, but it was narrower and its contours different from what they had been mere moments before. He squinted into the unexpected sunlight and wiped water from his eyes.

Ethan looked around at the virgin forest, untouched shore, and nonexistent city skyline. The sunlight was blinding in its purity. He looked down at his soaked clothes, then at Rachel standing nearby.

A family of ducks passed before them. The ducklings regarded them with something like disdain. In the distance, a drum began to beat.

Ethan wiped water from his eyes again. "What the hell?"

He looked at Rachel. Water ran in rivulets down her body, and the sun glistened from her curves. He'd seen her naked but never like this, in bright light that made her breathtaking. He was momentarily speechless.

Then a shadow passed over them, and for a moment Ethan thought it was a small airplane flying too low. Then he realized it was an enormous black bird, with wings nearly twenty feet across, sailing in silence toward the far side of the lake.

He turned back to Rachel. "Okay, that's not right."

She ignored him, squinting against the glare as she scanned the shore. Suddenly she pointed and cried, "There!"

Kyle Stillwater strode toward shore, down the spring stream's channel. The tree that stood over the water source in their own world was a mere sapling here, barely ten feet high. All the trees, in fact, were smaller, and there were a lot fewer of them. The forested Arboretum hill was bare of grass on top. There was no trace of the little observation deck.

Ethan was used to acting before he had all the information; as a soldier, he had learned to trust his instincts in a crisis. "I'll get him," he muttered, and swam hard for shore.

In moments his hands felt the bottom, and he rose to his feet. He tossed his waterlogged shirt aside and sloshed through the knee-deep water until he reached the bank. He ran from the water and saw Stillwater halfway up the slope through the trees. "Stop!" he bellowed.

Stillwater looked back at him in surprise.

Ethan froze. The man's face was no longer human but pointed and black-eyed like some devil. Stillwater's voice was high and shrill when he cackled triumphantly.

He shook the plastic bag with Garrett Bloom's heart. "Too late!" Then he resumed his climb.

"Like hell," Ethan muttered to himself, and followed. His wet jeans made movement difficult, but he used the trees to pull himself along so that he quickly closed the gap between him and whatever Stillwater had become.

WHEN ETHAN TOOK off after Stillwater, Rachel swam at an oblique angle toward a different part of the shore, intending to approach from a different direction. She doubted she could physically overpower Stillwater, but she might be able to surprise him at a crucial moment.

She reached a spot on the shore about thirty yards from the mouth of the channel. She slipped through the weeds, trying not to think about what might be under the water. As she was about to step onto dry land, a movement to one side caught her eye.

A man stood down on the shore, staring out at the water. He was tall and slender, and wore only a long loincloth made of some sort of animal skin. His profile was the most noble thing she'd ever seen. And his hair was long, snow-white, and braided down his back.

He turned and looked at her. At the instant their eyes met, she saw something familiar—a kindness and compassion that resonated within her. "Hello," he said.

She recalled that she'd had no difficulty speaking with the old woman before either. "Er . . . hello." She swallowed hard. "You're, ah . . . one of them, aren't you?"

"One of who?"

Wait, she thought, *he can't be. This is Lake Wingra, where the evil ones go.* But his smile was so warm, so without guile, that she said, "You don't belong in this lake, do you?"

He looked intently at her, and suddenly she remembered she was stark-naked in broad daylight. She felt the blush creep up her neck and face.

He laughed. "Oh, I see. You're not supposed to be here, are you? In your world, I'm already . . ."

"A spirit?"

He shrugged modestly. "If I'm good enough. But there *is* something familiar about you. Sometimes, as we get closer to joining the spirit world, we get a sense of both the future and the past. That could explain it."

"So why are you here?"

He nodded toward the lake. "My father is here. He was a man of singular vision and drive, and he accomplished a great deal. Except he never had the first bit of compassion for anyone else. So his spirit is here. You understand about that?"

"Some." She nodded toward the hill. "I don't mean to be rude, but I'm kind of in the middle of something. In the future . . . will you remember this?"

"I don't know."

"Well, if you do . . . say hello."

He nodded.

She headed up the hill, hunched low to stay out of sight and trying not to wince at the sharp-edged grass and briars that nicked her bare skin. This slope was steeper but also shorter, and she made good time. But the contradictions ran through her head. If the man became one of her spirits in the future, then wasn't he also trapped inside the heart? And if she was here, and had now spoken to him, would that change anything in the future?

Sarah Connor, where are you when I need you? she thought.

She reached the top of the hill and peeked around the trunk of a large tree. She saw a circular clearing. In the center stood a flat, simple stone altar almost identical to the one shown in the old illustration Betty McNally had given her. Rusty trails at the corners showed where sacrificial blood had run down to the ground. Three sharp, long knives rested in notches cut along the edge; the blades reflected the sun.

Stillwater emerged from the trees at the same moment. His whole being was distorted now, drawn tight and wiry over bones that seemed extra-knobby at the joints. His knees also now pointed backward, the way satyrs looked in old drawings. Whatever disguise he'd used in her world, he couldn't hide his true form here. She couldn't believe he'd ever been human.

Fear knotted her stomach. What could she possibly do? She was helpless in every sense, huddled naked behind a tree in a strange place and an unknown time. And yet she couldn't stand by and do nothing.

Stillwater was halfway across the clearing when Ethan tackled him from behind. The impact knocked them both down, and they struggled for dominance. Stillwater was hampered as he tried to hang on to the plastic bag.

Rachel saw her chance. She dashed forward, staying low to keep the altar between her and the men for as long as possible. Then she snatched the bag from Stillwater's hand.

He turned toward her and screamed. It was a cold, inhuman sound that sent shivers up her spine. He got his knobby feet against Ethan and kicked. Ethan flew through the air and landed on his back a few yards away, the impact knocking the wind from him.

Rachel lost crucial moments making sure Ethan was okay. By the time she turned her attention back to Stillwater, he was nearly on top of her. She tried to run, but his long fingers had grabbed a handful of her hair, jerking her to a halt.

"First my brother presents me with a gift," he hissed, "and now you do as well. Your death will only add to the agony of your spirits before they meet their own destruction."

He dragged her effortlessly to the altar. She fought, but his skin was now thick and leathery, immune to her assault. He slammed her head down hard against the stone, and she saw stars for a moment. He twisted one arm behind her and forced her to stay bent over the altar, her cheek pressed against the layers of dried blood left over from previous ceremonies.

"Let me go!" she snarled, kicking uselessly. She yelled in pain as he wrenched her arm even more. She expected to feel him move behind her, to take advantage of her helplessness the way cruel men always did with women at their mercy. Rage and adrenaline rose in her.

"I lived in that lake for centuries," he hissed. With

his free hand he slammed the bag containing the heart onto the stone. "I was once a man, with a man's desires and dreams. Now look at me!"

He shook the heart from the bag. It rolled perilously close to Rachel's face, and she scrunched her eyes shut. But it didn't touch her.

"They kept me there, until a moment of weakness let me jump into that stupid boy," he continued, breathing heavily. "And my brother. I thought he was truly dead, but they cast him into the body of a *woman*!"

"You bastard," Rachel hissed. She felt his deformed foot beside her own. "I'd say your brother was the lucky one."

Before Stillwater could answer, she slammed her heel down with all her strength on his instep. He howled, and his grip on her lessened enough for her to wrench free, although she left some hair in his hand. She turned, put her back to the altar, and kicked him again, hard, in the groin. When he doubled over, she brought her knee up into his face.

He staggered back, and she grabbed for the nearest of the three knives. It was just out of reach, but before she could lunge across the stone, a crack of thunder split the air, and she felt something warm splash on her back.

Birds shrieked and fled from the trees. She turned and gasped in surprise.

A hole marked the center of his chest, blood just starting to ooze from it. Behind him, Ethan stood with Rachel's gun, the barrel still smoking.

Stillwater made a sound like broken glass in a blender. She assumed it was a scream.

"Grab the heart!" Ethan cried. "Go back to the lake and try to get them home!"

Rachel grabbed the bag, rolled the heart inside with just her fingertips, and headed back down the hill through the woods. She prayed that whatever passage brought them here was still open.

STILLWATER TURNED AND hissed at Ethan. His tongue lolled out, longer than a man's and forked. He raised his hands and charged.

Ethan fired again.

The new hole appeared an inch beside the first. Stillwater looked down at the wounds, then back up in confusion. Blood coughed from his mouth.

"It's over," Ethan said. His heart thundered with adrenaline, but his aim was rock-steady.

"Do you know . . . what my existence . . . has been like?" Stillwater croaked.

"No, but I'm pretty sure you deserved it," Ethan said.

As he rushed at Ethan, Stillwater again screamed, a nails-on-chalkboard sound that made Ethan wince. But his next shot found its mark, right between the creature's eyes. Stillwater fell dead at Ethan's feet.

Ethan closed his eyes and sighed. His own heart felt like it might split in two on its own. He lowered the gun to his side.

When he looked back at Stillwater, instead of the white-haired creature, a young man with black hair and a Native American complexion lay at his feet.

Ethan knelt and rolled him over. His face was fully human, and blank with the peacefulness of death.

A new voice said, "That was unfortunate."

Ethan jumped to his feet. An old woman stood a few paces away, watching them sadly.

"You speak English," Ethan said.

"I speak what I speak. You understand it; that's what matters."

"I didn't have any choice, you know."

The woman's expression did not change. "There's always a choice. But this did what was needed. The spirit inside him is gone. It had no time to prepare a way to return to its former home."

Ethan wiped at the blood streaking his sweaty chest. "My name's Ethan, by the way. Rachel told me about you."

"Are you her human lover?"

"Er . . . yes."

The woman looked him up and down. "She has chosen well."

"Thanks, I guess. . . ."

"Don't thank me. Your path will be difficult—more so than hers. You will have to share her with her spirits."

"I know."

"Do you?" She nodded toward the trees behind him.

He turned. Two dozen men and a few women had emerged from the forest. They were all beautiful specimens, lean and handsome and well formed. Some wore loincloths, some full coverings, and two were nude. All sported long, straight white hair.

He met their eyes. In them he saw strength and re-solve but also compassion. They were warriors who fought the battles they chose, not soldiers who merely took orders. He understood that.

"So you're the spirits," he said.

One of them stepped forward. "In time, we will be. We have a lot in common with you."

"I'll say."

The man smiled. "I don't mean merely the woman. You, like us, wish to make things better. You are will-ing to do what is necessary to protect the weak. Or," he added with meaning, "avenge them."

"You fucking traitor," he'd been called when he re-ported a fellow soldier for the rape and murder of a lit-tle girl. *"Keep looking over your shoulder,"* they'd warned. Even his commanding officer had said, *"This is a war, son. People get a little carried away."*

"You did the right thing," one of the young women said.

"So you can read my mind?" Ethan said.

The first one who'd spoken laughed. "No. At least not with any detail. We have not achieved the enlight-enment that awaits us, and believe me, it's tempting to ask what the future is like. But we can't."

"And you," the old woman said to Ethan, "can't stay any longer. But you need to know what to do to release them safely back in your time."

RACHEL CLIMBED THE hill to the little observation deck over the spring and leaned on the rail. She was ex-hausted, yet there was no sign of Ethan emerging in her wake. The return dive into the pool had been a reflex, and it had occurred to her in mid-motion that if she was wrong, she was about to go headfirst into six inches of water over a bed of hard, smooth rocks. But no sooner had the thought flashed through her mind than she emerged back into her world, still clutching the plastic bag with its grisly cargo.

Belatedly she looked around. There was no sign of Betty McNally. Everything was gone except for Rachel's discarded clothes. She gazed into the dark woods, and then out at the lake, wondering where the woman—or was she a woman?—had gone. The Lady of the Lakes would have a hot tip for the police, if Rachel could figure out a way to keep her and Ethan out of it.

She stared down at the pool. All she could really think about was Ethan battling that creature. Surely the gunshots had been enough to stop him? Surely he hadn't turned and slain Ethan?

Please, she begged the universe, *please send him back to me alive.*

She shrieked when he suddenly burst up from the water and sat sputtering in the spring. Her heart pounding, she rushed around the tree, jumped into the water, and threw her arms around him.

"Oh my God, I was so afraid you weren't coming back," she cried as she flung herself against him.

He put his arms around her and drew her into a kiss. Then he looked around in sudden confusion. "Where is she?"

"I don't know," Rachel said breathlessly. "There's nothing up there but my clothes."

He looked down at his chest. Passing through the water had washed away the blood. "I need a shirt."

"Not from where I'm sitting," Rachel said, and began to giggle.

THEY WALKED BACK to Rachel's car and drove across town to Hudson Park.

As they got out of the car Ethan said quietly, "Have you seen a ring of small rocks anywhere around?"

"Yes," Rachel said. "Why?"

"Show me where it is. Your friends told me what we need to do."

When Rachel did, Ethan kicked the stones aside, dispersing the circle. Then he picked up the individual rocks and threw them as far as he could into the water.

The circle had been a lock, the old woman told him, placed there by Artemak to isolate the good spirits in the lake. As long as it remained intact, they could influence nothing beyond their watery confines, nor communicate with their avatar when she came to them. Once they were weakened in this way, Artemak planned to trap them in Rachel's heart, after which he could then destroy them utterly. This would free his fellow evil spirits in Lake Wingra.

But his brother Teculor, locked in his own bodily prison by the good spirits, got there first and trapped them in Garrett Bloom's heart. Teculor hoped the gift of the captive spirits would induce Artemak to help break the spell that confined Teculor. But Artemak had been unable or unwilling—not even the old woman knew which—to help, and in the end neither brother got what he wanted.

Rachel and Ethan snuck quietly down to the water, and Rachel looked up at him doubtfully.

"You're sure?" she said. "We don't have to cut it open?"

"Not according to what they told me."

She looked down at the bag. "So you saw them. You talked to them."

"I don't know exactly what happened. Maybe it was all in my head. But if it was real, then yes, I did."

Despite everything she'd been through, Rachel felt a surge of self-pity. "Why didn't they come out while I was still there? Why didn't they talk to me?"

"I don't know."

She choked down her tears and wiped her eyes. "What were they like?"

"Young, mostly. Very good-looking. They all had white hair. And . . ."

"What?"

"It's hard to describe, but you know how sometimes you just instinctively know something about someone?"

She grinned slightly. "Like the hot guy who just appears in your diner one day?"

"Something like that. Anyway, I just knew they were good people. Are good people. Are good . . . whatever they are."

Rachel handed him the bag and quickly disrobed. She looked out at the water, her emotions a swirl of desire and apprehension. "I hope so. I hope they still . . . like me."

"I think they do," he said, and opened the bag.

She reached in with both hands and lifted out Garrett Bloom's heart. It felt strange and disgusting as she cupped it in her palms.

She looked up at Ethan. "I'll be back soon. One way or the other."

He nodded. "I'll be here."

She stepped into the water and walked until it reached her elbows. Then she took a deep breath, lowered the heart to the water, and opened her hands.

The heart floated for a moment, then sank.

She stood there quietly, waiting.

The hands pulled her under slowly, into the wet darkness. They caressed her the way a diamond cutter might worship a valuable gem. She held her breath, afraid to trust them, but eventually she had to breathe again and found she could. She began to cry, and as the touches grew more erotic and insistent, she felt lips on her ear, and a voice, familiar from her recent adventure, said, *Hello again.* She could feel the lips form a smile, and she turned to let them kiss her.

ETHAN SAT ON the wet grass and watched the surface of the water. He was more tired than he could ever recall. He felt a sense of triumph, but it was tempered with the feeling that events were still out of his control. After all, the woman he loved was in the water, indulging in a supernatural orgy.

The skyline along the opposite side of the lake sparkled with light. It was the world he knew: concrete, steel, wood, blacktop. In the army he'd destroyed them;

as a civilian he built them. There was little room for talk of spirits.

He watched the lights of a plane as it rose above the city. How would this relationship play out in the long run? Would they get married, have children, grow old together? Would he be parked here in a wheelchair someday, watching Rachel use a walker to reach the water? That seemed implausible.

That is, unless the rules were a little different.

He stood up and undressed. It was time for the spirits to understand that they didn't always get the final say-so.

He waded into the water, took a deep breath, and fell slowly back into the water. He'd done this once before, to communicate with the spirits when Rachel had been kidnapped. They had welcomed him then. Would they do so now?

The air began to burn in his lungs. He would have to surface soon. He reached out but felt only water and the silty bottom.

Okay, guys, it's me, he thought. *I know you didn't pick me, but we're part of one another's business now, and we might as well get along. If you've got a shred of compassion in you, you'll give Rachel some peace away from the water as well. I promise I'll never make her choose between us, if you do the same.*

He waited for a response, but there was none. When he could stand it no more, he put his legs beneath him and pushed. He burst from the chest-deep water and took a long, desperate breath.

He shook his head in disappointment until Rachel's voice cried, "Ethan!"

He looked up. She stood on the bank, fully dressed, her face wrenched with concern. "Jesus, I've been out of the water for almost half an hour! Are you all right?"

I was underwater for half an hour? he thought. It had seemed like the length of one breath. He said in wonderment, "I'm fine."

"Well, come on, it's nearly daylight. You don't want anyone to see you!" She laughed, amusement mixing with concern. He walked toward her through the water.

CHAPTER THIRTY

MARTY WALKER LOOKED down at the body draped across the same picnic table where Garrett Bloom had died, beside the half-demolished mental hospital. The sunrise cast amber beams through the treetops and turned a wide swath of Lake Mendota bloodred.

The corpse was nude, unmarked, and intact. Beside it on the ground were a pile of clothes, a purse, and a canvas satchel.

He'd examined the ID and knew the woman's name. It was the only certainty in the whole thing. "Now who in the hell," Marty asked no one in particular, "is Betty McNally?"

"She ran an art gallery and was obsessed with the Lo-Stahzi," Julie Schutes said as she came down the hill.

Marty turned and scowled at her. "And how do you know that?"

"I have sources."

"Or a police scanner."

"Well, that too. But once I got the name, the rest was easy. She teaches pottery, reads tarot on the side, and sells bad art at good prices. And she was once arrested for trying to steal a rare book on the Lo-Stahzi from campus."

"And she's dead in the same place we found Garrett Bloom," Marty said, and shook his head. "Don't suppose you know how they're connected?"

"Hey," one of the technicians said, "this satchel is soaked with blood. And look at this." He carefully held up a long, thin knife before slipping it into an evidence bag.

"If the blood's human, get it typed right away," Marty said. He looked steadily at Julie. "Do you happen to know Garrett Bloom's blood type as well?"

"No, but I can find out."

"Don't bother. It's A-negative."

Julie's eyebrows went up. "You think this woman was killed by the same man who killed Bloom?"

"No," Marty said, and held up an evidence bag with a pill bottle inside. "This woman killed herself with an overdose, I'm pretty sure. This bottle was in her hand, and she'd thrown up some of them. And she did it at the same place Garrett Bloom was killed, with a knife that could've killed him in her possession."

Julie said, "Okay, wait, I want to get all this down."

"Oh, no," Marty warned. "This is all off the record. I could be way off base. But *if* the knife matches the stab wounds, and *if* the blood in that satchel turns out to be Bloom's, then we may have his real killer."

"Not the Matre woman?"

"No comment," Marty said, "until I get the forensics report."

"So where's his heart, then?"

Marty turned and looked out at Lake Mendota. "Maybe she dumped it out there."

His cellphone rang. He answered and listened in growing disbelief at the report from officers at Lake Wingra. Two morning joggers had found the drowned body of the actor Kyle Stillwater.

RACHEL AND ETHAN arrived at the diner just after the doors opened at 6 a.m. They had not changed or showered, and Ethan was still shirtless, so they drew stares when they entered. Helena looked them over and said, "I don't want to know about it right now. But I *do* want to know. Especially since I've had to get ready to open by myself."

"It's a fair trade," Rachel said with a smile. "Just . . . can you call Clara or Roya in to help this morning? I'm beat."

Helena looked at Ethan. "Have you two worked out your issues, then?"

Ethan, his arm across Rachel's shoulders, pulled her close against him. "Negotiations are proceeding."

"Uh-huh."

The door slammed open, and Patty cried, "Rachel!" Before Rachel could react, the girl wrapped her in a hug and spun her around. "I've been trying to find you!"

She scrunched up her nose at the muddy smell and stepped back. Then she took in Ethan's bare-chested presence. To Rachel she said, "Are you okay?"

"I'm fine," Rachel said with a laugh. "I'm glad to see you too. I was worried about you. You said you met someone and then you never answered my calls."

She blushed. "I'm sorry, I was just . . . I want you to meet somebody," she said, and ran back outside. A moment later she brought in a tall, dark-haired boy.

"This is Andrew," Patty said. "Everybody calls him Ace."

"Hello," Ace said, looking down nervously. Rachel realized that thanks to her disheveled appearance and his own nervousness, Ace didn't recognize her. She went along with it, saying, "Nice to meet you. I'd shake your hand, but I might leave a tadpole in it."

"Oh, you'll be seeing plenty of him," Patty assured them. "This one isn't made of water vapor and silt."

"She keeps saying stuff like that," Ace said. "I have no idea what it means."

Rachel winked at him. "It's all right. It's a private joke." Then she turned to Ethan. "I'd offer to make you breakfast, but if the health inspector came by and saw me in the kitchen in this condition, he'd close us down."

"That's okay," Ethan said.

To Helena, Rachel said, "We're going upstairs to take a shower. You sure you've got it under control?"

Helena couldn't help smiling. "I'd say all's right with the world."

RACHEL AND ETHAN lay in bed beside each other, their noses touching, her leg across his waist. The sheets were damp with sweat from their exertions. She sighed and ran a fingertip along his jaw, feeling his stubble.

"Did that really just happen?" she breathed.

"You'll have to tell me."

"That's the first time I've ever . . . ever come away from the water."

"How was it?"

She closed her eyes and sighed with amazed contentment.

"I'll take that as a positive response," he said, and kissed her. "Give me about twenty minutes, and we'll try it again."

"You know, you were very brave last night," she said.

"Bravery had nothing to do with it. It was instinct."

"Right," she said mock-knowingly.

"Besides, *you* saved the day. You dove in after him. I just followed you."

"I don't know what I was thinking. Instinct?"

"Instinct. Still, without you, we'd be dead. You saved both of us, just like you did those girls in the cellar."

They kissed, their tongues caressing as their hands sought familiar areas. With a soft trill, Tainter jumped onto Ethan's side of the bed and nuzzled the top of his head into the man's neck.

Ethan broke the kiss and laughed. "Is he trying to get me out of bed?"

"I think he's saying he accepts you."

He reached over his shoulder and scratched the cat behind his ears. "I like you, too, Tainter." He kissed Rachel. "And I love you."

"I noticed. I love you too."

He stretched, and Rachel luxuriated in watching the muscles of his chest and arms flex. "I don't ever want to get out of this bed. Except to go to the lake with you."

She felt a little twinge of the old fear. "You're still sure you don't have a problem with that?"

"Still sure. You never lied to me, and you never kept secrets. I don't have a problem."

She kissed the tip of his nose. "I don't know if I'll ever give them up. I don't know if I'll ever want to."

"I'll never ask you to."

She was about to tell him her other secret, that she was the mind behind the *Lady of the Lakes* blog, but before she could, he kissed her again. She slithered closer and pressed her body to his, and was surprised to feel him stir against her again. She would take that as a sign that, for now, she should keep that secret. Although she might leave him a clue here and there.

Besides, like her mother always said, every relationship needs a little mystery.

POSTED BY THE Lady to the *Lady of the Lakes* blog:

Take a moment to thank your partners today, people. Finding someone loyal enough to follow you down into hell and then make sure you both get back is a rare and precious thing. Don't take it, or them, for granted. And remember that the world you see around you might not be the only world out there. Tread lightly, do good for others, and cherish the ones who love you.